HEY
LENNY,
HEY
JACK

Other books by Alan Brody

COMING TO

THE ENGLISH MUMMERS AND THEIR PLAYS

By ALAN BRODY

HEY LENNY, HEY JACK

William Morrow
and Company,
Inc.
New York
1978

Printed in the United States of America.

1   2   3   4   5   6   7   8   9   10

Library of Congress Cataloging in Publication Data

Brody, Alan (date)
    Hey Lenny, hey Jack.

    I. Title
PZ4.B8638He [PS3552.R624]   813'.5'4   77-24389
ISBN 0-688-03249-4

BOOK DESIGN   CARL WEISS

FOR

MY BROTHER,

GENE

HEY LENNY, HEY JACK

Gainesville, Georgia
July 25, 1975

Dear Lenny,

Got your letter a couple of days ago. This is the first chance I've had to answer. Honest. I hope I can finish it in one sitting. The phone hasn't stopped ringing since the strike started. Every call means another emergency meeting —or management trying to take me out to lunch. They still can't get over the idea that a whole orchestra could get itself together like this. You'd think they hadn't heard us getting ourselves together for the past ten years. Yesterday Ed Lewis said to me, "A strike, Jack. A strike. I still can't believe it. For a whole symphony orchestra to strike. It's like a sin against God." So I said, "What else could we do? A job action? How do you manage a slowdown on Mozart?"

We're in our second week. Molly left for Europe a couple of days after you and Edith visited. She's delivering a paper on infant frustration threshold in the anal stage, then going to the Edinburgh Festival. The children are gone. Anna's taking summer courses in women's studies at Tulane to find out how she's oppressed. Marty is an apprentice at a summer stock company someplace in New Hampshire. Can you imagine? Fifteen years old and he's traipsing all over the country with degenerate artists. I warned him. I said, "If you don't watch out you'll end up like your father." I told him he should do something normal, like hanging around the pool halls in Gainesville. Then he could end up like his Uncle Lenny. He said something about a divinity shaping our ends, so I smacked him in the mouth. (Talking like that at fifteen.)

So I'm alone now for a couple of weeks with no rehearsals, no Molly, and no Marty. I've got no ruts to wish I was out of, meetings and phone calls every hour of the day and night. Everything's disorganized. And that's why it's taken so long to answer your letter.

Congratulations! I was so excited when I read the good news I didn't even finish the letter. I picked up the phone and wired Molly. "Lenny at it again. Economic advisor to the President. Tell no one in Vienna that you have connections. Love. Jack." It was over ten words, but who could be cheesy at a time like that? Besides, it was after eight o'clock so I sent it night letter.

It really is something. Economic advisor to the President of the United States. Momma would have said, "Only in America," so I'm saying it for her. I'm thrilled and proud.

You and Edith must have known when you were here. In fact, I know you did. You wouldn't talk politics. And when Leonard and Jack Fleischman see each other for more than two hours at a stretch and don't talk politics at the tops of their voices, then either chaos is come again or one of them has just been appointed economic advisor to the President of the United States.

Besides, Edith looked radiant. After you left I said to Molly, "She's pregnant. I swear it. She's blooming like she did when she carried Lisa." And Molly said, "A forty-two-year-old woman doesn't bloom when she's pregnant. She droops." So I said, "If she's not pregnant with a baby, she's pregnant with something."

Every time I looked at Edith I thought of an expression that used to come over Momma's face when she carried around a secret about one of us. Remember when I got the scholarship to Juilliard and she decided not to tell Poppa until after coffee? Do you remember how she wiped her fingers on her napkin after each bite of food and how she kept pursing her lips as if she was shushing herself? Or when you told her you were valedictorian at the Wharton School and she did the same thing? Come to think of it, I can't remember Poppa ever getting good news *before* dinner. Only deaths and divorces. *Naches* after coffee. Anyway, that was what I kept remembering when I looked at Edith.

I said that to Molly, too. I said, "You know, Edith never reminded me so much of Momma." She said, "Why are you surprised?" She said it like an analyst, so I answered like a patient. I shrugged. "I always thought it was the youngest who was supposed to marry his mother." She said, "You mean you? Don't be a dummy. You married your father." And, you know, she had something. Molly *is* like Poppa.

By the way, have you written to him? He asks for news of you and I've been dying to tell him. But I didn't know whether you wanted to write—or call—yourself. It would be funny if you already did and he's not sure if he should tell me. I've been seeing him every day since Molly's been away. He's alert and back on his feet after a siege of real weakness. The doctor says he's fine. "Got a lot more time yet to listen to Beethoven" was how he put it.

His room at the home is incredible, thanks to you. The

stereo with the headphones was exactly what he needed. He's got a huge, gorgeous collection of records, wall-to-wall bookcases full of them and as many scores as I could find. Whenever I come to visit I find him with the 'phones on, following a score in his lap. He doesn't hear me come in, so I can look at him the way I never could before. When he's concentrating on a score like that he looks so young. I have visions of what he and Momma must have looked like before we were around.

That's one thing about this strike that makes me unhappy. Poppa loves those concerts—especially in summer when we play the Peach State Arts Center. Of course, that's exactly why we planned it for summer. The outdoor season is the orchestra's biggest money-maker. But Poppa understands, God bless him. Every day he asks how the negotiations are going and reminisces about the U.H.T. strike of '26, when all the leatherworkers were out for four months. Sometimes he gets mixed up, but he's usually clearheaded. "It's one thing when those bastards exploit skilled labor," he said to me the other day. "But when they get their grimy hands on the arts . . . !" And his eyes lit up for a new fight. Then he sighed and said, "Still, I miss the music and the air."

I'm sorry you didn't get to see him when you were passing through. I would have liked to know what you thought about how he looked. And he would have been pleased. You know, I was thinking the other day that when we were younger you were always the one who talked about how important family was and I was the rebel, talking about dead institutions. I should be embarrassed that Molly and I have stayed together for over twenty years and had Poppa down here with us for six.

O.K. Enough beating around the bush. I'll get down to business. I finally did read the rest of your letter. In case you didn't guess, that's the real reason I'm writing. At the end you said you were saddened by your visit with Molly and me. You felt that you and I were growing apart. It's the first time you've ever said anything like that to me. I was a little surprised. I've always thought you didn't pay much attention to that kind of thing. I've thought about it a lot—our relationship, I mean. But I figured it was just because I'm younger than you, and that's the kind of thing that only the younger brother bothers his head about. Maybe it's only that the younger brother starts thinking about it sooner.

I guess what surprised me most was that you said you felt we were growing apart. I'm not sure we were ever close. I think that what's kept us in touch for the past fourteen years, and what kept us together so long before that, was a *yearning* to be close. There's a kind of love in that, but it's not a closeness. Even when we were working together, when you were managing me—and when's the last time we mentioned that part of our lives to each other?—even then it was more a struggle for both of us to understand each other than closeness.

I've always wondered whether you knew that. And now your letter comes. "I feel as though we—and our families— are growing apart and it saddens me." I guess I know what made you feel that way. I've been pretty guarded with you for a while, now. This time, with the strike in the offing and Poppa so ill, I guess it was more obvious than ever.

But underneath it all I've also always wondered if a real closeness was possible—even this late. Maybe it's *only* possible this late.

What if I took your letter as a start? How could I answer? It could take a whole novel to explain about us . . . and even then . . .

But what the hell, I'm on strike and alone. I can't imagine those two things ever happening together again, so I'm going to try to tell you a little about us—you and me—and see if it helps. You think we've grown apart. I think we were never close. We both think we love each other. So let's see what's doing.

. . . Wouldn't you know it? Called away to the phone just when I was getting to the good part. Executive committee meeting in half an hour. So I'll put the letter aside and come back to it in a couple of hours. Don't go away.

July 26, 1975

Finally have a chance to get back to you. This strike is really something. The meeting went till two in the morning. Roast beef sandwiches on white bread for dinner. It's eleven now. Phone calls since seven-thirty. Jerry Frank, the first horn, woke me up to find out what happened. I said to him, "Are you sure this is the way Petrillo started?" He said, "Who's Petrillo?" Twenty-three-year-old pisher.

There are five of us on the executive board. Phil Carnovsky, cello; Eileen Simpson, harp; Dudley Rogers, oboe; Tony Querault, percussion; and me, first violin. If only we could bring our instruments and talk to each other that way.

Everybody's got his own *schtick* to go through before we get down to business. Tony gives us the history of the orchestra and ends up on the verge of tears. "To have it come to this . . ." And his lips tremble and he drops his head in his hands, which is Dudley's cue to remind us he's only the house nigger, after all, but . . . which stops everyone else from listening while he tells what conditions were like when he played the Hollywood Bowl. Eileen feels compelled to announce she played the Albert Hall and Phil, who's been sitting tight-lipped for an hour, can't stand it anymore and explodes. "Burn the place down. Burn them all down. Give the fucking music back to the people!" Eileen takes exception to Phil's language. Dudley takes exception to Eileen. Tony pulls himself together, says something like "Well, where are we then?" and smiles at me. I'm supposed to synthesize.

Review of the grievances. We took forty-five minutes on the hot-plate issue. Management doesn't want us to overload the circuits with hot plates in the dressing rooms. Eileen talks about how important it is to have nourishment during intermission. She uses Lipton's Cup-a-Soup. Dudley mentions he sometimes only had soup for dinner when he was a kid. Tony brings out *Consumer Reports* and reads comparative hot-plate voltages and Phil yells, "Fuck it! Overload the fucking circuits! Burn the place down!" at which Eileen takes exception . . . and I synthesize.

When we finally get to the non-negotiables it's midnight. Three basic demands. No mandatory retirement, 10-percent pay increments, and full artistic control of the repertoire.

The retirement issue is the most important right now. Arthur Quasnosky, the first bass, is sixty-three. He's got bone cancer and he can only manage to play about every fifth note. The rest of the bass section has been covering for him for over a year. Lewis wants to retire him, but the orchestra's all he's got. A lot of the strike is about that. At least it's what finally got us moving.

Funny thing is, nobody likes him. He's a miserable human

being. A couple of years ago we were taking up a collection for an air conditioner in the dressing rooms. What with the dinner jackets we wear onstage and the Georgia summer, things get pretty ripe down there. When Eileen approached Arthur in the green room, he announced publicly, "We don't need an air conditioner. Just get rid of the niggers. That'll clear the air." Born in Gainesville. Never left it. Spent thirty years teaching music in the Gainesville public schools until the orchestra happened. Every other word out of his mouth is poison. Carries a rifle in his car and sleeps with a pistol under his pillow. But the sounds he used to get out of that bass . . . you could hear the seventh sphere turn tender. So go explain art.

And go explain strikes. That we should finally go out because of him. Phil tried once—to explain, I mean. When we first found out about the cancer, he said to me, "Maybe that's why he's such a prick. Maybe he knew all along he was dying." I said to him, "Who doesn't?"

I had a terrible time keeping my mind on the deliberations. Once I decided to go through with this letter, the floodgates opened and the memories poured out. I sat there with the other four and kept scribbling down snatches on my pad so I could make some kind of sense when I got back here.

I think my mind's been on this letter a lot longer than the past couple of days. Maybe about twenty years. Marty would probably say it's that Venus is in the ascendant, aligned with Mars, at an oblique angle to Saturn, and that's why I got your letter and happened to have a couple of pads of yellow foolscap and a box of Flair pens lying around. Molly would say the strike is the manifestation of a repressed id and it's activated my superego, which, since Poppa's got his headphones on all the time, I'm projecting on you. Anna would say I'm evading my political commitment and trying to salvage the nuclear family because the larger unit is turning classless. Whatever. I say it's maybe that I was forty-two last April and I've got more memories than prospects.

I've also got my pad of notes from last night's meeting sitting in front of me. Every other page there's a scribble that says something like "Riding my bike with one hand. Lenny proud." Does it ring a bell? It's one of my earliest memories of us.

Listen, I've never been sure whether I'm cursed with total recall or an abnormally vivid imagination. Neither is Molly. But I'm going to share my memories with you—as many as I can—and we'll see if you can recognize any of them. If you can, you'll be right. We have grown apart. If you can't, then maybe you'll understand that we were never close.

Either way, if we're both honest, we may end up finding a place to start. And that wouldn't be such a bad thing either.

RIDING MY BIKE

I was coming home from Hebrew school in the late afternoon in spring. I couldn't have been more than ten. Do you remember how it worked? From third grade until our thirteenth birthday all of us would spend the day at P.S. 197, tear home, hang around the street for an hour, then take our bikes to the synagogue on Nostrand Avenue for Hebrew school. At least that's what everybody else did. I needed the hour to practice for practicing. Momma would say, "Practice a little now, Jackie, so when Poppa's home your practicing will sound good." I used to put up a fuss and complain that I never got a chance to go out on the street. But I was really just as glad. By ten I was already the sissy of East Twenty-seventh Street. Nobody ever really wanted me on his side for punchball, stickball, ring-a-levio, or grounders—which didn't even *have* sides, for chrissake. But I figured there was something wrong with me for not wanting to go out, so I was just as happy to blame Momma, put up a fuss, and lose.

The one thing that assured me I was normal was that I hated Hebrew school as much as anyone else. That was comforting. I was lucky to have Mr. Cohen. I have a feeling that if I'd had a less oppressive, less ignorant teacher I might have really gotten into it. Then I would have worried. I was enough of a freak as it was, with my violin, an overhand throw that looked as if my arm was attached to my shoulder with a paper fastener, and a preference for *Looney Tunes* over *War Comics*. Mr. Cohen was just what I needed. He wore a black wool suit that smelled as though he'd been caught in a drizzle, had a beard line that made him look positively Hassidic by four-thirty in the afternoon, and a thick German accent that confused me terribly. The only other German accents I ever heard were in the movies on Saturday afternoon. They belonged to Otto Kruger and all those other Nazis. The idea of a Nazi teaching Hebrew school was not an easy one for a kid of ten to field. Especially in 1943.

Our classes fell into three parts: history, ritual, and the reading of Hebrew. In the first part we were taught our cultural heritage, all the Jewish overachievers from Abraham to Ted Williams. Mr. Cohen also had evidence that Galileo and Christopher Columbus were Jews. I didn't know much about Galileo at that time, although it seemed logical to me that a Jew would be watching a chandelier swing while all the Catholics around him were praying—at least that's the way Mr. Cohen explained it. I did wonder about Columbus though, and once had the gall to ask why, if he was Jewish, his parents had named him Christopher. Mr. Cohen explained that the Sephardic Jews were always the most cunning. A few minutes later he yelled at me and slapped me on the side of the head for chewing my pencil. He said it was a sure way to get lead poisoning and if any of us died we wouldn't be able to grow up and be the messiah, which was always a possibility in our religion, kind of a sop for not being able to become President. Mr. Cohen was very big on the idea that one of his pupils might be the messiah, so I thought about it a lot, too. Every time he mentioned it, I thought, If it *is* me, buddy, you're the first one I'm going to get.

The third part of the class was reading. Mr. Cohen would get out old, worn prayerbooks and each of us had to sound out paragraphs of Hebrew. We understood every ninth word, except for Deena Frisch, who we all hated because she read fast and with expression, and had fat thighs. He always gave her the longest paragraphs, but she would zip right through them. If the next person stumbled, he'd bang his ruler on the desk, shout that we were letting women take over the world, and warn us that we'd spend the rest of our lives reading transliterations. "Is that what you want?" His voice would be like the God of vengeance. "To have to go to *shul* on Yom Kippur and ask for *transliteration?* You deserve it! For the rest of your lives you deserve such humiliation."

At five-thirty he'd release us and we'd scramble to the bike rack behind the synagogue. The bike rack was a gift of the graduating class of '34. There was a big commemorative plaque on the wall behind it, a daily reminder that we should think about what we would give when we were finished at thirteen. I once suggested we have Deena Frisch bronzed.

One day I got out of class and found my bicycle basket broken. I suspected gentiles, which meant that at least some of Mr. Cohen's training was getting through. I thought about going to the rabbi. He always welcomed complaints like that, but I noticed the rust flaking off the broken ends of the basket attachment and figured I didn't have much of a case. I left the basket under the plaque. We always carried books home from Hebrew school. I can't imagine why. I never looked at one in the house. Still, we had to shlep them back and forth. I carried mine in my basket. Now I had none.

I'd never ridden a bike one-handed before, but I had no choice. I hopped on and took a couple of turns around the yard behind the synagogue before trying to cross Nostrand Avenue. I was shaky at first, until I figured out I was working the handlebars too much, that it was really all in my body, the balance of weight. It was getting dark by the time I started home. Some of the cars on Nostrand Avenue had their headlights on. I rode across, even managed to handle the trolley tracks, and started home down Avenue P.

Do you remember what the spring twilight felt like in Brooklyn? The trees that lined the sidewalk were just starting to leaf. The blossoms looked like little fuzz balls. Sometimes the street would still be wet from a sanitation truck. Your bike tires made little crackling sounds and left prints, and the gutter smelled like after a rain. Down the cross streets you could see the shapes of kids trying to get one more inning. And you wore your lightweight jacket a little cockily. If you were really lucky you would be out when the streetlights went on.

It was like that on that night I rode home one-handed, feeling pretty good that necessity had taught me something new and terrific. I'd never before known it was all in my body, not the handlebars.

I turned into East Twenty-seventh Street. You were finishing up a game of stickball. You saw me. Usually when that happened you tried to avoid me. My reputation on the street was a terrible burden to you. There you were with the whole world opened to you. You were Junior Varsity basketball at James Madison High School; already shaving; you carried yourself as if you'd been laid more than one experimental time; you had your own fake I.D., which meant you could play pool whenever you wanted; and you had the most taped hockey stick on East Twenty-seventh Street.

And you had me. I was your signal to the world that all was not well, a skinny little kid who spent three hours a day with a violin tucked under his chin. With all those other things you simply had more of what everybody else wanted. That made you more like everybody else than anybody. But nobody had anything like me. I was your fatal flaw, your Oedipal limp. I knew what a burden I was to your career on East Twenty-seventh Street. Sometimes, when I was working on scales, I would daydream that I was mild-mannered Jack Fleischman whose concealed identity was Super-Fiddle. One day I would reveal myself, in tights and a mask, and destroy all the evil in the world by fiddling it to death. Then everyone would understand why you had put up with me for so long and admire you even more for keeping the secret.

I owed it to you. You see, as much as I was a burden to you, you were a kind of salvation for me. You were the only thing in my life that touched the world of everybody else. If people were suspicious about what kind of setup you could come from that could produce me, too, I was reassured that at least the setup that I had come from had also produced you.

So that late afternoon when I turned into East Twenty-seventh Street I expected you to give me the same worried nod you always did and I was prepared to respect it. But you didn't. You looked straight at me and all of a sudden there was this huge grin on your face. I was so surprised I nearly lost my balance. You flagged me down at the top of the ramp to the basement of our apartment house. That was where we kept our bicycles. Six floors, five apartments on each floor. A hundred and twenty bicycles, 250 strollers, twelve scooters, and eighty-five sleds.

You caught me at the top of the ramp and asked if I was riding one-handed.

I said, "Yes," and I was about to explain about the broken basket, but you said, "No shit! Let me see," and had me circle the concrete backyard once.

When I got back you had such a look of pride and pleasure on your face that I wondered if maybe you didn't really love me. It may have been the first time I was conscious of the possibility. And that may be the reason I remember it so well.

You said, "That's tremendous. You know that? That's really tremendous."

I tried to be nonchalant, but my face was flaming. I was about to offer to go around the backyard again when you said, "You're really growing up. You're really fucking growing up. Soon you'll be doing *everything* like everybody else."

You told Momma about it that night but she wasn't as impressed. She told Poppa about it before dinner. No. She didn't exactly tell him about my bike riding. What she said was "You want to hear what your oldest thinks is important?" Then she told him.

Poppa said, "Important is as important does," with a very wise voice, and Momma said, "What does that mean?"

I didn't care what they thought about it, though. I knew what was important to me. You had been proud. There was hope for me. I had learned to do something like everybody else.

The next day I hopped on my bike, eager to look normal

all the way to Hebrew school. I even hitched up my pants before I got on.

Well, I made it to Nostrand Avenue one-handed all the way, but nothing felt the same. I had a terrible, tense time controlling the bike. By the time I hit Avenue P, I was panicked. I wanted so desperately to look like everybody else I couldn't find my balance. I wobbled all the way, hung between doing what felt right and looking like I was supposed to. I walked across Nostrand Avenue, furious at myself and desperate. My first chance at the big time and I was killing it.

After Hebrew school I waited until everybody else had left the courtyard behind the synagogue and tried to find my way back to control. I couldn't break away from trying to look right. My face must have looked eighteen. No less. But I couldn't find my balance. The more I lost control the tenser I got. I gritted my teeth and started home. If I just made it home this one time, I told myself, I'd be all right. It was just a bad day, nothing to worry about.

I weaved across Nostrand Avenue and up Avenue P. Every time I settled back I'd remember what I should look like. The bike would veer and I'd pull it back with blind control, determined to make it home. I was all over the road by the time I hit Twenty-seventh Street. I tightened my grip on the single handlebar, eased around the corner, and skidded against the curb. The bike went under me; my books flew into the gutter, and I slid across the curb on my stomach. The palms of both hands were torn and the slide scratched holes in my shirt. My nose was bleeding. I wiped it with my sleeve and cursed myself for crying.

I collected my books and walked the bike into the storage room. You and Momma were in the kitchen. I tried to sneak by but Momma spotted me. She washed my face and hands in the kitchen sink. As she was patting them dry, she asked what happened. I said I had gotten into a fight.

Her mouth went tense. Your face lit up.

She asked who I had fought with.

"Gentiles," I said.

She smacked me and said, "From now on you stay out of trouble," and checked my fingers.

But you were looking at me with even more pride than the day before.

I never rode to Hebrew school one-handed again. I rigged up a strap for my books with an old belt and attached it to the handlebars. When I saw you, I would let go with one hand and miraculously keep control until you were out of sight. You never suspected anything.

It's five o'clock. I've been up and down with the phone while I've been writing this. Dudley stopped by for an hour to rehash what happened last night. He's afraid that Tony Querault is leaking our meetings to Ed Lewis. I made some lunch and we talked.

He kept looking over at this letter. I think he suspected I might be writing reports on our meetings. Everyone's getting a little paranoid.

"You writing your memoirs?" he asked.

I laughed and said, "No. Just a letter to my brother."

He gave me a funny look.

A couple of new developments in the strike, but I'll tell you about that later. There's another committee meeting at eight—here—and that gives me another couple of hours to talk about us.

OUR ROOM

We lived together in that room for fourteen years. There was just enough space for two beds, a desk between them, a radio on top for listening to "Inner Sanctum" in the dark, a dresser made out of some kind of orange wood near the closet. The window looked out on Kings Highway. The Madison Park Hospital was across the street—with blue lights in its windows.

There was an overhead bulb in our room, but by the time I finished sixth grade we had wooden wall lamps over our beds. We'd made them in shop class. Mine was in the shape of a shield, with an oak stain. It lasted until I moved out to Juilliard, but the varnish never dried. I still rub my fingers together after I turn on a lamp. Yours was a blob that was supposed to be round with a decal of a P-47. One wing was torn.

On school days Poppa woke us at seven, just before he left for the leather factory. Momma's one great indulgence was that she always got up after we made our own breakfast and left for school. She couldn't bear us in the morning—and do you blame her? The problem was that we didn't have to get up until eight. Poppa never needed an alarm; it never occurred to him that it might be useful to anyone else.

The only clock was in the kitchen. Every five minutes after he woke us, I would stumble out of bed, pad into the kitchen, check how much more time we had to sleep, race back to bed, and use as much of it as I could. At five to eight I would shake you, tell you it was eight and you could use the bathroom first. Then I'd jump back in bed and relax for the duration of your piss. I encouraged you to drink enormous amounts of liquid at night to ensure a little extra rest for myself. It was usually incredibly long and loud—and that early in the morning you knew no shame. You always left the door open. I would fall back into a half-sleep, one ear on the familiar orchestration. One small, tentative splash, pause, Niagara Falls for thirty-two bars on a good day, then a retard, pianissimo, silence, a splash coda, silence, trickle—and a flush for the big finish. Once, for about a month, you got into this John Cage thing of aiming for the side of the bowl. It ruined my mornings.

I remember weekend mornings best when I was nine and you were fifteen. We always ended up wrestling. It wasn't as though we planned it. It just happened. And it took us by surprise each time. We'd find ourselves thrashing around on somebody's bed, then rolling onto the floor. Your breath smelled terrible. Mine did, too—and that lent an extra discipline to the fight. We had to avoid face-to-face contact. Ever since then I've been suspicious of movies where the stars wake up after a whole night's sleep and go into a big clinch. If it hadn't been for you that would have been another thing I might have mistrusted about myself. And it's thanks to you I wasn't surprised at Molly's morning breath either.

My most intimate memories of you are those wrestling matches. You'd be sitting on top of me, your knees clamped tight to my sides, deciding whether to finish me off by dropping your full weight on my stomach or tickling me to death. Your pajama tops hung by only one button. There was a beauty mark just over your left pap and I was always amazed at how unconcernedly you carried it around. I had one that I hated just at my waist, on the right side, and I was *always* concerned about it. Even when I was dressed. It was just another sign of how much better prepared for the world you were than I. By fifteen you also had a thin line of hair up to your belly button and an almost full armpit which I envied. It was also my secret weapon. Whenever you had me straddled like that, I only had to free one hand, reach up, and pull the hair under your arms. You would fly off me and I'd scramble back to neutral territory.

Once I tried it and didn't get away in time. Do you remember that morning? Just as I was pushing off the floor you came back down and crushed the fingers of one hand with your knee. You somehow managed to concentrate all your weight on that one spot. I let out a scream that was only partly pain. I pulled away on a reflex while you still had your knee locked down. The real pain shot through my whole arm; my hand went numb. That was when the fingers must have broken.

It woke Momma up. She'd slept through a lot louder noises, but the message of this one must have cut right through. She was in our room before we even got to our feet.

She grabbed my wrist without thinking. I let out a yell that reached every apartment on Kings Highway. The second and third fingers were already bigger than my thumb.

She took just enough time to smack you onto your own bed, then bundled me up, still in my pajamas, and carried me across Kings Highway to the hospital.

They splinted me up and put on a wrist cast. Momma was a little relieved when she realized it was only my bowing hand, but not enough to forgive you for days.

Poppa stayed home with you. I don't know what you two did together, but by the time we got back you were able to take Momma's tongue-lashing and the week-long silence that followed.

I couldn't understand that. I didn't think it was your fault. Usually, even when you were justly accused, you would lose a temper that was the only match for Momma's in the house. This time you just took it. I wanted to talk about it with you, but I was too ashamed at not defending you. You had every right to despise me for my cowardice. Besides, I wondered just around the edges whether you might have done it on purpose.

* * *

There's another scribble on my pad that says "Advice in the Dark."

ADVICE IN THE DARK

At night, after our radio programs, we would talk to each other. We must have picked it up from Momma and Poppa. When the whole apartment was dark their bed would creak and they'd whisper in Yiddish. We'd listen for a while, then retaliate with pig latin.

When we got tired of talking for spite we'd talk for real. Then you would show me what the world would be like for me in six years. You were so much wiser than Momma and Poppa. You'd suffered more. They never got yelled at, or lost a basketball game by two points in the last thirty seconds of play, or got detention for smoking in the bathroom. How could they know what life was really like? I never felt more secure, more sure that the world was a sane, logical place than when I lay on my side with your voice floating across the dark to me. You were my only connection with the lore of the street.

Down here people remember learning about real life from their black housekeepers or their grandfathers. Dudley once showed me how he had learned to read the future with an ordinary deck of playing cards from a mulatto neighbor in New Orleans. He read mine once. It kept coming out fame, fortune, friends, lovers, and power until we realized it was a pinochle deck.

You never taught me how to read the future, but you gave me pointers on how to handle it.

You explained about masturbation a lot, how it wasn't good for you. We were too progressive for you to pull any nonsense about going blind or getting warts. But you did explain that it would stunt the growth of my penis. You even gave scientific support. It had something to do with sailors, who never masturbated, and that was why girls liked to go out with sailors. Because they had big penises. And the proof of it was their peculiar flies. You must have been about fifteen and we lived in Flatbush, which was miles away from the navy yard. I got over the taboo about masturbation, but I never could take sailors seriously.

You also taught me about winning. By that time you were on the Senior Varsity basketball team and heading for all-borough. You told me how, whenever you had a game, you spent the whole day working up hostility, that you only played really well when you convinced yourself that you hated the other team. When you made all-borough, then all-city, I knew you were right. You assured me that Jascha Heifetz did the same thing when he played. That was why he was in the big time. If I wanted to make the big time I'd have to learn to be hostile, too.

For about a year, I remember, I was working on a Wieniawski concerto. First I would practice the music, then I would practice my hostility. But I could never figure out who to be mad at. Heifetz? Wieniawski? Mr. Resnick, my violin teacher?

It never worked for me. My bowing would turn harsh and my fingers would jam. I'd always end up hating *you* for convincing me I was doomed to be a loser.

You were different. I knew it worked for you. Sometimes I would pass the school yard where you scrimmaged and watch through the fence. The sweat would run down your neck and spray off when you turned. You kept your dribbles low. When you drove in for a lay-up it was like watching the BMT express run through a local stop. No one could take the ball from you. You plucked rebounds like ripe oranges.

Once you had the ball in your hands they couldn't stop you. You charged down the court free and clear, Arnie Finkelstein, Fred Schuller, Melvin Roth, Stanley Mandell, Ronnie Feinberg, all of them following behind. You looked driven by demons.

I watched, and I envied you your demons. All I had were these sissy angels hovering around my music stand, and they weren't even visible the way Finkelstein, Schuller, and the others were. It took twenty years for me to discover that I had my own host of demons, and that you had a couple of angels, too.

You fought with Momma about your friends a lot. It happened on weekends while she was changing our linen. She would appear at the door to our room with a stack of clean sheets. We'd both clear out of our beds and she'd go to work. Just as she snapped the bottom sheet open, she'd say, "What are you doing today, Leonard?"

I disappeared fast when she called you Leonard. She was the only person in the world who could make your name sound like a rattled spear. I fled to my violin. Your voices would cut through, but I never heard the words.

Once I stayed in the hall and watched the two of you play the whole scene out. It went something like this.

"What are you doing today, Leonard?"

"I don't know."

"You're just going to hang around?"

"Not around the house."

"Of course not. You've got the poolroom."

"You going to start, Ma? I'll go now."

"What do you do with yourself? You hang around Dubrow's and smoke cigarettes and think you're Robert Mitchum."

"What do you want me to do?"

"Find friends who are going to amount to something."

"I don't want to go through this every goddamned Saturday, Ma!"

"You use one more word like that with me and I'll throw out every pair of pegged pants in the house. I swear it, Leonard. I'll burn them."

"Burn them. See if I care."

"You don't care about anything."

"I care. I care plenty."

"About what? Eight ball in the side pocket? Put the ball in the basket? You're seventeen, Leonard. Seventeen. Stop playing with babies. There are nice boys around here. Bright boys. Boys who are going to amount to something. Make friends with them. Learn something. Be somebody."

"I am, goddamn it. I am somebody! Who do you mean? Lowell Miller? Larry Cohen? Just because they get good marks in school? They're still jerks."

"Big shot. You think I don't know what's going on in your head? You hang around with bums and jerks so you can be a big shot."

"You'll see."

"What? You're going to be the big star of the Knicks?"

"Mr. Kramer says I could make the Knicks if I practice."

"I'm not raising my son to be a basketball player."

"What do you want me to do? Hang around the house all day with a fiddle under my chin? Have everybody in the neighborhood laughing at me like they do at Jackie?"

She dropped the blankets. You knew exactly what was coming. You watched her approach and took the smack. You didn't even put your hands up to defend yourself, or touch your face afterward. I wanted to run away down the hall, but I was afraid you'd both hear and know I'd been there the whole time. Momma went back to the bed and you said,

"Sure. Sure. It's O.K. for Jackie to think about being famous. It's not crazy for him to care about something. Only me."

And Momma said, "What are you going to wear today?"

That night, in the dark, I told you I thought you'd make the Knicks.

You said, "What do you know? You're only a kid."

July 27, 1975
Late afternoon

Well, we had one hell of a meeting last night. Got to tell you about it.

Tony brought in the union representatives. Poppa would have plotzed. One young guy, about twenty-nine, thirty, with a crew cut and a three-piece suit. Mouth like a baby's. His name is Gwynne. Laurence Gwynne. Spent the whole meeting on the edge of the sofa with this attaché case affair opened on his lap. The other is Hebert Dowd. About my age, round-faced, with a brush moustache and the most incredibly pudgy fingers I've ever seen. He settled back in the armchair as soon as he came in, never moved.

They're the representatives for all the southeast area, spend most of their time working with country and western artists, keeping the peace, taking a rake-off from management to look the other way. You couldn't miss it. Every time one of us asked a question Gwynne adjusted his glasses with two fingers and Dowd's face went blank.

Up until now we've been working with Vic Jenkins, our local lawyer from Atlanta. The union was just as happy. They still can't figure out how the Gainesville Symphony ever happened. The whole thing was such a miracle from the start, and unions today are so out of touch with their own history they don't know how to deal with miracles anymore. So when the strike began I had a couple of calls from the national office. "I suppose you boys know what you're doing . . ." "Our men have a pretty full roster, but if you need any help . . ." "Give 'em hell . . ." and good-bye.

That was the first couple of days. I think they hoped the whole thing would stay buried. But all the Atlanta papers are carrying the strike on the front page. *The New York Times* and *The New York Post* picked it up last week. The *Times* ran it in the amusement section; the *Post* ran it under the labor news.

By then the union knew it was out, so they sent Dowd and Gwynne.

They had the list of demands and grievances. They'd already looked them over. Phil Carnovsky wanted to know where they'd gotten them. Dowd said they'd already talked with Vic Jenkins.

"We didn't know anything about that," Phil said. He was suspicious from the minute they walked in. We all were, but Phil's a barbarian. He doesn't know from handshakes and curtsies.

"It looks like there may be more trouble than you bargained for," Gwynne said.

"Why isn't Vic Jenkins here?"

"He's turned the negotiations over to us."

That didn't sound like Vic to me. "Don't we have anything to say about that?"

Dowd smiled at me. It wasn't exactly the kind of smile that

smooths things over. It was the kind we always get from management, full of respect for our art, and compassion for our innocence. The smile of the realist. It does incredible things to my adrenalin. "Of course, it's finally your decision. But the way things are moving I don't think Jenkins is going to be able to handle the action. We've got some compromise suggestions that should get you just what you want . . ."

"Wait a minute." That was Dudley. "What's this about compromise?"

"That was a bad word, Hebert." Gwynne to the rescue. He adjusted his glasses at Dudley. "In negotiations like this it's always a matter of give-and-take . . ."

"Don't forget this strike is the first time for you fellows," Dowd said. "You've got the cause, and we're behind you all the way on that. But we've got the experience."

Then this little voice from the armchair comes through. "Excuse me." Eileen's been sitting with her hand up for a couple of minutes and no one's noticed. Her *hand* up, for chrissake. "I'm sorry for interrupting, but . . . about your experience." She flashed this southern-trained smile at Dowd. "How many other symphonies have you worked with?"

Dowd shrugged. "A musician's a musician."

"I see. Do you play?" Dowd tuned out so she turned to Gwynne. "Do you?"

"A little banjo . . ."

Eileen smiled again. "Well . . ." She wasn't used to having us all listen to her that way, so she was very nervous. "It seems to me that we're all a little inexperienced in this kind of thing." You wouldn't believe how small her voice was. "And the only thing that's different about you and us is that we know it." Then she paused and shook her head. "No, I think maybe you two gentlemen know it, too."

Now Tony was up. "This isn't getting us anywhere." We

were arranged in a circle and he started pacing in the middle, all the time squeezing his handkerchief in one hand. You know the size of my living room, so you can imagine the teeny-teeny steps he had to take in order to pace. He wanted to look distraught, but he only looked like he had to go to the bathroom. "These men came all the way from Nashville to work with us and all we have to offer are hostile questions. I've never been so embarrassed. For fourteen years the orchestra has been a family. For fourteen years we've brought music to lift the hearts of all the people in Georgia." So help me God, that's the way he talks. "For fourteen years we've played together, rehearsed together, cried together, laughed together. That it should come to this . . . this . . . wrangling and suspicion. It was fourteen years ago . . . fifteen—fifteen come September—that Jack Fleischman and Ed Lewis began to realize a dream in Gainesville, Georgia . . . a small community ensemble . . ."

"Sit down, Tony," Dudley said. "You're only going to end up crying."

"And shouldn't I cry? To see it . . ."

Dowd and Gwynne looked like they'd stumbled into Walpurgis Night. I figured it was time for me to synthesize again.

I told Tony to sit down. He didn't want to at first, but I explained it was my house and Molly would kill him if he wore out the rug. Then I told Dowd and Gwynne what was going on. They had to understand that the union's track record with us was not terrific. I explained that Vic Jenkins had been with us from '61. We trusted him and we were suspicious to see him suddenly out of the picture.

You should have heard me, Lenny. I was the voice of reason. You would have wanted me on your staff. Everyone calmed down. Gwynne admitted they had seen Lewis the night before, but it wasn't a meeting. They ran into each other by accident in the hotel dining room.

"It was a good thing, too," he said. "Because we found out that they're going to try to get a restraining order out on you."

Even Tony wasn't ready for that one.

"I thought they only used those on miners and train conductors."

I got mad. The law was the first thing Ed Lewis pulled out of the hat when the orchestra needed something. I'd been up in his office too many times with smaller grievances. It was always the same. "It's not like the old days, Jack," he'd say to me. "We've got a board of trustees now. We've got to find out if the charter . . ." And "There's always the danger of a lawsuit if . . ." It always worked, too. Until I started educating myself about labor law with Poppa's help.

"They can't get a restraining order out on us," I said. "Even with Taft-Hartley. The only justification for a restraining order would be the threat of violence, danger to personal property or life and limb."

"They think they can prove the danger of violence."

Tony sat up. "From us?"

"Lewis says some of your people want to burn down the orchestra shell."

We all looked at Phil Carnovsky. He was sitting like a yogi next to Dudley. "That was rhetoric!" He trembled self-righteously. "Lewis knows empty rhetoric when he hears it."

"That's right," Dudley said. "We all know Phil is ineffectual."

Eileen asked what a restraining order was.

"They can get a judge to send you back to work," Dowd said.

"If we don't go?"

"He sends you to jail."

"The whole symphony?" Tony's lips started trembling.

"Only the strike leaders."

"But that's us."

Dowd nodded.

Eileen laughed a little hysterical laugh. "I didn't study harp for ten years to go to jail."

"None of us did."

"Yes, but the harp is a *string* instrument."

I thought about Molly coming home and finding a note on the refrigerator with my forwarding address. I looked around at the other four. They were looking at me. My face got very wise all of a sudden.

"How do we fight it?"

"You can settle."

"How come you're suddenly talking 'you' and not 'us'?"

"We think you should settle," Gwynne said.

"And give up what?" Dudley asked.

"Practically nothing." He shuffled his papers.

Dowd moved in fast. "Ten percent increment across the board. Twelve for soloists."

"What about artistic control?" I asked.

"Set up an advisory committee."

"And who does this advisory committee advise?"

"Lewis."

"So the control is still his."

Tony shook his head. "When I think of how you two loved each other," he said to me.

"We still do," I said.

"Advisory committees can have enormous influence," Gwynne said.

"So can housewives," Eileen put in. "What do we do about retirement?"

((39))

"We can get that for you, too."

Dudley looked surprised. "No mandatory retirement?"

Dowd nodded.

"You mean that?"

"You see?" Tony said. "All we had to do was give them a chance."

Dowd smiled.

"The management will have to make a study of present conditions . . ."

"Where does that leave Arthur Quasnosky?" I asked.

"Who?"

"First bass."

"He's sixty-three," Tony added.

Dowd shrugged. "You might have to figure him as a casualty of the war."

"He's the *reason* for the war," I said.

"Well, if he's that good, I don't see why we couldn't work something out."

"He's not that good," Tony said.

"Then why—"

"Because he was that good," I said. I was angry.

Dowd and Gwynne were waiting for an explanation. I have a feeling that all of us were thinking about the same day six years before, at a rehearsal of the Brahms Concerto for Bass and Orchestra, when Quasnosky filled the shell with a sound so rich, so astonishing and tender that each of us remembered that secret, lonely moment when he realized his own mortality, and made his decision for music. How do you explain a memory like that? How do you say to the union men, "The shit has a soul. That's why."

"I tell you what," I said to Dowd. "You get them to keep Quasnosky and we'll settle without a retirement clause."

"And what happens next time?" Dowd said.

"We'll worry about that when it happens."

((40))

"That's suicide," Gwynne said. "It's legal suicide."

"The union doesn't make deals on individuals," Dowd added. "You know that."

Gwynne looked around the room. "What do the rest of you think?"

Phil said, "Nothing happens without Quasnosky."

Dowd said, "It's crazy, you know."

Tony said, "The symphony wouldn't be here if we were sane."

Then Eileen. "And you boys wouldn't have as much work to do."

Gwynne shook his head uncertainly. "That would affect the increments, you know."

"Let it," I said.

"But that's the key issue."

Dowd leaned his head back in the armchair. For a moment I panicked about grease stains, but then he said, "Let me give you fellas some advice," and the weirdest thing happened. I started to giggle.

Eileen said, "Jack."

And Tony said, "Jack!"

I think Dowd checked his fly. It was something about the way he had leaned his head back and offered advice. For a second I was sure he was going to explain to us why girls liked to go out with sailors. I got control of myself and kind of apologized without explaining.

Tony said, "We certainly have our company manners on."

And Eileen said, "Don't, Tony. You'll just set him off again."

I said, "No. It's O.K. I'm all right now." Then, to Dowd, "You were going to give us advice." I chuckled a little, but that was all. I did have a fantastic impulse to turn off all the lights and lie on my side on the sofa.

Dowd picked up as though nothing had happened. "We've

been through negotiations like this before. Whatever you think about this Quasnosky fella, increments are the key issue. Everything works from there."

Phil said, "Why?"

"That's the way it's always been. It's the only language management understands."

"Why can't we teach them a new language?"

Dowd laughed. "Well, you'd have to teach us, too."

"O.K."

Dowd shook his head. "The world doesn't work that way."

All the others were getting edgy. Phil was chewing on his beard. As soon as anyone comes along and explains how the world *really* works we lose our nerve. And I thought, You were right, Jack. He's going to give us advice in the dark, after all.

"So. . . what do you think?" Phil said.

Dowd could tell he was listening. He suddenly got casual, as though he was improvising. "I think your best bet is to call a meeting of the whole orchestra. We'll get facts and figures from management so you can lay it all out. Then we'll see where they want to go."

None of us looked at each other. Tony shifted in his seat again. "I sure would like to get back to the music." He said it almost to himself.

"This meeting," I said. "Do we call Quasnosky, too?"

Dudley sighed. "I think we have to."

"That should be terrific for healing old wounds."

Eileen said, "Maybe if one of us spoke to him first, explained the situation. I mean, he knows the whole action is about him."

"That's a good idea," Dowd said. "Just ask him not to come."

"Sure," I said. "Hey, Arthur, baby, we're selling you out.

You're invited, but it'd be easier if you didn't come."

Tony jumped in. "You'll be able to come up with something better than that, Jack."

Nobody contradicted him.

"How did I get elected?"

"It's your Jewish charm," Phil explained.

Gwynne put his papers together and closed up his attaché case. "Well, it's settled then. We'll see Lewis and his cronies tomorrow."

Now they were cronies. The national was alive and well.

"When can you call a meeting?"

"Better do it before the weekend."

"Thursday, then."

"That's two days."

Everyone looked at me. "Will that give you time?" Tony said.

I shrugged.

So there we are. The cavalry from Nashville is in town and I'm going to see Arthur Quasnosky tomorrow morning.

I just took a look at the pile of paper I've already covered. It's getting pretty big. I didn't expect that. I suppose I could put down "Love, Jack," right now and shove it off in a big envelope, but it'd feel unfinished. That'd be just another sample of the reason for this whole thing. I feel as if I always want to tell you things and always leave them unfinished. It'd be stupid to do it again. Besides, if you want to know the truth I think I don't have much choice. I've got to finish this time.

I didn't expect to spend so much time talking about the strike either, but it's on my mind—and, besides, I have a suspicion that what's going on here is, as Marty would say, relevant.

So I'll just keep going. And if you've gotten this far, you keep going, too. And we'll see where we come out.

Spent an hour with Poppa this morning. I wish I could get him out of that home and here with us, but he needs too much attention. He's weak, Lenny. That's what's so hard about visiting him. His mind is still as strong as it ever was, but his body just can't respond to all the orders he gives it. He once told me that he felt like Mozart composing on a harpsichord with every other key missing—and the others shifting out of tune. "The music's there, Jack," he said, and he knocked on his head. "And it won't go away." From the way he said it, I couldn't tell if that was something good or not.

I told him about last night's meeting. He was in his chair near the stereo with the headphones down around his neck. He hadn't turned off the record when I came in, just took off the headphones and let them hang. Every once in a while a snatch of Beethoven would come through as if from a great distance. He closed up the score when he saw me, but he kept it on his lap.

I told him about the meeting.

"It wasn't always like that." He sounded as if he were apologizing for all the change in the world. "In 'twenty-six the union would have told you what to pack for jail and let you know they were ready to come, too. I swear it to you."

I told him I believed him.

"I wish I could get in there with you. I could let your committee know things about the way it was . . ."

I felt like Hamlet on the ramparts.

"Don't let them get away with it." His voice was weak, but I could hear the effort behind it. "If we haven't had music for two weeks, at least there should be a reason for it. You know what I mean?"

I said to him, "How would you feel about having a son in jail?"

He grinned. "We could compare notes."

Did you know that Poppa had been in jail for two months? "Just like Eugene Debs," he said.

"You never told me anything about that."

"Momma—she should rest in peace—made me promise never to tell the children." He chuckled. "First she was afraid it would warp your characters. Then she was afraid it would ruin your careers. Then it was for the sake of the grandchildren. By the time she died I almost forgot about it myself. You just reminded me." He paused. "You feel warped?"

"Not any more than usual."

"She was really worried about the neighbors, anyway. When I went in we lived on Coney Island Avenue. When I came out she'd moved to Twenty-seventh Street. That was the way she was. That was the way I was. I don't know how we stayed together for thirty years. Same thing with you. She liked the idea you'd be famous someday. I liked the idea you'd make music." He shrugged. "So who was right? We were both proud."

"How do you think she'd feel about jail?"

"She'd have a heart attack. Then tell you to do what you want. Only not to write letters on company stationery."

We grinned at each other, but behind his eyes he was worried. I couldn't tell if he was worried about me or the strike. I could hear the needle scratching the end of the record in the earphones. I got up to turn it off but he said, "Turn it over. I like it going. Even when I'm not listening."

He was quiet for a long time. The music sounded as if it was coming from his throat. I thought he was listening, but he was thinking. I could tell because his face always changes with the music when he listens.

"I guess they had to come after you sooner or later," he said.

"Me?"

"The orchestra." He nodded and looked up. "Just about the right time, too. Thirteen, fourteen years since it started? It figures."

"They didn't come after us. We struck. We started it."

"Don't give me that guilt *dreck*. Did you make up the issues? Or were they there? They started coming after you six years ago." He shook his head, so lightly the headphones didn't even move. "I should have warned you. I saw it coming. But I was selfish. I listened to your music instead. *That* was your fault. If the bunch of you didn't play like such angels . . . But I saw it. Just like the union." He looked up at me. "My union. Not yours." Then he corrected himself. "Maybe yours, too. I only know from mine."

I thought he was going fuzzy, but his eyes were still clear, and he kept them steady with mine. "The best was the beginning, Jack. 'Twenty-six, 'twenty-seven, 'twenty-eight. No one was sure of anything, then. Even *we* thought we were crazy. If somebody told us then that we would be paying off Presidents to take care of us, and they'd be paying us off to take care of them, we would have laughed. Nobody was sure of anything. That's how we knew we were right. There was no one to give us permission. We had no one to imitate. Then we were a community. An orchestra, like yours. We had to work to stay together. We had to tackle actions the way you tackle Bartók. Each of us—every one—by himself, had to decide. Then we were like that." He made a fist. It was weaker than the memory in his face. "And when we started to win, they came after us."

"Who's they, Poppa?"

"From so far off we didn't even see them. We were still so busy fighting we didn't even see we were winning. Or that they were coming. Then we heard voices. Like Jacob at Beth El. Even in jail we heard them. All around us. 'You're right,' they said. 'You're right. Come join us. Be right with us.' " He paused for a long time. He looked like he does when he talks about Momma in the hospital. "We were tired, Jack. There was a lot of blood. Real blood and real hunger, with all the fighting, and the sadness because we knew we were right, and the anger because we were never sure. So you hear voices from all around you like that, from the very people you fought and frightened last week. With the little energy you have left you celebrate, you offer your hand and believe you can make an even bigger community. And you don't pay attention to the other voice, the one inside that's warning you, 'They don't understand. They don't know how to make a union. They think the union will make them.' So you settle and so pretty soon the younger ones come along and they're right about new things, and angry because they're not so sure. You want so badly to join them, to have their energy again, but you can't. You know why? Because this time it's you they're fighting. And you hear your own voice saying, 'You're right. Be right with us. Settle.' Then you know you're old." For a minute it was so quiet I could hear the piano passages in the Beethoven. "Don't settle," he said.

I told him I thought we were still in control.

"Don't settle. I remember once when you must have been nine or ten and Lenny was—what?—sixteen—I was still going to meetings, still organizing. Momma said to me, 'Why don't you relax, Sy? It's over already. We've got Social Security. The work and the fighting are over. We're getting old.' I said to her, 'We'll get old, anyway. And the work is never over.' Don't settle." He leaned back in the armchair and closed his eyes. His eyebrows are white now, and his lids are thin like cigarette paper.

"Are you tired, Poppa?"

"You see what I mean? It used to be I could go on like that all night. And louder."

I said, "I know. I remember."

He smiled. "What do you hear from Molly?"

"Nothing yet. Transatlantic mail takes time. Marty called last week."

"You told me. Collect, right?"

I nodded. "And Anna won't call until Molly's back. She doesn't want to perpetuate the patriarchy."

"She's one of the new young ones."

"I'll tell you something, Poppa. So are you."

"And Lenny? Do you hear from Lenny?"

I hesitated. "He's a busy man."

"Busy, busy, huh?"

"Busy, busy. But I'm writing him. A long letter."

"That's nice."

"No," I said. "It's peculiar. It's a really long letter." Then I explained what I'm doing here.

He seemed to understand. He asked if I'd told about my bar mitzvah yet, about what happened. I told him I was planning to write about that next. And I was, too. And I will.

We were together for an hour. Driving home, I kept thinking about Marty and Anna. I wondered if one of them would someday be with me like that—and if they came to visit me in my last room with the music coming from so far away, if I would be able to tell them, "Don't settle."

Same day. After a break.

THE BAR MITZVAH

It was your idea. You were the one who convinced them I should play the violin instead of making a speech.

((48))

The bar mitzvah speech terrified me. I didn't mind the *b'rucha* and the *haftorah* at the service. That wouldn't be easy either, but I said to myself, You made it through your circumcision. You can make it through this. The speech was something else. There were three other boys being bar-mitzvahed that same morning. The rabbi had already told us there was no time for speeches. We'd have to give them afterward, each at his own party. I could see me, standing behind the dais, the top of my head just clearing the cake, my knees trembling, my voice choosing octaves with a will of its own. I knew I couldn't go through with it. I had dreams of doing it naked, of standing on the cake by mistake, of Uncle Oscar dissolving in gales of laughter.

I remembered when I was seven, helping you to rehearse your speech. "Sit on the bed and be Grandpa," you said to me. Then you stood in front of the dresser and turned to stone. You clamped your arms to your sides, palms at your thighs, feet spread slightly apart—a statue waiting for someone to measure your inseam. You forced your lips back in a smile and swiveled your head once, slowly. Your eyes were an inch behind. You looked at me. "Revered *zadeh*." The first time I giggled, but you jumped on the bed and punched me in the stomach. Then you went back to the dresser. After that, I tried to look old and nod. "Revered *zadeh*." You looked at the window. "Honored parents." You looked at the radio. "Rabbi Tannenbaum." You looked at your wall lamp. "Loving relatives and friends." Breath. "Today I am a man."

I couldn't. I knew I couldn't go through with it. I tried to rehearse in the room the way I'd seen you, but I ended up trembling and crying. One day you found me that way and I told you.

"I can't do it, Lenny. I'm not like you. I'm not brave.

They'll laugh at me. I'll forget everything. I'll disgrace us all. I'll get kicked out of being Jewish."

You said, "I felt the same way."

"Nobody would laugh at you. You play basketball. And my voice hasn't changed yet. Every time I answer the phone they say, 'Is your mother home, little girl?' How can I say, 'Today I am a man,' with a voice like that?"

You were nineteen and you understood. You could tell it was more than normal terror. And you came up with the idea of having me play the violin instead. It was the first time you tried to promote me. I loved you for it.

Poppa liked the idea from the first, but Momma was frantic.

"My sister Sarah will have gallstones. Right there in the hall."

"Why?"

"It's sacrilegious."

"It's holy," Poppa said. "It's a holy idea."

"If it's holy how come nobody's ever done it before?"

"That's what makes it holy."

"What does that mean?" She was always asking Poppa what he meant.

You said, "It's never been done before because nobody before Jackie ever had the talent to do it. The God-given talent, Ma."

"Sarah's expecting a speech."

"Esther, my darling. Your sister is not the high rabbi of Flatbush."

"My oldest sister—"

"If she were, she would clap her hands and dance in celebration because a new man can make a joyful noise."

"Don't get Old Testament with me, Sy. This is serious. We're talking about Jackie's bar mitzvah."

You said, "Do you think ice swans are wrong, Ma?"

"That's not a question."

"They didn't have ice swans before freezers. Somebody must have been the first to have ice swans at bar mitzvahs. Do you think it was wrong the first time? Every bar mitzvah has one thing special, one new thing. You expect it. Right?"

"I was thinking of flowers at each setting instead of a centerpiece." She knew it sounded lame.

"Ma, Ma! You're sitting here with something no one can match. It doesn't even cost. It's beautiful. It's an *expression* of something. Of your own son. He can get up and make the same jerky speech I made . . ."

"Your speech was beautiful. I could cry just thinking about it."

"It was a jerky speech, Ma. The same jerky speech every bar mitzvah boy makes. You cried because it was me and you were afraid I'd be a bum."

"And next year the Wharton School." She patted your face.

"We're not talking about me now. We're talking about Jackie. He can really say something. With his fiddle."

"Violin," Poppa corrected.

She thought for a moment. "What would you play?"

"I thought . . . some Bach."

Her lips quivered. "He wasn't even Jewish."

Poppa said, "We're talking about music now. Not tickets for the High Holy Days."

"Don't get socialist with me. If Trotsky wrote music you'd probably have Jackie play that."

"At least he was Jewish."

"All right. That's enough. Let me think about it. Only *you* have to tell my sister." In all my life I can't remember Momma ever saying, "Yes." She always let us know she'd committed herself without committing herself.

((51))

Aunt Sarah never even made it to my bar mitzvah. I think I conflicted with a wedding on Uncle Meyer's side. You know how that works. Weddings take precedence over bar mitzvahs; funerals over weddings; natural catastrophes over funerals. *Briths* are a sport. So she wasn't there.

Everyone else was, though.

We had a luncheon reception in the room upstairs at the synagogue. There was an even larger room in the basement, but the Pearlmutters got to it first. Dickie Pearlmutter was another bar mitzvah boy. Joel Townsend was the third. When the rabbi called our names at the service a buzz ran through two-thirds of the synagogue. "Townsend? Townsend? What kind of name is Townsend?"

I wasn't allowed into the reception right away. The caterer pulled me into a side room and told me to wait for my mother and father. We would make our entrance together. I tried to explain to him that I was a man, now, and could do what I wanted, but he screamed at me and said something about the affair downstairs being bigger.

I was alone for a long time. I practiced putting my hands in my pockets and walking without getting my jockey shorts caught. The bar mitzvah suit was a size too big because Momma figured I could wear it for affairs through 1948, but my underwear was tight and I had sweat a lot during the service.

By the time she came in with Poppa I was pretty much in control.

I put a hand in my pocket and said, "Hi," as though they were business acquaintances. "Some affair, huh?"

Momma said, "Take your hand out of your pocket. You look like you're playing with yourself."

The caterer came in and said, "Now? You ready?"

Poppa nodded.

The door swung open. The caterer stood in front of it, blocking us.

"Ladies and gentlemen," he said. "The bar mitzvah boy and his parents!"

He stepped aside. The crowd had organized itself around the tables. The center floor was empty. Across it was the dais, a long table with three vacant chairs dead center. Beside them, on one side, were you, Sammy Waldbaum, and Mitchell Cohen. Momma had told me I could invite two friends. They were the closest I could find. On the other side were Grandpa, Uncle Alex, and Aunt Florence. They were standing in for Aunt Sarah and Uncle Meyer. Grandpa should have been making the entrance with us, but his sight was starting to go from diabetes, and he said it would take forever to get across the room. It couldn't have taken longer than it felt.

Momma smoothed her dress just below the bust line and pulled herself up. Poppa put his hand on my shoulder and we were off.

The accordionist hit a fanfare, then broke into a harmonic minor. He played something that sounded like an Eastern European version of "Three Little Fishes."

The more we walked, the longer the room felt. The dais floated farther away with each step. Momma's face was grim, her lips locked tight. She thought she was smiling. Poppa kept his arm on my shoulder and once, when I thought my legs would give out, he patted me. Faces blurred. We passed Uncle Oscar's table six times. We're lost, I thought. We'll never find our way to the dais. We did, though. And when I was safely behind my chair I realized everyone was applauding. That made me tremble more. I still couldn't distinguish faces. All the guests were a mass of clapping hands and clutch bags and beaded sweaters.

The caterer stood in front of the dais.

"Ladies and gentlemen, the bar mitzvah boy will now say the *b'rucha* over the bread!"

Another fanfare from the accordion.

He handed me a big bread knife.

Fanfare.

I piped the blessing. The bread was a *chaleh* that looked like a huge tight hairdo. I cut into it.

Another fanfare and a collective "Ah!" Then everyone sat down to the fruit salad.

Once they stopped looking at me I was able to see them. Ten large round tables. Now I understood the folded diagrams Momma had carried in her pocketbook for six months and the incomprehensible conversations at the supper table.

"Meyer can't sit with Ben because Ruth and Ida don't get along."

"Since when?"

"Ida went to Florida and brought Ruth a coconut instead of oranges. It wasn't even the kind you could eat. It was one with a face. So Ruth says she's thoughtless and has no taste. Then Ida got mad because Ruth didn't put the coconut in her living room. So I'll put Ben and Ruth with Al and Millie and I'll put Meyer and Ida with Solly and Harriet. No. I can't do that. Ida's Howard got into Yale and Harriet's Arthur works for his father. I'll put Solly and Harriet with Ben and Ruth, too. That'll be Ben, Ruth, Al, Millie, Solly, and Harriet. That's six. There's room for three more at that table. Then I've got to find seven more to sit with Meyer and Ida. I could put them with your aunts and uncles, except they're very sensitive about age. They'd think I put them at the old people's table."

"My aunt Selma's younger than Ida."

"That doesn't matter. She's an aunt, not a sister."

"Oscar and Naomi! I can put them with Oscar and Naomi. Then the Pinkuses."

"Who are the Pinkuses?"

"Lorraine and Harvey. Oscar's daughter."

"How come Lorraine's invited and not Arthur and Howard?"

"Lorraine's married. Which reminds me. I'm putting Eva with Dave."

"My brother Dave does not want to get married again. His first marriage is still costing him."

"He hasn't met the right woman yet."

"He's met Eva. Don't put them together."

"Are you going to start on Eva's wen?"

"I didn't say anything about Eva's wen."

"If she were married she could afford some cosmetic surgery. Did you ever think of that?"

"I don't think about Eva's wen."

"Well, where should I put them then?"

"Put Eva at the table with my friends from the factory."

"With the *goyim?* I can't have Eva representing us. I'll put Dave with your friends. He can talk to *shvartzas.*"

"Juan Concepcion is not a *shvartza.* And please don't use that word in front of the children."

"All right. All right. And I'll put Eva with Ben, Ruth, Al, Millie, Solly, and Harriet."

They were all there. Momma's diagram had come to life—the apartment-house table, the married children's table, the socialists' table, three tables for good relatives, two for bad, one for neutral and emergencies. All the little boxes with names that had been penciled in, erased, written over, and erased again—they had turned into real tushies on real chairs and their owners were eating real grapefruit sections. It was as if Momma were a kind of composer. I'd been seeing her score on crumpled paper without understanding. Now they were playing it. This was the fruit-salad movement.

Toward the end you leaned across Poppa's back and punched me in the arm to get my attention. You pointed toward the accordionist.

"I set everything up over there. The music stand and the music. Your fiddle's near the wall. How do you feel?"

I nodded.

"You'll be great. Listen, when you dance with Momma, don't worry if she starts to cry."

I didn't know what you were talking about. No one had prepared me for that part. I'd forgotten it from your affair. It was only when the caterer reappeared and the accordionist hit another fanfare that I remembered. Momma was already adjusting her dress. All my body fluids rushed to my head. I wanted to leap across Poppa and plead with you to take my place. "I'm too short. I can't. I don't know how to . . ."

"Ladies and gentlemen, the bar mitzvah boy will dance the first dance with his mother."

Momma was up before he finished. I followed her to the huge empty dance floor. My knees had melted. We confronted each other, Momma and I. The accordion played "Always." Momma smiled proudly and waited for me to put my arm around her waist.

"That's by Irving Berlin," I said.

From behind her smile Momma said, "Dance."

I put my hand around her waist and she grabbed my other one. Everyone said "Ah" again.

I started to move. Momma was a rock. I froze. She was waiting for me to lead.

Her smile got tighter. Under her breath, she said, "One-two, three. One-two, three," and nodded. "Just push me. I'll go."

I put some pressure on her back and she moved her feet. I had never been in charge of so much living flesh in my life.

I shuffled around the floor with Momma nodding and keeping time in a whisper. Everyone applauded. Momma's smile relaxed; then, just as you predicted, her eyes filled with tears. She still whispered, "One-two, three," but there was a little catch in it.

Poppa cut in. I backed off and had to keep from running to my place at the dais. Poppa held her closer than I did. He managed her better, too. But as I left I heard her whisper "One-two, three," in his ear.

The floor was filled with dancers by the time I got back to the dais. Mitchell and Sammy were trying to squirt each other with leftover bits of grapefruit. You had gone to talk to Uncle Oscar. Alex and Florence were dancing. Grandpa leaned over and said, "Poppa says you're going to play." He had gotten into the habit of talking to people sideways, as if he was trying to see with his ear.

"Yes, sir."

"Something good?"

"Bach."

He considered it. "One of the violin sonatas?"

"The Second. Is that all right?"

He nodded hesitantly. "Bach is good." Then he fumbled for my knee and patted it. "Only they'll have to listen to that."

It was supposed to happen just before the cake. The caterer wheeled in the cart with an eight-layer frosted monument. On top stood a little boy doll, dressed in a blue suit, yarmulke, and tallis, holding a prayer book.

I started to get up. Poppa put a hand on my shoulder.

"I have to tune up," I said.

"After I introduce you."

"But . . ."

"They'll wait."

Momma rested her forearm on the table, trying to look relaxed. She was smiling, but she kept collecting crumbs with the edge of a matchbook, then dipping her finger in the pile and eating them. Every once in a while she would sigh.

Each table settled down and turned in our direction as the caterer passed with the cart. When it was almost quiet you grinned and locked your hands at me in the sign of the champ.

Poppa stood up. He looked around the room and nodded, smiling, at everyone. His voice was very soft, but they heard him in the back. I wasn't nervous anymore. After all, with Bach *and* Poppa behind me . . .

"Ladies and gentlemen," he said. "There's *naches* and *naches*, right?" A warm murmur came back, low laughter. One person clapped. "A lot of you know what's doing with Esther and me up here. You've been up here yourselves, so you know what's doing in our hearts. Right? And some others of you will. Soon. So you can imagine. A boy gets up in the temple and does what all of us did a hundred years ago and you know that his children will be doing it in a hundred years, too. And that's right and it's good. Especially in times like these. With what our people have been through. And what we have to look forward to. Now we can even dream of children doing what my Jackie did today in a place that's our own Jewish state. That's something, huh? After a nightmare to have a dream like that? So now it's time for Jackie to make a speech. That's like a hundred years ago, too. Right? First, when he reads the *haftorah* and says the *b'rucha,* he's saying, 'Today I am a Jew.' Then, when he makes a speech, he says, 'Today I am a man.' And when the bar mitzvah boy says he's a man, what does that mean? It means that he's a brother to every other man, Protestant, Negro, Chinaman, Hindu—a comrade."

Everyone shifted. There was a smattering of applause from the socialist table and Momma said, "No Trotsky, Sy."

"So Jackie understands that. And so Jackie is going to make his speech in a language that all his comrades will understand. And Esther and I would like to thank you all for coming today to share our joy and our pride and now we can say, 'Next year in Jerusalem,' with a special kind of hope. Yes?"

There was another murmur. Poppa started to sit. Momma poked him in the hip.

"Oh." He straightened up. "Jackie's going to play the violin." He sat down.

The voices swelled. Aunt Millie said, "I thought he was going to make a speech in Yiddish." Uncle Al said, "Right, Millie. That's just what a Chinaman needs." Someone else said, "He must have practiced."

I tuned the violin quickly. The hall's acoustics were flat. When I bowed the strings for tuning it felt as if the cake and coffee and the tablecloths soaked up the sound. That bothered me. There were special moments in the Bach, some of my favorites, that needed a live room. I loved the sonata, and I wanted them all to hear it. One movement especially, the third, was the most beautiful music I'd ever played. It was the reason I'd chosen the Second Sonata.

I finished tuning and cleared my throat.

"I'm going to play the A Minor Solo Sonata. By J. S. Bach. In four movements."

There was another, low "Ah," but it wasn't for the piece. It was a murmur of approval for the way I said it. I wanted to say, "No, no. Don't listen to me. Listen to the music," but

I knew that wouldn't help. Besides, I was sure that when I started the music would take over.

The first movement flowed. Once I had the instrument under my chin there was only the music. I was even glad my suit was too big. It gave me freedom in my bowing arm. A couple of times someone coughed or clinked a coffee cup, but none of it got in the way of the music. Even in the dead room the Bach sailed out to the farthest table.

At the end of the first movement someone applauded. Someone else shushed him. I'm used to that now, but it surprised me then, and I looked up during the rest. Aunt Millie was smiling and crying. I was baffled. The first movement was somber, yes, but it was nothing to cry about. Or smile about. All the others were smiling, too. Uncle Ben made an impressed face at Momma. No one had heard the music. They were all looking at me. Their smiles were smiles of approval for a little boy who was doing well. They weren't listening.

I raised the violin to my chin again. The second movement, the fugue, had the most complex development. They would have to hear that. My bowing was more insistent, too insistent. I was so determined to make them hear what I heard that I turned it harsh and lost control. It was a shambles. It felt interminable. I cut through every repeat.

At the end they were still smiling. There was a larger smattering of applause. I wanted to simply bow and leave it at that. If Poppa hadn't been there, I might have. But he knew there were two more movements to go. I glanced up at him. When our eyes met he closed his lightly and nodded assurance. I clamped my jaw and raised the violin again. A couple of faces stopped smiling. They hadn't realized it would go on so long.

I tore into the andante. They couldn't miss that one. It

had the richest melodic line, the kind they could go home humming. Before it was even established, the shuffling and coughing began. They'd had enough of me and had never wanted the music. If I'd made a speech it would have been over already. Ten minutes. No more than that ever. Just enough time for the aunts to coo and the uncles to approve. With a speech there was no time to listen, nothing to listen to, and the bar mitzvah boy never knew what he was saying anyway. I knew what I wanted to say—and no one was hearing. I wanted to turn invisible, to become transparent so they'd have to hear the sounds they were killing now with the shuffling, coughing, whispering. I didn't even take the rest between the andante and the last, allegro movement. I paused just long enough to reposition my fingers, then attacked. I sped through it, fumbling, slurring. My fingers jammed, and I had to force back the tears to keep the notes on the page from blurring. I didn't even care about Poppa anymore. I cut through to the end, botched the last run, and ended up playing just like the little boy they had all been smiling at in the beginning.

They burst into applause. I let go of the tears and ran through the noise to the little room where I'd waited before. I slammed the door and sat huddled on the floor in the farthest corner of the room. I kept my hands over my ears until the applause stopped. I stared at the violin and bow in my lap, trying to work up the courage to break them both on the table.

That was how you found me. The accordion had started again. It suddenly got very loud and the laughter and clatter of tableware with it. You had opened the door and poked your head in. Your face was flushed with excitement. You didn't see me at first. "Jackie?"

"Leave me alone, you fucker."

It helped you locate me.

"What the hell are you doing there?"

"Leave me alone."

"Everybody's asking for you."

"Close the door."

"Jackie?"

"Close the door!"

You shut it and got on one knee in front of me. "What's the matter, babe?"

While I was alone I'd gotten control of myself, but the excitement and utter lack of comprehension on your face released another angry flood of tears. "It's your fault!" I tried to punch your face, but I was still all huddled up and hampered by the violin. I just kind of pushed your jaw with my knuckles. You grabbed my wrist. I snatched it away and banged my elbow against the wall. Then I pulled the violin to me and cradled it in my arms.

"You nut."

"It's your fault."

"What did I do?"

"It was your idea. You talked them into it. You talked *me* into it."

"But you were terrific."

I held the violin tighter and made a growling noise.

"Everybody's talking about it. They want to see you."

I shook my head.

Even on one knee you were a foot above me. You wore a gray gabardine suit. It was your Burt Lancaster period so you had this great pompadour wave in your hair and a very fat knot in your tie. You kept puffing liquor at me. You were the man I was supposed to have become.

"Poppa wants you."

"No!" I practically wailed it.

"What's the matter with you?"

"You don't even know," I said. "That makes it worse."

"You upset because you made a couple of mistakes? Jesus, you can't be such a perfectionist, Jackie."

"You're as bad as the rest of them."

"Everybody out there thinks you're terrific. You *are* terrific. And you sit in here like a little baby, sulking."

"Sure. Sure. Everybody thinks *I'm* terrific."

"What's wrong with that?"

I clenched my teeth and growled again. "They didn't . . . They didn't hear the music."

There's a certain look you get on your face. I've only seen it happen with me. It's a mixture of confusion and anger— and sadness when I do things that are absolutely incomprehensible. Your lips get tight. Your eyes look as if they're about to laugh—but they flash instead, and your forehead wrinkles. That happened to you then. "I'll go get Poppa."

"No."

"Goddamn it, Jackie, you want everything at once. You think you can have it all. Just because you're a little special you think you can have it all."

"Leave me alone."

"What about me?"

"What do you have to do with it?"

"It was my idea. Remember? And I'm proud of you."

"That's 'cause you're like the rest of them."

"And you're a little snot."

"That's tough."

"Why don't you grow up?"

"Why don't you all let me?"

"How? Leave you alone here to sulk?"

"Yeah. Just don't pay any attention to me."

We were both quiet. I hugged my violin. You were deciding whether to slam out of the room or try to reach me again. You went to the door. "You know, you made a lot of people really happy out there."

"Poppa's not happy."

"Why don't you ask him? And what about all the others?"

"I know *I* made them happy." I tried to keep my face from crinkling. "Not the music."

"You're a spoiled brat."

"And you're stupid."

"You think you have a right to decide what makes people happy? You're a spoiled brat."

"You just leave me alone."

"You're spoiling everything for everyone."

"I don't care."

"You can't have it all your own way."

"Then what's the use—" I gulped and shrugged again. "I'm just not good enough. That's all. I wasn't good enough to make them hear."

"You going to get better in here?" That made me look at you. It was the first time I'd ever seen your face so tough, and heard your voice so sharp.

I looked down at the violin and fingered it a little.

"You want me to wait for you?"

I shook my head and you left me alone.

I finally made it out. For the rest of the afternoon uncles came up to me with checks in their hands. Some stuffed them in my pockets; some shook my hand and left them crumpled in my palm; a few congratulated me, then deposited their gifts with Momma. Aunts kissed me, older cousins patted me. Nobody said a word about the performance.

When they were gone, Poppa told you and Momma to drive Grandpa home. He asked if I'd like to walk home alone with him. "It would be a nice way to end," he said.

We took the same route I'd taken on my bike for four years. It was another spring.

On the way he said to me, "It wasn't just a celebration, Jackie. You learned a little something today. Yes?"

I said, "Yes."

"From your audience?" He put his arm around my shoulder.

"From my brother," I told him.

It's noon. I'm in the dressing room at the Arts Center. I just left Arthur Quasnosky's house and I've got an hour or two before I go see Poppa. Figured I'd duck into the hall and keep writing this letter instead of wasting the time it would take to go home.

I tell you, Lenny, this thing is getting to be a little bit of an obsession with me. I carry around pads and pens wherever I go—just in case I have a little time. Everything I do, every phone call, every time I go out to buy a bottle of Cremora, I ask myself if I should include it in the letter. Stray bits of memory float up when I don't even think I'm thinking about you. And last night I had a dream that was a doozy. It would have given Molly a month of laughs. No, I'm not going to go into the whole thing here. If I started telling you my dreams we'd never get anywhere. I just want to record one remarkable thing. You weren't in it at all. I know. That's not so remarkable. Except it was about you. All the time I was dreaming I was thinking, Where's Lenny? This dream is about him, but he's not here. Where is he? *Nu?* Where were you?

Arthur Quasnosky is in bad shape. When I called last night to ask if I could come over he started snarling. When I got there this morning he was in the middle of the same snarl.

He's a fat man. Always has been. The only place his sickness shows is in his face. So he's got this drawn, thin man's face on a fat man's body. His eyes are hollow, but he shifts them as if they were still narrow. Nobody's sure which bones the cancer's affected already. Ed says it's pretty much spread through his whole body. He's in pain every time he moves. He won't let it show, though. He still walks and he still plays, but it's all incredibly stiff—except for his wrists. When he bows the bass and even when he fingers it, more and more slowly and stiffly each concert, his wrists still flow.

His house is a huge old Victorian on a street full of them. All the others were turned into boardinghouses sometime in the Thirties. They all look held together by hooks and eyes, with sagging wraparound porches, broken rockers, scratched VACANCY signs, and tired, dirty magnolias in back. Arthur's is the only house without a sign. The porch has collapsed. A narrow set of steps leads to a kind of platform in front of the door.

I waited a good ten minutes before he answered the bell. He stared as if he was trying to place me, then turned away and started down the hall. "Housekeeper's gone," he said, and disappeared into the music room. He'd left the door open. That was his way of telling me to follow him.

I guess he's taken to pretty much living in that room. The drapes are closed over a huge bay window that looks out on the collapsed porch and Orange Street. His bass and his music stand are near the window, next to a magnificent

Steinway. There's a daybed against one wall with an Oriental spread, and he's got a stereo system that makes Poppa's look like a crystal set. I figured the housekeeper must have just left after vacuuming, making up the daybed, and polishing the piano. I stopped at the door. It was like one of those rooms they rope off in museums.

Arthur was inside, heading for another door. "You're here on business," he said. "We'll go into the kitchen. This room's for the music." And he disappeared again.

When I got to the kitchen I knew the housekeeper hadn't just left. There were dirty dishes scattered over all the counters. Bags of garbage leaned against the sink. The floor crunched underfoot. The room smelled of cigarettes and rotting fruit. When he said the housekeeper was gone, he meant for good—and she'd left weeks before. Whatever energy he had for keeping himself together he'd put into the other room.

There was a huge oval table in the center of the kitchen with one overflowing ashtray. He picked it up to empty it. I went to help him but he pushed away my hand and spilled the ashes in the process. He glared at me, then limped to the sink to get a sponge.

"Just sit down. I'll take care of it."

He had to make two trips to the sink. First to collect all the butts in the ashtray and empty them on top of one of the garbage bags, then to wipe up the ashes. He left gray streaks on the tabletop. When he got back the second time he was wheezing.

He eased himself into a chair across from me and waited, just wheezing and staring at me. All the ways I'd planned to break in, all the small talk and hearty questions fell out of my head. All I could do was stare back and wait for the wheezing to stop.

He put his arms on the table and said, "Well? Do I go back to work?"

I started thinking Ed Lewis was right. We'd all been out of our minds to make Quasnosky the issue. The man was dead on his feet. Maybe the best thing for him, after all, was to get him the hell out of the orchestra, get him the hell out of town and into a hospital, where he could wheeze away and die in some kind of peace. I'd come braced to talk to the bastard I'd always known. Now all I had on the other side of the table was his pain. I couldn't imagine how he'd make it to a rehearsal even if there was one.

He waited for me to say something. His face was a mixture of expectation and contempt.

I shook my head. "Not yet."

"Well, why don't all you bleeding-heart liberals get on the stick?"

"It takes time," I said.

"I don't have any time."

"We've called a meeting for tomorrow."

"A meeting's not music."

"I know."

"What do you know?"

There was a long pause. I filled it by thinking what I would say if he offered me coffee. He never did.

"Well, what's going on?"

"The union men are in from Nashville. They're taking over for Jenkins."

He nodded. "Jenkins never knew what the hell he was doing."

"They've got ideas for a compromise settlement. They want a meeting of the full orchestra."

He shot me a suspicious look and pulled a cigarette out of his shirt pocket. I've never seen a cigarette look as deadly as it did in his mouth. He never took it out either, just let it dangle there, dropping ashes on his shirt and pants.

"You didn't get your ass all the way over to Orange Street to tell me there was a meeting. What do you want?"

What I wanted was to kill him. I'll tell that to you, Lenny, and not to anybody else in the world. What I wanted was to find some way to make all that wheezing, wincing, angry flesh just disappear. He sat there with this cigarette dangling from his mouth, his stained white shirt pulling against his stomach, and I couldn't imagine what the negotiations were all about.

I told him about the meeting with Gwynne and Dowd. It was insane, talking about pay increments, artistic control— even retirement. His face contorted once, as if he was wincing, but he never finished. He just stayed all pinched and concentrating on whatever it was that was happening inside him. And I went on like a madman, explaining about restraining orders and feasibility studies.

When I finished, Quasnosky said, "So?"

"So the meeting is to vote on whether we want the package —or if we stay out."

"If you take the package Lewis retires me."

I nodded, trying to avoid his eyes.

He gave a short, bitter laugh. "And if you stay out. Does that give me a chance to play?"

"Well, at least there's a chance."

"What are you telling me about, Fleischman? Hope?"

"Arthur . . ."

"What did you come here for? You still haven't told me why you're in my house."

"The strike committee asked me to . . . find out if you're coming to the meeting."

"Are you going to everybody's house?"

((70))

I shook my head.

"Why mine?"

"It hinges on you. You know that."

He made a snorting sound and took the cigarette out of his mouth with his first two fingers. It was one of those dainty gestures only fat people can make. "You guys are really something, you know that? Querault, Carnovsky, Rogers. All of you. You're really something. Nobody asked you to go out in the first place."

"We know that."

"I wouldn't go out for a dying man who can't play worth a damn anymore, and hasn't for three years. I wouldn't stop the music for that."

"We know that, too."

"What's it supposed to prove? That you're all better than me?"

"No, Arthur." His pain and his bile were starting to exhaust me.

"All you loose-assed liberals get your rocks off showing how much you care about people. Whacking off on your own charity. Holland and Cross have been doing it for three years, covering for me. And you want to know what I think about you and your committee and Holland and Cross and all the rest of you? I think it stinks." He was wheezing again, but he lit another cigarette. "The music's more important. And if I had someone sick and useless in my orchestra I'd do just what Lewis is doing, only I'd do it sooner, the first time he missed a bar. Because the music's more important." He shifted stiffly. "And if I come to the meeting, that's what I'll say."

"Are you going to?"

His eyes shot up at me. There was a look on his face I'd never seen before. No matter how many ways his face changed for the rest of the morning, that was the look that stayed with me. It was a look of fear and of yearning that cut through all the pain and contempt and bitterness that had filled his eyes before. It lasted only an instant, then all the rest flooded back, but it told me the one thing Quasnosky would never have been able to. He wants to stay. He knows he's useless, he sneers at us for fighting to keep him and despises us for caring about a disruptive and incompetent dying man more than the music, but he wants to stay. Maybe because he's afraid and carries that fear around with his rotting bones wherever he goes, and maybe because it's only when he's in the middle of the music that he's a little less afraid.

"I don't know," he muttered. "I already made some appointments for tomorrow."

I nodded as if I believed him.

"I might, though. I might . . . cancel my appointments." He glanced around the kitchen. "Little nigger kid's supposed to come later and clean this up," he said. "I don't know, though. You can't depend on them."

He straightened up with one sharp movement. It was a pain that must have jolted through him. He reached into his pocket and pulled out a bottle of pills. "Get me a glass of water."

I went to the sink and found a clean glass.

"Hurry it up."

I cleared the sink enough to fit the glass under the tap and filled it.

He took the pill. His cigarette had dropped from his mouth when the pain hit him. It was smoking on the floor near his feet. I picked it up and held it, waiting for instructions. Both of us waited for his body to relax back. He motioned me to stub the cigarette out, then he caved back in the chair.

"I'm supposed to take it every two hours. But I like to see how much more I can go. Waited too long." Then, after a minute, he said, "You know why I like you, Fleischman?"

"I didn't know you did."

"You know your music. You're soft and you've got a lot of half-baked yid-liberal northern ideas—but you know your music."

I thought about saying, "Thanks."

"You remember when I did that string sonata? What's-his-name's? You know, the nigger composer. Ulysses Kay."

It was in 1965, a memorial concert for Martin Luther King.

"Afterward everybody was carrying on, all the liberals were crying and Carnovsky was clenching his fist and the house with the red carpet looked like the inside of a water-melon. People were shaking my hand, even Lewis was dewy-eyed. Well, in the middle of it all you passed by me on the way downstairs. You remember what you said?"

I remembered. "You missed a G sharp in the second movement."

He nodded. "That's when I found out you know your music."

I'd lost three nights' sleep over that. I'd said it for spite. The whole concert was one of those charged affairs. Arthur had been poisoning it for weeks. We played Scott Joplin, Kay's sonatas, W. C. Handy, and ended with Ellington's *Mass*. And Arthur had a lot to say, loudly, about the color of the scores. At the same time he wasn't letting anyone else solo. He played magnificently. I hated him for it, and I hated myself for wanting all his meanness and ignorance to be exposed in the music. So when it was over and I saw him getting his due as a musician, I couldn't stand it. I said it to him. "You missed a G sharp in the second movement."

"Nobody else heard that note," Quasnosky said.

"Maybe they did."

He took another cigarette and pointed it at me. "But you said something about it."

There was a short silence.

"Well, what time's the meeting?" he said.

"Two-thirty. At the hall."

He nodded.

"What should I tell the committee, Arthur?"

"Let 'em stew." He paused. "I'm not making it easier for anybody."

I gave a short laugh. "Which would make it easier? Coming or staying?"

He stared at me. "I got to lie down, Fleischman. You want anything else?"

I stood up. "No. I guess that about wraps it up." I wanted to ask if he needed help, if I could send someone in to look after him, but his whole face warned me. He lit another cigarette and I found my own way out.

I called Dudley as soon as I got here. Told him I wasn't sure, but I thought Arthur would be there.

Later

Back home after some time with Poppa. The meeting's at two-thirty tomorrow. The rest of the committee's contacting everybody else. I don't have to call anyone. They all agreed my one visit was worth ten phone calls. I'll tell them sometime who got the old fiddle bow on that bargain.

The house hasn't been so quiet since the strike began. I thought everybody would have been calling me to find out what happened this morning, but I guess they're treating it like a crime of violence—everybody's curious but no one wants to ask for particulars.

Poppa did.

His eyes were twinkling the old Sy Fleischman twink, part mischief, part fight. He said he hoped Arthur would come tomorrow. "So the action can start making some sense," he said.

I said I wasn't so sure it didn't make sense now.

He said, "No action makes sense till it's over. That's when you see what you've done—and why you've done it. And I'm starting to wonder if you all know why you're fighting for Quasnosky."

"He was a gorgeous musician."

"Feh. That's not a reason."

I looked at him, shocked.

"Stop bulging your eyes. Tell me something. No. Don't tell me. Just ask yourself. Why are you fighting for Quasnosky? If it's because he was once a good musician you're in trouble, because he's not now and even he knows that—and that means you're fighting for a thing that's already a corpse. Do you understand what I'm saying, Jackie? You'll lose. You'll compromise. You'll settle, if that's your reason. Nobody wins actions for corpses. But if you're staying out because he's still alive, because he's a human being who needs something to give whatever is left of his life some dignity, some sense of community, even if he hasn't asked for it, even if he throws it back in your face, then what you're doing is going to make some sense. And if it's the live human being you're fighting for, then he should be there so you can all look at him and listen to him, and despise him and still decide to fight for him." He pointed his finger at me. "*That's* a radical action, Jackie. You know what I mean? And only radical actions win."

And if that's not enough to field for one day, guess what's waiting for me when I get home. A letter from Molly. It's dated the eighteenth, which means she probably carried it around for a week in her briefcase on top of the infant-frustration paper. She must have written it after she got my night letter about you. I'll Xerox it tomorrow and put it in right here. You'll see. She talks about you—almost predicts this whole letter.

Vienna
July 18, 1975

Darling,

I don't know how it works, but they already know about Lenny over here. The first day of the conference people kept coming up and congratulating me. As if I had anything to do with it. I was a little pissed because some of them thought I was his mother. It made me decide to lay off the strudel for the rest of the conference. I think probably the Washington contingent let the news out. Maybe something happens to the patient-analyst privilege when you cross the international date line. Mouths are flapping about everything. Gossip, state secrets, unpublished manuscripts, new information on Judge Crater. The bar at the cocktail hour is a Dionysian orgy, analyst-style. Everyone's letting out repressed session notes. Some are making them up, too, I think. The news about Lenny isn't supposed to go public for another two or three weeks and it's supposed to be a big deal because of a couple of other shifts and resignations that are going to go with it. So it's really a tribute to you that he said anything so early.

My paper went well. They gave me a very big room and the audience was divided in four sections. Freudian, Jungian, Adlerian, and Others. A lot of the Others were TA barbarians who didn't listen to the paper. They just kept watching everybody else listen. Anyway, the Journal of the American Academy of Child Psychology *(which is mainly this one little man in a walker) wants to publish it. So you see? Five years of research were worth it. They'll publish it, everyone will footnote it, no one will read it, and analysts will go on thinking everything is Oedipal, anyway.*

What I know about Vienna right now is what I see through the doors of the hotel lobby. It was a mistake getting a room in the same hotel as the conference. The sessions will be over in a couple of days, though. Then I can get to the concerts and parks and museums. Everybody's making big moral decisions about whether they should go to Freud's house. One group calls it fetishism. Another calls it historical fixation. I'm going. I want to see how many rooms his wife had to keep clean.

Which reminds me. I got a letter from Anna. Her big news is that her summer course helped her stop having menstrual cramps. She also says we should learn to be sisters. I wrote her back, "It took twenty years to learn how to be a mother. Don't confuse me. P.S. Your patriarchal oppressor is on strike. You could call and find out how things are." Also a card from Marty. With writing up the side. I couldn't read his handwriting but it was nice to hear from him.

I'm happy for Lenny. I think he's getting what he always wanted. Assurance. And I think there's enough of your father still in him to keep him human. I'm glad I don't know all our world leaders as well as I know Lenny. I love him, Jack. You know that. Because he's your brother. And because I know how vulnerable he is under all that nervous brilliance. I know how you confuse him and how much he needs your admiration and approval. Did you know that? I've told you before, but I don't know if you ever heard.

((77))

*I've seen my patients tune out on what they can't believe
—or can't afford to—so I can tell when you do it. That's
why I thought I'd mention it again. For your sake. And
for his. He wrote and told you before it was official. That's
a big opening for communication. I think it's an opportunity. For both of you. I think you'll do something with
it.*

*I hate writing letters, Jack. Remember? That's why I
told you not to write me. So I wouldn't have to answer.
The only reason I'm writing this is because you broke the
bargain first. But enough is enough. In two weeks I'm off
to Edinburgh. I'll send you a card. With writing up the
side.*

Love,
M

*P.S. Dr. Lampert and I had a long discussion about what
it means when a man sends his wife a night letter about
his brother's new job and doesn't say a word about his own
strike negotiations. Think about it. We'll compare notes
when I get home. In the meantime, don't write. I get the
Atlanta papers from an international kiosk in the hotel.
I'm proud of you.*

M

I don't think she'll mind if I put her letter in here. If I
know that woman's mind, she expects me to do something
like that. That is a person and a half, that lady. Someday,
maybe, you'll get to know her. I mean really know her. Then
you'll have such a treat. I always wondered if the only reason
you were never able to let yourself get close to her was because she was an analyst. People get so nervous when they

find out somebody's an analyst, as if all their deepest, most incestuous secrets are going to come out from the way they sneeze. Don't think I didn't have trouble with that at first, too. It was even worse then. She was still a graduate student so she thought she *could* know everything. Did I ever tell you about our courtship? The whole story? No, it's not time for that yet. I'll put it down on my little pad as a note for later.

Anyway, what she says about you in her letter isn't a professional diagnosis. It's a sister-in-law's affection. Believe me. And a wife's love. I'll tell you something, Lenny. I miss her.

First phone call since I've been home. Dowd and Gwynne want the committee to meet at noon tomorrow to prepare for the big meeting. Until then I'm on my own. So here's what I'm going to do. I'm going to slip a Swanson into the oven and have a forty-five-minute bourbon while I listen to three Mozart concerti which just happen to have been recorded in Vienna. Then I'm going to unplug the phone, pull all the drapes, turn out all the lights, and take you upstairs with me where we can be alone and undisturbed.

You see, I think I know where this letter is going now. I'm pretty sure of what's going to be with it. And as I get more and more sure of that, I get less and less sure of what's going to happen tomorrow afternoon. And I'm getting a little nervous. So at least if I don't know where I'll be in a week or two, it's good to be sure I'm starting to know where I've been for the past forty years.

When I start up again here I'm going to tell you about all those years you were away from home and I was growing up. The way I figure it, sitting upstairs at my desk with the one secret light on in an empty house, it will be like writing a novel. Which is something I've always wanted to do.

((79   ))

GLIMPSES OF LENNY

You were gone so suddenly. Two months after the bar mitzvah it was summer and we were off to separate camps, you to be basketball coach at Wa-na-ha-ta-in-the-Catskills for overweight boys, I to an experimental camp Poppa had found where the campers did all the farming and building and were told we owned the camp. They also taught us home crafts in a huge cabin that another summer of owners had built. There was a big picture of William Morris in it, hung over a loom. On Sunday nights we pushed the loom and the pottery wheels to one side and learned to be creative through modern dance. Naomi Fenker gave us a demonstration with a thing she called "Self and Society." The center of the floor was "Self," and the walls of the cabin were "Society." She put a 78-rpm record of *Rite of Spring* on the Victrola and ran back and forth between the walls and the center of the floor with her eyes very wide to show she couldn't decide. Sometimes she would run to the Victrola to change the record and then she was terrific because she danced on the soles of her feet, but she ran on her heels, and when she ran her boobs bounced under her leotard. Watching Naomi Fenker run to change records is my first clear memory of lust. That's why I mention it.

After the summer you were home two weeks. I started at James Madison. I was always the youngest in my class, so I spent most of my elementary and high school career trying to avoid being squashed by my classmates. I was so nervous and excited about starting high school I didn't realize you were actually leaving home. It seemed as though you had just enough time to count your tips from the summer, hint darkly about a few new positions you'd learned, and you were gone.

Poppa drove you to Philadelphia. Momma and I had been planning to go, too, but by the time you loaded the old Packard with your suitcases, cartons, sports equipment, Benny Goodman, Harry James, and Bunny Berigan records, there was no room. We waved you off down Kings Highway from the bedroom window.

Momma turned away and started for the door without letting me see her face. "I'm going to strip the sheets," she shouted over her shoulder. "From now on don't mess up the bedspread." I realized the room was mine.

I ran to the living room, gathered up my violin, my music and my stand, and brought them in. Now I could practice anytime I wanted. I could close the door and even if my sounds seeped through, I still wouldn't have to think about Momma, only two arches away, writing reviews for *The New York Times* in her head. I pushed the dresser to one side and cleared a practice area. I went to the desk and slid the radio to the side near my bed. I rearranged the drawers. I had one deep drawer, the one that pulled out sideways and stuck. All my books and old decoding rings, loose-leaf papers, recital programs, a walkie-talkie from Captain Midnight, a folded, full-color picture of Roy Rogers on Trigger that I got for being 252d runner-up in a contest to name Trigger's new colt, my ball of silver foil that I'd started six years before as my contribution to the war effort, three boxes of broken colored pencils, and a book on muscle building I'd sent for from a Donald Duck comic book, all lay jumbled in the one drawer that only came halfway out, anyway. Now I could sort it out and arrange it. All the drawers were mine.

I was just trying to decide which one to use for miscellaneous when Momma finished smoothing the spread over your empty bed. She looked at me with cold eyes. "Vulture," she said, and gathered up the sheets on her way out. I shrugged and went back to work. I was thirteen and a half. For the first time in my life I had a room of my own.

It was only that night, when I lay in bed in the dark, that I realized having a room of my own meant not having you in there with me. I thought about you and sniffed. I wasn't crying. I was checking to see if the room still smelled of your feet. You always wore athletic socks and left them lying on the floor inside out. Over the years the smell had permeated the room. Every night you gave it a little booster as you padded around barefoot, wafting the day's exercise. It was all that was left of you. In a few months that would probably be gone, too. I tried to see your face but I couldn't. That made me feel terrible. You hadn't even been gone a day and I couldn't remember your face.

I remembered coming into the room for the past two years and finding you scrunched over your desk. At the beginning of your senior year in high school you decided to get serious about school. So there you'd be every night, struggling to concentrate on your homework over the music from WNEW. Sometimes you'd even have your hands over your ears. Once I asked why you didn't turn off the radio, and you explained that even though you were getting serious you had to keep up with the real world. I would miss finding you like that.

I would miss finding saucers filled with orange peel and pits on the desk, and an old T-shirt or purple knit tie of yours lying on my bed, which meant that you had no more use for it. You were never able to actually offer me anything, but somehow the signal had been arranged. If it was on my bed, I had inherited it. Once I tried giving you an old loose-leaf binder because I knew you needed something to keep all your basketball clippings in. I left it on your bed. That night I found it back on mine.

I would miss watching you shave twice a week. It took a

half hour each time. You laid out the mug and brush Poppa had given you, the safety razor, a face towel, and a styptic pencil. You treated it as a ritual. First came the Slow Preparation of the Soap, then the Lathering of the Face, the careful scrape, scrape of the razor, the Washing and the Drying, and the Stanching of the Blood where you'd opened up pimples. I thought about you shaving but I still couldn't see your face. I could see the way the lather made your teeth look yellow and the soapy rectangles you drew with the razor. I tried to imagine you shaving, step by step, until all the lather was gone. But your face always disappeared with it.

Once I caught a glimpse of your eyes in my head. For an instant you were there, your whole face and body, but it was gone just as quickly. I had thought of you, two years before, on a Saturday morning after a fight with Momma. I came in and found you holding tight to one of the knobs on the bedstead. When you saw me you said, "I gotta get out of here." Your eyes were haunted. They were usually soft and cool-looking. Someone once told you your eyes looked like Robert Mitchum's. After that you learned how to look heavy-lidded and ironic. This time, though, they were wide, with a little white showing at the bottom. Your mouth was tight. I couldn't understand why that was the only image of you I could summon up. "I've gotta get out of here," you said. "This room is too fucking small."

Now you were out, but as I lay there alone in the dark I couldn't imagine anyplace bigger or emptier. I promised myself I would study your face, store it away, the next time I saw you. Then, on other lonely, frightening nights like this one, I could take it out and have it.

Thanksgiving was my first chance. Momma had written to ask you home for at least one of the High Holidays; you wrote back you were already over your head in work. You promised you'd cut classes, though, and fast on Yom Kippur.

By Thanksgiving I'd taken possession of the room. I followed Momma's orders and never messed up your bedspread, but your bed had become a very small island in the middle of my own new life. I had put up a bulletin board with school posters and pictures of friends, also a picture of Joan Leslie, whom I had fallen in love with one Saturday afternoon at the Avalon. My music lay scattered over the top of the dresser. Three small plaster busts of Bach, Mozart, and Beethoven surrounded the radio. Momma and Poppa had given me a typewriter for my bar mitzvah. That was on the desk, too, and I had taken to typing out wise sayings and Scotch-taping them to the walls around my bed. I woke up every morning to things like "Human kind cannot bear very much reality. T. S. Eliot," and "Beauty is truth, truth beauty. John Keats," and "The weed of crime bears bitter fruit. The Shadow." Momma would yell at me for that sometimes. "If you want wisdom for frontlets between your eyes, I'll get you *t'fillin,*" she said. "But your signs are ruining the paint job." I kept being stunned by new, deep ideas, though. So the signs kept going up.

I hadn't realized how much I had made the room my own until you came home. You bounced in and plunked your suitcase next to the bed. You didn't seem to notice the changes. You said, "Hey, Jackie, how you doing?" and shifted the radio back to your side.

We stayed around the kitchen table a long time after supper. Momma worked on preparations for the next day, hauling out pots and serving dishes. You and Poppa talked over coffee and schnapps. I watched, remembering my vow to study your face.

It wasn't easy. The Lenny who had left three months before was not the Lenny who'd come back. I suppose you had

((84   ))

been growing and changing all the time we lived together. Seeing you every day, though, and changing right alongside, I hadn't noticed. As I sat at the kitchen table I knew that the Lenny I had tried to remember was gone. There was no reason to remember the new one.

You had, for instance, grown handsome. Your nose had always been a little too big for your face. You tended to hold your head at a slight droop, partly because it was the style, more, I think, to hide your nose. It didn't work. It only made it look as if your nose was pulling your whole face down. You must have been fleshing out for over a year without my noticing. The rest of your face had caught up with your nose. Your good, strong mouth and brown eyes had come into their own. You were a college man.

I have a snapshot that was taken the next night. I just pulled it out to verify my memory. You're sitting between Aunt Sarah and Momma, smiling at the camera. You look like a pimply sophomore. Your hair is short and your ears stick out and your smile is fatuous. It doesn't matter. As far as I was concerned, you'd taken care of all your rites of passage. You were as tempered as Thor Heyerdahl, as wise as my English teacher, as suave as Ronald Colman. The only thing youthful about you was your eyes. They were bright and excited that first night as you answered Poppa's questions. I stared, trying to decide whether to use your face to reconstruct the old Lenny or to work at memorizing the new.

Sometimes I glanced at Poppa. I thought he looked puzzled. You were telling him about your economics courses, using college language. If I'd been a little older I would have known he wasn't puzzled. He was worried. You had discovered Adam Smith and Keynes. You were telling him about *The Wealth of Nations*. He kept nodding. He saw how excited you could get about ideas; and if there was one thing he cherished more than Momma, it was the minds of his children. He saw yours come alive that night in ways he had never seen before. He wasn't about to interfere with that. But every once in a while, as you talked about haves and have-nots, free enterprise, capitalism, self-interest and the profit motive, Poppa would raise his eyebrows and ask, "You believe that?"

You would stop a second, then you'd say, "It's in Adam Smith."

It seemed like a good enough answer to me, but Poppa's eyes looked distant, even behind the nodding, and once I saw him wince at Momma.

Then you said, "But I'm not just learning in my classes," and it looked as though he was going to relax. "It's the whole life there. When I got down there I thought I was really a big shot, you know? I was from Brooklyn and I thought that was a pretty big deal. You know what I mean?"

"It's not a small deal. It's not a big deal," Poppa said. "It's not a deal."

"You know what I mean. All-city basketball. James Madison High School. Brooklyn, New York. I thought I had everything." You looked at Poppa the way I'd seen certain teachers look at kids they were going to punish for their own good. "Poppa." You said it very seriously and sadly. "You don't know it, but we're outsiders."

Poppa said, "What is it you're trying to tell me, Leonard?"

"I thought Brooklyn was the whole world. I thought being king of East Twenty-seventh Street was the most important thing you could be."

"You're king of East Twenty-seventh Street?"

You blushed. "I was a pretty important guy in the neighborhood."

Poppa looked mystified, so I explained. "Lenny was the

first to wear blue suede shoes." Momma tapped me on the head with a basting brush.

"I was always a part of the inside crowd. You know what I mean?"

Poppa shook his head.

Momma said, "Dubrow's and the poolroom."

"I see now that was stupid. I mean, Momma used to fight with me about that. But she was right." You turned to her. "You were right."

She and Poppa looked at each other with wide eyes.

"What's wrong?"

Momma shrugged. "I always dreamed someday you'd say that." She threw another glance at Poppa. "I just figured you'd suffer more when you did."

You turned back to Poppa. "The point is, I never realized that I was only an insider in a group of outsiders. There's a whole world out there I never knew about."

"In Philadelphia?" Poppa said.

"At the University. And especially at the Wharton School. That's one of the terrific things about where I am now. The University of Pennsylvania's an important place. You know that. But, boy, you should see how important the Wharton School is. It's like being on the inside of the inside. You see what I mean? When I was at James Madison and City College, that was nothing. That was just being on the inside of the outside. Now I'm really right, smack where it counts. And I never knew about any of it before."

Poppa blew some air out through his mouth.

I jumped to your defense. "You don't understand." He couldn't. Not like I did. You were saying things I'd been trying to say to myself for a long time, but you'd been to college. You had the words. Insiders and outsiders. That was what it was all about. You glowed as you explained to

Poppa. I stored it all up. In a couple of hours we'd be alone in the dark again. I couldn't wait.

"Everybody thinks they're on the inside all the time," you explained. "Or even if they're on the outside, like Jackie, say, they think they know what inside they're out of." I nodded. You understood everything. "But that's only because they never get a chance to see all the other places they could be. The bigger ones. The *real* ones, like I'm doing. It's only the people who have been *all* around who can choose where to be. They're the real insiders. Like the people at the Wharton School."

"And what's there?"

"At the Wharton School?"

"On the inside. You're being theoretical, let's keep it theoretical for the time being. What is it that's so important on the inside?"

Your eyes were serious and certain. "Poppa," you said. "When you're there you know you're right."

"How do you know that?" Poppa asked. "That you're right?"

"Because everyone around you knows it. You can't miss it. You're surrounded by it."

"You mean everyone goes around reassuring everyone else and that's how you know?"

"They've got traditions, Poppa."

"And we don't?"

"Different ones."

"So maybe we're the insiders."

I was getting angry at Poppa. He was purposely not understanding. I wanted to say, "You're old. You're already set in your ways. My brother is the future. Learn from him, like me." I didn't. But it showed.

Momma said, "Your face will freeze like that."

"Or maybe there is no inside," Poppa continued. "Maybe there's just people, Lenny. Some of them a little more frightened than others."

"What's there to be frightened of?"

He shrugged.

"There's nothing to be frightened of." You sounded puzzled.

"Some people are frightened of nothing. Some people, when they have nothing to be frightened of, they make things up."

I said, "Lenny's not afraid."

Poppa looked at me with these sad, reassuring eyes. "I hope not."

You said, "I'm doing very well, Poppa." It sounded as if you were trying to change the subject without anyone noticing. I was puzzled. "I mean, really well. I'm working hard. My midterm grades were the best. And I *like* working."

He nodded.

"I'm going to keep it up for the next three years, too. You know what I'm learning, Poppa? Really learning? I'm learning how to be successful."

Poppa didn't answer right away. He threw Momma another look and she started to laugh. She planted a wet smacking kiss on your forehead. "Don't worry, Lenny," she said. "Your father will love you even if you *are* a success."

That night I took a lot of time to just enjoy having you across from me in the dark again. I lay quiet, listening to you breathe and trying to sniff without your noticing. You'd brought back your old smells, but they were fainter and mixed with new ones. I had to work to find my way around the Old Spice shaving lotion and Ammens medicated powder. After a while I was afraid your sleeping pattern might have changed, that you were going to go off before we'd talked. I pushed up on one elbow and peered through the dark. I could barely make you out, lying on your back. That meant you were still awake.

I whispered to you and you said, "Hey, Jackie," as if you were just greeting me. It was a habit of yours.

"You notice how the room's changed?"

"You brought in your music stuff."

"You don't mind, do you?"

"No." I waited for you to notice more, but you didn't say anything.

"It's funny, you know? I feel a little funny," I said.

"Why?"

"It's like you're my guest or something. In your own room. Don't you feel funny?"

"No."

"It's good having you back."

You made a little embarrassed laughing sound. After a second you said, "How's the victory garden?"

I blushed in the dark. My pubic hair had been very late coming in. The year before I had started worrying and asked you how you got yours to grow. You couldn't give me any advice on that, but you told me not to worry, that nature would take its course, and you always referred to it as my victory garden. Every couple of weeks, just about the time I would start to relax, you'd ask me how it was doing. It always started me worrying again. Now there was no problem. "Terrific," I said. "You want to see?"

"I believe you."

"You were right. I had nothing to worry about."

"That's great."

"Hey, Lenny?"

"Hmmm?"

"I understood what you said to Poppa tonight. I mean,

I know what it must have felt like to realize you were an outsider. But why'd you change the subject all of a sudden?"

"When?"

"Right in the middle. You were explaining how you knew when you were on the inside and then you were talking about your grades."

"Oh, yeah. I remember."

"Why'd you do that?"

You hesitated. "You promise you won't say anything to anybody else?"

"Sure."

"Sure?"

"I never said anything that time you thought you had the clap, did I?"

You chuckled. "You remember that?"

"I mentioned it, didn't I? And it turned out you were only chafed from the bleach Momma used on your jockstraps. So why did you change the subject tonight?"

"I didn't want to hurt Poppa's feelings." You propped yourself up to face me. I could almost make out your face. "See, there's another way you know you're right if you're an insider and I didn't want to mention that to Poppa because it would really upset him."

"What way?"

"You've got power. That's the real secret, Jackie. The guys I know at the Wharton School, their fathers *control* things. Businesses, money, people. They're the ones who make the decisions about everybody else. About us. That's why their fathers sent them to the Wharton School. Because they know that's where they'll learn how to handle the power. And some of them are dummies, Jackie."

"I thought it was hard to get in there. Remember how worried you were about applying even?"

You nodded in the dark. "That proves my point. These guys are dummies and they never worried. You know why? Because they knew their fathers had power. I didn't want to tell Poppa he had no power. A man doesn't like to hear that. You know what I mean?"

"Poppa has power over me," I said.

"Because you have no economic mobility."

"No what?"

"Economic mobility. It's something I learned in my political-science course."

It sounded athletic, so I figured you were right. I didn't have any.

"How much allowance do you get?" you asked.

"A dollar a week."

"Who decided that?"

"Poppa," I said. "But Momma gives me extra for lunches, so it's all I need."

"That doesn't matter. The point is, you don't decide. You couldn't just one day go up to Poppa and say, 'From now on, twenty dollars a week,' could you?"

"What would I do with twenty dollars a week?"

"That's not the point, Jackie. You couldn't do it."

"I guess not." There was a pause while I thought about what I would do with twenty dollars a week. I was stunned by the size of your vision. Then I said, "I suppose I could find a way to use it."

"Don't daydream, Jackie. I'm trying to teach you something about reality."

"The dummies at the Wharton School don't tell their fathers what they want for an allowance, do they?"

"Not yet. They don't have economic mobility yet. Only their fathers do. We don't have anything negotiable yet."

"Like what?" I asked.

"Like a degree from the Wharton School. Or a big business. Or a lot of land or things people need. Or a special talent. You, for instance. You can play the violin. Right now that's non-negotiable. But if you become a star, say, and a lot of people want to hear you play, then your violin playing would give you economic mobility. Then you'd be on the inside because you'd have power. See? But if you're just a so-so fiddler, then you'd be in somebody else's power. That's why you have to work so hard."

I frowned. "I don't know, Lenny. I mean, I believe you," I said quickly. "I know you're right. I just don't know if I can think about music that way."

"You can't be too idealistic."

"I'm not. Honest. It's just . . . I can't think about it that way."

"You've got to learn." You lowered your voice. "You don't want to end up like Poppa."

I lowered mine. "What's wrong with Poppa?"

"That's what I've been trying to explain, Jackie. I mean, I love him. He's a really nice man. That's why I didn't want to hurt him tonight. But somebody else decides what goes into his paycheck."

"Momma says he's a fighter."

"You don't have to fight when you've got power."

My head was reeling. You'd only been away three months but you'd come back like Marco Polo from Cathay, with new and exotic stones. You were spilling them into my lap. They were too new and too many to take in at once. And the jeweler's glass I needed to assess them hadn't even been invented.

"You know why you know all this," I said. "Because you know what it's like to be on the inside and the outside. You're lucky. I only know what it's like to be on the outside. I don't know if I'll ever be able to get in."

"Sure you will."

"I don't know, Lenny. I'm worried."

You pushed yourself up farther. I had gotten used to the dark and I could almost see your face clearly. You were smiling and your eyes were very warm and proud. "You don't have to worry about anything," you said. "Whatever happens I'll take care of you. You're my kid brother."

That was the last conversation in the dark we had for over two years. Your visits home were spotty after that. At Christmas you went sailing with your roommate in Palm Springs. You came home at Easter, but you spent most of your time at the library. Momma couldn't decide whether she was pleased about that. "I don't know," she said to Poppa once. "He's making all my dreams come true. And still I'm nervous. Am I ungrateful?"

Poppa said, "No, Esther. You're just complex."

At night you would go to Manhattan to visit friends from school and their friends from Columbia. I would be asleep when you came home.

During the summer you worked for a professor, doing research and mowing his lawn in Bucks County.

The next year you started bringing girls home. You never came for the holidays, but on some weekends you'd call from Manhattan to let us know you were in town and to ask if we would like to meet the girl you were staying with.

Momma said, "Do you mean staying with, Leonard? Or do you mean 'staying with'?"

You would reassure her. "I mean staying with, Ma."

"All right, then. Come for dinner."

I think it was the same girl with a different wig each time. That may be because I was learning taste from you. It happened seven or eight times and I was trying to find the thread so I would know what qualities to look for. I wanted to fall in love with someone you'd approve of.

They all had twinkling eyes, not the kind of twinkle Poppa had when he was thinking two steps ahead of us; it was more a kind that looked as though they'd been practicing. They had firm, perky cheeks, as if they had stuck little apples inside, and hair that bounced. And they had funny names. If it hadn't been for you, I would have gone on thinking the only girls' names in the world were Deborah, Barbara, and Joan until I left James Madison. You brought home a Darlene, a Penelope, a Thea, a Veronica, and a Cynthia. It was when you brought home Cynthia that I found the thread. You introduced her like this: "This is Cynthia. She plays the bagpipes."

Momma said, "Oh," then whispered to me, "She's musical. You talk to her."

I had made the connection. They all looked alike because you went after girls with a single outstanding achievement, something you thought could help keep the conversation going. It all clicked into place. Darlene was a champion dressage rider; Penelope had been to Turkey on an archaeological dig. Thea had been editor of the student issue of *Mademoiselle*. Veronica was the Middle Atlantic freestyle swimming champion. I could hardly wait for the next girl to check out my theory. Sure enough, Melisande had been an extra in *Naked City*.

The visit always started out awkwardly. The girls would bubble in pretty much the same way they twinkled. They would ask Momma if she needed help in the kitchen, show keen interest in Poppa's work at the leather factory, and generally patronize us. Momma and Poppa would turn unnaturally courteous. Momma would develop what she thought was an Oxford accent. Poppa would assume a triple air of wisdom and quaintness that made him look enigmatically senile.

Actually, Momma was trying to find out if the girl was

Jewish; Poppa, if she had a sense of humor. It always turned out that she was and she did, but that both were deeply buried. Sometimes it was even a surprise to you. Momma had a genius for drawing out ethnic backgrounds, a carefully placed allusion to the food or the holidays, a word like *schmotta* or *mies,* and a hawk's glance for a flicker of understanding. She worked fast. She was usually able to drop her speech impediment by the time she was serving soup.

Poppa worked more slowly. It sometimes took a whole meal and a lot of peculiar silences and nervous smiles, but by the sponge cake and coffee that moment would happen. Poppa would tell a story, ask a particularly absurd question, or give a particularly absurd answer with a noncommittal face. The girl's twinkle would disappear. For an instant her eyes would go blank, then a flicker of real intelligence would shoot out. She would make a lightning reassessment of Poppa. Her face would start to split. It was all instantaneous, but Poppa never dropped his own, enigmatic face until he saw that reassessment. Then he would let go and the laughter would percolate around the table.

I loved the laughter at our dinner table. It was like the wildest Hassidic dancing. It would start with wit. Often Poppa's. Sometimes Momma's. She astonished us so many times it's a wonder we were ever astonished at all. Yours or mine as we grew older, less innocent, and got the knack. The others would appreciate, chuckle, build on the witty notion until the sheer joy of laughing took over from our minds. Then the laughter became shouts of celebration that fed on themselves and possessed us. Someone would shout "Enough!" but there was no controlling it. We laughed ourselves out of breath, swept into tears, flurries of breath-catching, and Momma would always run to the bathroom. They were our most deeply religious, mystic times.

((96))

The girls would get caught in it with a kind of amazement behind their tearing eyes. Only Margaret could never participate. She made jewelry in Bucks County. You brought her home over Christmas of your senior year. She was the quickest to laugh, but she never gave herself up to it. Her laugh was always beautiful and throaty. It sang but it never danced. It never turned grotesque. After you left with her, I realized for the first time that you would graduate that spring, that you were old enough to get married. I'm not making that up just because she did turn out to be your first wife. What I'm not sure of is whether I figured it out on my own or picked up the worried signals from Momma and Poppa.

That was 1950, the same year I played Brahms with the Brooklyn Symphony. It was my first solo with a full orchestra. I was sixteen, a junior at James Madison. It was also the year I became a rebel.

Being a rebel wasn't easy in our house. If I rejected Momma's values and railed against bourgeois materialism, Poppa was always there, lending silent support. If I rejected notions of self-sacrifice and universal brotherhood, Momma would disappear into the bedroom, where she muffled groans of relief.

Luckily, my rebellion had no ideology at all. It took the form of wearing ropes instead of belts, sneakers with everything (which was bad for my arches and made me look Orthodox on Saturday), spending my allowance on paperback books, haunting the apartment instead of living in it. It was enough to send them both up the wall the way you had done six years before—which was all I think I was after, anyway.

The truth of it is, I was horny and frightened. I felt as if I would go on wandering the halls of James Madison all my life, searching for a Selena or a Britta or a Juliette with fat cheeks and One Outstanding Achievement to keep the conversation going. There was one, Thelma (not Selma, Thelma) Moskowitz, who had broken her leg cheerleading. She probably never would have gone out with me, but I was the only one who asked her to a Saturday-night hop while her leg was still in a cast. We stood on one side of the gym all night. She had a lot of friends who would dance up and write funny things on her cast, and I would absentmindedly stroke her crutch. We tried to talk about her One Achievement, but I was mainly interested in how it felt when her leg went, and what they did to set it. The only thing she remembered was that it had happened in the middle of a cheer she had composed.

> Rah, rah, radison
> James, James Madison
> Rah James
> Rah James
> Ma-di-son

I remember it so well because she did it a lot that night. It had already become the important part of the story in the school. When friends came over they would wink and say "Rah, rah, radison" to her and she would wink back and everyone would laugh.

I hobbled her home and kissed her good-night. I knew she was expecting me to try and she had been preparing to put up with it as a sign of gratitude for taking her. We stood together, our lips touching fiercely, locked just as fiercely closed, breathing fiercely through our noses, for about five minutes. When I couldn't stand it anymore, I said, "Your cast must be killing you."

She said, "Yes," very passionately, and "Thanks for a lovely evening," very brightly, as I held the door and she swung inside.

I walked home in a panic. Thelma was the kind of girl I should have been attracted to. She had all the qualifications. All night I had been trying to feel something uncontrollable for her. The only thing I couldn't control was my indifference. When I held her to kiss her, after I had worked my way through her crutches, which she hung on to through the whole ordeal, it was like hugging a giant loaf of Wonder Bread in an angora wrapper.

I was miserable. How was I ever going to make it through life if my crotch went to sleep at the right kind of girl? The only girls who interested me were the ones with No Outstanding Achievement At All, like Carol Bernstein, who was very intense and dark, a loner like me, a little overweight, and who held her books under her arm like a boy; or Joan Greene, who wore sweaters that showed she was flat-chested and didn't seem to care, and whose voice was as husky as a woman who'd been smoking and drinking for years; or Marcia Kauffman, who carried a copy of *No Exit* the whole of our junior year. They aroused me. Cripples all.

I decided I had to do something, fast, to change the desperate course of my life. From now on I would change my fantasies when I masturbated. No more Renaissance Virgin with the Unicorn, which was becoming pretty standard for me. From now on I would imagine Thelma Moskowitz. The closest I ever got was a virgin under a willow with her leg in a cast, murmuring "Rah, James, Rah, James," to the unicorn in her lap.

So I became a rebel. It was a pretty incoherent program. The only controlling principle was the fear that someone would discover I was still a virgin myself. I advocated free love loudly at the dinner table and announced that Momma and Poppa had disillusioned me by getting married. I threatened to run off to Paris and become an existentialist. I bought Juliette Greco records, which I played very loudly, to prove I was serious. When I got tired of that I went Oriental. I struggled through the *Bhagavad Gita* and announced I was going to India to transcend my body, which was only an illusion, and merge with the Universal One. In those days I would have given anything for my body to be an illusion.

I railed against hypocrisy in general and talked for hours about lack of communication.

It wasn't all deep and intense, though. I hedged against it periodically by deciding to be brittle, superficial, and intellectual. I memorized the first act of *The Importance of Being Earnest* and went around dropping epigrams as if they were my own. I bought *The New Yorker,* read the cartoons and snotty fillers, and stacked my copies on the dresser, where anyone who wanted could be impressed. I developed an Oxford accent that made Momma's sound like Dame Edith Evans'.

That phase ended when I discovered Philip Wylie. He'd just written *Generation of Vipers.* One night at the dinner table, without any provocation, I turned on Momma and screamed at her for strangling me, poisoning my life, emasculating me. Then I turned to Poppa, figuring he would be my ally. "She's a viper," I said. "All this time you've been living with a viper!"

His hand shot up for an instant and I started to flinch with relief. But he checked it and ended by scratching his nose. The fire went out of his eyes. "You mean like a vindow viper, Jackie?"

It was hard to take myself seriously around Poppa, but I managed. Through the rehearsals with the Brooklyn Symphony I had made friends with a lot of musicians, most of them five or ten years older than I. They helped. They spent a lot of time in Greenwich Village. Some of them lived there. Every weekend I would hang out in coffee houses, go to jazz concerts, chamber music recitals, or parties. I even had my own fake I.D., just like you. On the subway I would read some esoteric paperback, always with the cover prominently displayed. Secretly I would pretend I was on my way to Columbia, where I was meeting friends from the Wharton School.

It was hard to tell how much you saw of all this. It seemed to me that the only contact we had after that first Thanksgiving visit and through the next two and a half years was an occasional puzzled glance you would throw in my direction. Most of the time you were preoccupied with keeping conversation going, with what kind of impression Momma and Poppa were making, with studying, with your clothes. Clothes had become important to you. I can't remember you ever arriving home without a copy of *Esquire* under your arm. Momma's brother, Oscar, was a haberdasher, so you, Poppa, and I got our clothes from him. Before we went shopping you would pull out your copy of *Esquire*. "Does Oscar carry this?" you would say to Momma.

"White-on-white? Sure. Everybody carries white-on-white."

"But I mean the style. This cut. With the extra-short sleeves."

"You use a jacket with white-on-white. The sleeves don't matter."

"And the wide collar. That's the only kind that can take a Windsor knot."

"With a forty-percent discount, you take the tabs out. Any collar will stretch."

So you would buy from Oscar and try to match what you

saw in *Esquire* as closely as you could. Sharkskin for silk, 60 percent wool for cashmere, and special instructions to the alterer that he never followed.

"Someday," you said to me once, "someday, I'm going to buy only retail. And from strangers." That was one of the times you threw me a puzzled look. I was wearing my checked flannel shirt of the year with an imminent hole in the elbow, baggy gabardine pants polished to a high shine, my rope, and sneakers.

I was using my outfit the way I was using my rebellion—to support the lie. I thought my studied negligence suggested sexual confidence. I have the feeling it worked on you. Over those two years your glances became more complex and troubled. You stopped talking to me about sex. It had been one thing when you could tell me about your sex life. The idea that I might be gathering some information of my own to add to the pool of knowledge seemed to disturb you. You seemed to be telling me that over the years you'd been giving me all that information only for general, disinterested purposes, that my actually using it was some kind of betrayal. The mere fact of my growing up seemed to constitute a kind of rebellion; it seemed to threaten your power and position in the household.

And there I was, trapped in my own lie. I couldn't admit that beneath the rope I was still twelve years old, which would have been reassuring to you and probably to me, too, because we would have been able to talk. I had to carry on with bravado, pretending to be a threat while underneath I was painfully loyal and panicked at it.

The violin was my only anchor in reality those years. I practiced four hours a day. That time must have been precious to Momma and Poppa. It was to me. Once I had closed the door to my room and started tuning up, all of us were free of my irrational outbursts, my lies and confusion. The music demanded too much real concentration.

Mr. Resnick was working me hard for the concert. The music on the stand was too real and too demanding, my violin too finely tuned and responsive for any fantasies to get in the way. I couldn't be you, or Adam Smith (whom I always imagined wearing a fig leaf and checking into a motel), or Jean-Paul Sartre, or Lord Krishna, or Jerry Bettelheim, who played football for James Madison and had laid Thelma Moskowitz. I couldn't even worry about being me. I only had to get down the fingering on this run until *it* was me; the bowing on this passage for a richer tone until it wasn't even second nature, but *my* nature; the attack on *this* phrase. During those times I probably looked as committed as any existentialist, as transcendent as any mystic, as savage and sexy as Jerry Bettelheim, but I didn't know that. I was working.

The concert was to happen in April, about two weeks after Easter.

Mr. Resnick was responsible for it. He had been the first violin with the Brooklyn Symphony since 1940. He had emigrated from Poland in 1939, just a couple of weeks before Hitler marched in. He came to America alone, played at Radio City for a year, then moved to Brooklyn, where he taught in a public school, gave private lessons, and helped create the Brooklyn Symphony. It started out as a chamber group of refugee musicians and grew into the serious community orchestra it was when I played with them.

He was thirty-eight when he left Poland. He was just turning fifty the year I played. He never married.

I know all this because he talked about it that first day Momma invited him to the house to hear me. I had been studying with Mrs. Sales, who lived two floors below us.

When I was ten she told Momma she couldn't take me any further and gave us Mr. Resnick's name.

He frightened me when I met him. It was late in the afternoon and he had come over straight from P.S. 146. He seemed angry, distracted, and tired. I thought he was hoping I would make a scene, beg Momma to find someone else. "Prodigies," he muttered. "Prodigies. You know how many mothers in Brooklyn have prodigies?" Momma leaned back on the sofa and gave him a funny half-smile. "Well, let's hear him," he said. He stretched one arm over the back of the sofa and set his face in a stony stare.

I played the last couple of études I had worked on with Mrs. Sales. I played blind with terror. When they were over I dropped my arms, relieved.

"Never drop your instrument like that," he said sharply. "You start with pride and finish with pride. And keep your head up." He hadn't moved. His face hadn't changed. "What else?"

I was too frightened to understand.

"Play something else, Jackie," Momma said quietly.

I chose a little study by Vivaldi. I hadn't looked at it for a month. I was hoping he would announce I was terrible, refuse to take me on, and leave the house, jeering at Momma. But something else must have been at work in me, too. In my confusion I almost played well. When I finished, I dropped my arms, caught myself, raised my head, and lowered the violin and bow slowly.

He turned to Momma. "His articulation is sloppy," he said. "He hasn't had enough careful work with fingering. Intonation is fair. The bowing is harsh. That's partly the instrument, but even so, he should be able to find a richer tone. The phrasing is very erratic. He's had no experience with it at all."

I wanted to shout "I'm only ten!" but I had a feeling it wouldn't have carried much weight.

"And he's been given work that is much too advanced. Showpieces. He'll have none of that for at least a year. Maybe two. There are already too many bad habits. It will be scales, exercises, a little étude now and then. He needs to understand technique."

Momma said, "Would you like some coffee?"

It was over coffee that he told about Poland.

When he left, he said, "I'll find him a new instrument."

I went to his apartment in Brooklyn Heights every Thursday afternoon for six years. I'm not sure that I ever got over my fear of him, or that I ever really believed he thought I was anything but mediocre; even after I sneaked a look at his appointment book and saw that he had students crammed into every half hour of the afternoon except Thursday, which was blank; even after we started playing duets and instead of barking "No! That's legato! Legato!" he would say "Sorry. Can we take it back to D flat"; even after he told me he had arranged for me to solo with the Brooklyn Symphony.

He was a realist. That's what confused me. I was used to people dreaming on me, like Momma and Poppa—or paying no attention at all, like the kids of East Twenty-seventh Street—or swinging from one to the other, like you. I wasn't used to anyone seeing and hearing me clearly, working with me where I was, not where he wanted me to be, not where I had even been last week.

I know now how many dreams he must have had invested in me, how much pride. I know now how he must have loved me. I should have known it then. I had all the information to put the pieces together. But I was a student. He was my teacher. At that age it was inconceivable that students and teachers actually felt anything for each other.

I mention all this because of what happened at the concert.

It was my first taste of glory. I had been rehearsing the violin part alone in my room for over a year, then with Mr. Resnick doing a piano accompaniment. Just working with him, beginning to hear how the parts would fit together later, gave me a funny little chill. We started rehearsing with the orchestra in a little public school band room in Canarsie. The room was too small for me really to understand what we would sound like in an auditorium, but once, in the middle of a particularly grueling session, I realized for the first time what it meant when they talked about playing "in concert." I was excited. We moved into the Brooklyn Academy for the last rehearsals. Playing in the empty auditorium, I thought I had an idea of what the performance would be like.

Nothing could have prepared me for that moment when I stood beside Maestro Falconetti, with the orchestra behind me and an auditorium filled with strangers in front of me. The very air around me was thick and alive. The lights turned the audience into a single dark mass, shifting at first, echoing up an occasional cough or shuffle, then utterly still. Maestro Falconetti gave the downbeat. The strings struck out over my head and around my body, and sang into the waiting house. My legs went weak, my shoulders floated away from my body. I was standing in the center of Brahms. Then I was playing, not in the center anymore, in every part of it. My fingers felt light, as though they were racing through time, but they were firm on the strings, controlled. I was conscious of every articulated moment of the music, and of how quickly it was all happening.

When it was over the mass in front of me came to life, first with applause. A couple of heads popped higher than the others, a few more. They rose like a wave, starting close to the front, then swelling back. Maestro Falconetti hugged me and made me bow. He reminded me to thank the concert master.

I turned to Mr. Resnick. He was wiping the sweat from his forehead and eyes with a handkerchief. We shook hands. He was nodding hard, but he didn't look at me. The other strings tapped their instruments with their bows, then they rose, too, at a sign from the maestro. I was in the center again.

I found my way offstage, trembling and light-headed. In the green room there was another rush of people, not a dark, anonymous wall now, but friends, relatives, faces I knew, some I didn't. Individual faces. I didn't like that. Now that it was over I wanted to turn anonymous, too. I didn't want the responsibility of smiling, thanking, shaking hands, and I didn't want the risk of having someone smile at me the way they had smiled at the bar mitzvah. I was frightened of that. I was starting to feel a mild hint of nausea when you came into the green room with Momma and Poppa.

You had told me you wouldn't be able to come to the concert. You were graduating in a couple of weeks and you just had too much work to clear up. I was hurt, of course, too hurt not to show it. But I was also relieved. It had always been hardest for me when I knew you were listening. Now I wouldn't have to worry about the whole audience turning into you while I played. I had played with that freedom and I had played well. And it turned out you were there after all.

You grinned. I hadn't seen that look on your face since the day you discovered me riding my bike one-handed. I broke through the crowd around me and ran to you.

"You were great," you said.

"Did you like it? Did you really like it?"

"You were great."

"Did you notice in the second movement the place where I almost lost the harmonics? The bow slipped in my hand, so I had to change the position . . ." I babbled.

Other people came up to congratulate me. Poppa kept tapping my shoulder to make me notice. I would shake hands and turn back to you. I replayed the whole concert for you. I went over every passage, asking, "Did you notice?" and "Could you tell when . . . ?" and never gave you a chance to answer.

Mr. Resnick stood a few feet behind you, looking very old and tired. He kept wiping his hands with his handkerchief. Momma talked with him for a little while, but he hardly took his eyes off me. He was waiting for me to make the move I should have made, to recognize him, to thank him at least, to hug him at most. I know that now, of course. Then I only knew that you had been there in the dark mass out front and you were here now, still grinning at me proudly. He must have realized I wasn't going to move away from you. Sometime later Poppa tapped me on the shoulder and said, "Mr. Resnick, Jackie."

He had come over, still wiping his hands with his handkerchief. "You were very good, Jack," he said softly. His voice sounded unfamiliar and he was leaning toward me in a way I had never seen before.

I said, "This is my brother, Lenny. He came all the way in from Philadelphia. Can you imagine that? He's going to the Wharton School and he's graduating in a couple of weeks. They think he might be valedictorian. He came all the way in just for the concert. All the way from Philadelphia. He told me he wasn't going to be able to make it because he had so much work, so I didn't even know he was there. But he was. All along. Only I didn't know. I probably wouldn't have played as well if I'd known. He always makes me nervous. But I didn't know. Not until he came in with my mother and father. He's studying economics and he's going to be valedictorian." I turned to you. "I know you are."

Mr. Resnick shook your hand and said, "Laszlo Resnick." Then he disappeared into the crowd.

The night after my first concert at Carnegie Hall was the first time I dreamed I was kissing Laszlo Resnick on his cheeks, over and over. That was in 1956 and he had been dead two years.

You stayed with us in Brooklyn until Sunday morning. We were all a little surprised. Momma asked if you didn't have a lot of work to get back to, and you said, "My brother's just had a big event. I want to be around." You put your hand on my shoulder and pulled me to your side. It would have been O.K. if I died right there.

I think you meant it, too. But it wasn't the only reason you stayed, and the concert wasn't the only reason you'd come home.

It was a hectic day. The phone never stopped ringing. People kept dropping by with extra copies of *The Brooklyn Eagle*. My picture was on the front page with Maestro Falconetti's. We were both blurred and I looked as if I was picking my nose with my bow. Everyone said it was wonderful though, and Momma had to send me out three times to get Danish from Ebinger's while she put up another pot of coffee.

You stayed on the fringes of all the activity. You would sit in the living room for a while, then disappear into the bedroom. After a while you would come out. It almost seemed as if you were peeking around the archway to see how many were still there. I thought you were waiting for a chance to get Momma or Poppa alone, but every time there was a break in the traffic and you were alone with one of them, you'd find a way to get the rest of us together, too. You hugged me a lot and kept saying things like "I never see you. You know that, Jackie?" and "We've got to have a long talk," and "Every time I come home you're older."

We ended up having nine or ten people for dinner. Momma must have foreseen it. She had one of her giant pot roasts ready. The smell of the meat had hung thick in the house from the time we woke up. Now there were just enough slices for lunch left swimming in the orange gravy. Momma served coffee, and Poppa got out some brandy. He raised the bottle toward me and said, "For you, Jackie. In your honor," and everyone clapped and laughed. They all took their drinks into the living room while I disappeared into the bedroom.

You lay on your bed thumbing through an old *New Yorker*. There was a little stack of them beside you.

"You read all these?" you asked.

"Most."

You looked at me closely. "The articles and everything? Not just the cartoons?"

I shrugged. I had learned that the best way to lie was by being noncommittal.

You made an impressed face.

It was growing dark outside. The light in the room was gray, dim enough to soften your outlines as you lay there, still too bright to turn on the light. The noise from the living room pushed against the closed door and seeped through the cracks.

"Poppa just gave me some brandy," I said.

"How do you like it?"

"Sticky."

"Brush your teeth."

"The toothpaste would make it worse."

I sat on my bed and started cutting out the picture and article from the *Eagle*.

"Do you have enough light for that?" you asked.

"You're reading."

"I'm just browsing."

For a while there was only the sound of my scissors, the rustle of your pages, and the murmur of voices and laughter from the living room. I sneaked an occasional glance at you. Our eyes met a couple of times. Once we half-grinned, then looked away, embarrassed.

"Why don't you wear a belt?" It was one of those casual questions I could tell you'd been thinking about for a long time.

"I guess I don't care much about clothes."

"You should, you know."

"Wear a belt?"

"Care about clothes," you said.

"Why?"

"It's important. How you look. That rope makes you look like a jerk."

"I didn't wear it last night."

"You were in a dinner jacket."

"I still could have worn it," I said.

"You wouldn't do that."

I wished I had, just to prove I would.

You threw aside the magazine and said, "I'm worried about you."

You sat up and looked at me with these very concerned eyes. All day I'd thought there was something bothering you about *you*. I knew better than to ask about it. I always dreamed about someday being able to give you advice and reassurance the way you'd done it for me so many times. Every time I'd ever tried you closed up and reminded me I was your kid brother. I had just been thinking about offering help again when you said you were worried about me.

I stared back in confusion. I couldn't have felt better about myself that day. In the back of my mind I was afraid you might have seen through my disguise and figured out I was a virgin. If you asked point-blank I didn't know what I would tell you.

I finished cutting out the picture and asked "Why?" as offhandedly as I could.

"You're changing, Jackie." You fell silent. I held my breath. You looked around the room, then back at me. "You used to be so serious."

"I'm not serious now?" I asked, interested. Hearing you talk about me was always a little like having my palm read.

"You've got to start thinking about your future."

"I think about it all the time."

"Realistically, I mean."

"I'm going to play the violin." I was mystified. I'd thought you'd known that. It was as if you were talking to somebody else, or about somebody else; someone you'd never known very well. And it was as if you had just decided to look at him a little more closely.

"That's what I mean," you said. "Do you think that's serious? Or realistic?"

"I never thought about that. I guess you're right. I mean, I'm serious about playing. I just never thought about whether playing was serious or not. I never thought I had to. Maybe I should, huh?"

You nodded. "Especially after last night."

"Did I do something wrong last night?"

"No. No. You were great last night. You really were."

"What, then?" I asked.

"Well, it's just that a thing like last night—you could start to get the wrong ideas about what it's like."

"What what's like?"

"The real world, Jackie. It's not all applause and handshakes, you know. It's a lot of hard work."

"I know that."

"I'm telling you this for your own good," you said.

"I know that too."

"I don't want to spoil how terrific last night was for you. Because it was. And it should have been. You were great."

I said, "Thanks." It was almost automatic by then.

"But stuff like that can really confuse a person. I mean, everyone crowding around and reassuring you. It's as if they're all promising they'll take care of you. It's wonderful when they're all standing around and you're in the center of the crowd. But pretty soon the crowd goes home. You know what I mean? They've all got their own problems and their own lives. And what do you have then? Where are you then? You have to think about that, too. I mean, you've got a right to be excited. I wouldn't take that away from you. But I don't want you to think you can depend on all those people." You jerked your head toward the sounds on the other side of the door. "They've forgotten about you already. I'm telling you this for your own good."

I said, "Sure, but . . ." I fiddled with the scissors, then turned the picture face down on the bed. I wanted to reassure you that I hadn't even liked being in the center of the crowd the night before. If I had been glowing it was because of you, and because I had been in the center of the music.

"You've got to know what you really want, Jackie. That's the important thing. Otherwise you end up floating. And you can't depend on anyone else."

I said, "O.K."

The light was getting dimmer, but I could still see your face. It was troubled and urgent. "Momma says you've been spending a lot of time in Greenwich Village."

"A little. Mostly weekends," I said.

"What kinds of friends do you have?"

I shrugged. "Just friends."

"They smoke reefers and stuff like that?"

"No."

"Don't sound so surprised," you said. "That's the kind of thing that goes on there. You don't want to get mixed up with a lot of deadbeats."

"It's not like that."

"What do you do?"

"Go to concerts and stuff. Parties sometimes."

"You've got to have a sense of direction, Jackie. You can't hang around with a lot of drifters."

"They're my friends."

"Momma's worried about you."

"Why doesn't *she* tell me, then?"

"You know what I think she's afraid of most?" you said. "That you might end up marrying the wrong kind of girl."

"What kind is that?"

"I mean, it's O.K. if you fool around with anybody. You know what I mean? But it would break her heart if you ended up . . . you know . . ."

I didn't. I had no idea what you were talking about. You were getting more agitated though, as if you were doing something you didn't much like yourself for. I shook my head, bewildered.

"You wouldn't marry anyone who wasn't Jewish, would you?" You practically blurted it out.

"I never thought about it." If I'd been half a man I would have admitted then and there that I still hadn't gotten beyond thinking about getting laid.

"It would break her heart if you did anything like that, Jackie. Sometimes you have to think about things like that. About other people."

"You just said you have to know what you want yourself."

"That's different. I meant *other* people. Not family."

"O.K." It was easy to promise that. Marriage wasn't in the offing for another fifty years. What wasn't so easy was the feeling that you were dropping a load of responsibility on me, letting me know that from here on the well-being, the hopes, and the youth of the Fleischman family rested on my shoulders.

"Have you thought about college yet?" you asked.

"Mr. Resnick says I'll get a scholarship to Juilliard." You were unimpressed. "What's the matter?"

"What are you going to do with a degree from Juilliard?"

"Play the violin."

"You think you could be a star?"

"I don't think about stuff like that. I just want to play."

"That's what I mean about not being serious."

"I want to be the best violinist I can," I said.

"You should want to be the best there is."

"Why?" I asked.

"Then you'll be somebody."

I thought about that awhile. Mainly I thought about how we hadn't had a talk in a long time and how it felt different. "I guess I wouldn't mind being a star," I said.

"Nobody's going to help you, you know. No matter how hard you work."

"I know that," I said. It was almost dark.

"I'm only trying to help you out, Jackie. Give you some of my experience. You've got to work hard. But you've got to be ready for disappointment, too."

"Are you disappointed?"

"No. No. I'm not disappointed. I *could* be," you said quickly. "That's the point. I could be if I wanted to, but I understand what's happening. Like the job I have for next year . . ."

"You said it was a good job."

"It is. It's O.K. It's not the best though."

"It's your first one," I said.

"That's what I mean. You've got to learn what it feels like to start over again—all the time. I'm the best in the Wharton School, right? But when I'm finished there, I'll just be another outsider until I can prove I'm the best all over again. I understand that, so I'm not disappointed. I mean, the job I've got at the Holtzman Corporation. I mean, I know I'm just going to be a kind of glorified office boy. I'll admit that. I know it. It's just the way things work. But I'll be on Wall Street. See? That's what's important about it. So I can just start working my way up again, because I'll be in the right place again. Just like the Wharton School. I know I can do it. That's how it'll be for you, too. Like last night you were the best. If you go to Juilliard you'll just be another nobody unless you prove you're special. Then when you get out of Juilliard, no matter how good you were there, you'll still be a dime a dozen. So you can't depend on anybody, and you've got to be sure."

"Do those other guys have better jobs?"

"Some of them," you said. "Their fathers . . . See, we have no connections, you and me. We'll never really be insiders the way we should be. That's why we have to work so hard." You were quiet for a long time. I could barely see you. I went to turn on my wall lamp, then decided not to. I had the feeling it might be the last time we'd talk to each other in the dark like that and I wanted to hold on to it a little longer.

"Like Cynthia Dicks. You remember her?"

"The one who played the bagpipes?"

"You know her father wouldn't let her go out with me after I met him," you said.

"Why not?"

"He told her I wouldn't ever amount to anything."

"That's stupid," I said. "You're going to be famous."

"Everybody's family thinks they're going to be famous. But when Cynthia told me that it started me thinking."

"You mean she just told you? Just like that?"

"I said to myself, How could I prove he's wrong? How could I show I'm going to be successful?"

"You want it so badly," I said.

"That's not enough. That's what I realized. I thought about that a lot and that's when I realized how important it is to really have a sense of direction. So I was really very grateful to Mr. Dicks. See, it's not enough to want something for yourself, Jackie. That's what I'm trying to explain to you. You've got to want to *prove* it to everybody else, too. That's what I'm figuring out. And I don't get the feeling you want to prove anything to anybody."

"I don't think playing the bagpipes is such a big deal, you know." It was all I could think of to say.

"You've got to really know what you want, Jackie. That's what I'm trying to tell you."

I frowned. I could hear Poppa's low voice and Momma's laughter and the voices and the laughter of the others, still going strong in the living room. They all sounded as if they knew what they wanted and I was having a little trouble believing I didn't know, too.

"Lenny?" I said.

"Yeah."

"Do you know what you want?"

"You don't have to worry about me."

"I know that. It's just . . ."

"What?"

"This is the first time we've ever talked like this about you."

You said, "We're not. We're talking about you."

Then you flipped on your wall lamp and grinned at me. You looked just like Momma, especially those times she would smile at Poppa to show him that her headache wasn't bothering her.

That summer I figured out the real reason you had come home. You must have already known you were going to marry Margaret Fitzgerald. You were trying to find a way to tell us.

I don't know if Momma or Poppa noticed anything with all the excitement of the weekend. A month later though, when we went to Philadelphia for your graduation, they were pretty sure something was up. You didn't say anything then either, but Margaret was with you for the whole time. You had her sit with us during the exercises. When they announced you as valedictorian, Momma shot a worried look at her. Margaret's face was cool.

The day was hot. She was wearing a peasant blouse that left her shoulders exposed, sandals, a pair of dangling earrings that looked like chimes, and a lot of copper bracelets she had made. Her hair was piled up to expose the nape of her neck. It glistened with the heat and smelled of soap.

She was different from anyone I would have expected you to be interested in. She was more like the women I had seen on the other side of the room at parties on MacDougal Street, ones who used the word "bourgeois" a lot and carried leatherworking tools around in their shoulder bags. The smell of her soap was getting to me. It was perfumed, and I sat there having a whole sensual thing with it until she looked at me and smiled this little distracted smile. I blushed and smiled back, flustered, as if she'd caught me breathing her in. I was confused. If she had been my girl friend, I could hear your advice about getting mixed up with Bohemians. Yet you'd been with her for half a year, longer than any other girl had lasted, and here you were this weekend, practically dancing her around the whole time. It couldn't have been just the soap.

Momma and Poppa were quiet, driving home to Brooklyn. At about Elizabeth, New Jersey, Momma said, "What do you think, Sy?"

Poppa said, "We'll wait and see," and they were quiet again.

That's how I know they knew.

In the middle of the summer you called from Bucks County to announce you were married. You knew it was kind of sudden, you said. You had actually been planning to wait a little longer, but the Korean War was heating up and now that you'd lost your student deferment the draft board was breathing down your neck. Besides, this way you and Margaret could move right into a permanent place when you started with Holtzman in the fall.

Momma was spectacular on the phone. She told you she was happy for you and asked when the two of you would come to visit. Her voice was surprised and excited. She made sure that was all you heard. On our side her face had reservations. The only clue you might have had was the way she asked your wife's name. Three times.

Poppa got on and asked if you needed anything. That reminded Momma of questions she'd forgotten to ask. She hovered over Poppa and prompted him. He tried to wave her away, but she had to know if you had enough sheets and she finally yelled it into the mouthpiece. Her face was next to Poppa's ear and he winced with pain.

When he hung up, Momma's lips trembled. "She clanks, Sy. With all that jewelry. If only she didn't clank." Then she started to cry.

It was the only time I know of that she cried over your marriage to Margaret. Maybe Poppa helped her take it in stride, maybe she figured out pretty quickly it wouldn't last. Whatever, they kept their disappointment to themselves when you were around.

When you weren't, I was your staunchest defender. They were being provincial, I told them. Margaret was opening whole new worlds to you. She could open them up for us, too, if we'd give her half a chance. You were misunderstood young lovers. I was your only ally, the prince's friend, ready to whip out my sword at the hint of a sigh from Momma.

You took a first-floor apartment in a brownstone on Bank Street. It was convenient to Holtzman, you explained, and Margaret wanted to open a jewelry store in the Village. I was ecstatic. You were moving into my world. It meant in some way your love for Margaret was also your love for me. It meant you had come to understand the very people you had asked about so suspiciously the night after the concert. I had visions of welcoming you to my Village society, introducing you to all my friends, playing chess with you in a coffeehouse on MacDougal Street on Saturday afternoon, running into you by accident at Maria Theresa's, or calling you in the middle of a terrific jam session and telling you to come over.

I helped you move. I'd never been inside those old brick fronts on Bank Street. I expected the usual railroad flat with improvised furniture. Your apartment had a working fireplace, oak woodwork, embossed wallpaper, French windows in the living room that led to a patio with an actual garden.

Until then, when I walked through the streets with my friends, I'd had no idea there was a whole other life going on around me. I didn't know about the young men in rep ties, just out of college, who had landed jobs south on Wall Street or north on Madison Avenue, who had come with money or married into it, and who knew that Greenwich Village was becoming the right address to start with. That day it crossed my mind that you hadn't moved into my world at all, just behind a brick front near my playground.

I dropped in almost every weekend to invite you both to come along wherever I was going. Sometimes I wasn't going anywhere. I had really come to see you, but I made up a destination. I sensed I needed that. If you asked me to stay I would sink into your furniture and love the casual attitudes I could take. Margaret would make coffee. Sometimes the two of you would just go about your weekend business while I read or helped. I loved those times because they made me feel most like a part of your lives. If you didn't invite me to stay, I would wander around the Village alone.

When the jewelry shop opened I hung around that, too. The shop was as different from what I expected as your apartment. It wasn't another makeshift crafts center that helped the Village look like an open-air bazaar. It was elegant, with a coffee lounge and leather-covered chairs and counter stools. Margaret's customers were all from uptown.

It dawned on me that the two of you were not the struggling young couple I wanted you to be. I found out that Margaret was divorced—which was something you never told Momma and Poppa—and that she had used her settlement money to set up shop. I found out her father was Howard Fitzgerald, the architect, and that he still gave her a monthly allowance.

With all that, I still wasn't ready to give up my dream of sharing your lives. Each time I showed up on Saturday morning, your hesitation would grow longer before you smiled and said, "Hey Jackie," in the old way. I wouldn't let myself notice. I wouldn't notice how Margaret's mouth went tight when I came into the shop, or how the silences between you got longer and deeper as the weeks passed.

Momma forced the issue.

I was home from school on a weekday during my Christmas vacation. She had finally decided to take the screens out of the windows. Every year we offered to take them down after the first snowfall, but Momma said, "Wait. We haven't had Indian summer yet." Near Christmas she would lose hope. Then she would do the job herself—to show God how He'd disappointed her, I think.

We were in the kitchen. I had gotten up late and I was being sophisticated, which meant I was drinking black coffee and smoking a Pall Mall. Momma had the window wide open as she struggled with a screen hook. The room was freezing. It smelled of fresh air and ten months of city soot.

Your birthday was coming up. I was talking about what I should give you. Momma said nothing. Her silence always made me babble.

"You think about your brother too much." She said it simply, almost casually. Underneath it was sharp. It was what she used to call a *potch* on the *toches* when we were younger, the gentlest tap with just enough sting to bring us to our senses. That was O.K. for a nine-year-old, but I was seventeen. My dignity was ruffled.

"Just because you don't like Margaret," I said.

"I didn't say anything about her. I said about you. You think about Lenny too much."

"What's too much?"

"Be your own person."

"What's that supposed to mean?"

"You don't know what that means because you think about your brother too much." She freed the screen and worked it through the window. "You've got a life of your own, Jackie. Qualities of your own. Good ones." She shut the window and locked it. "I'm not saying that because I'm your mother. You do. You're special." She stacked the screen against the sink and shook her head.

"I'm not so special," I said.

"A scholarship to Juilliard? A concert violinist?"

I shrugged it off. I had kept up my practicing, but ever since our last conversation, my love for the work was tinged with guilt. "It's not important," I said.

She nodded. "If you want to think that, it's your business. But I'll tell you something that *is* important. You're a nice person. You're sensitive and thoughtful. And that's special."

"You mean Lenny isn't nice."

"Lenny's nice, too. In his own way."

"Boy, Ma. That's some way to talk about your own son."

"What do you want me to do? Make him up like you do?"

"You never had any faith in him. I don't even think you love him."

"I love him," she said. She opened the other window. "I love him plenty. You think I'd put up with his nonsense if I didn't love him?"

"You mean Margaret, huh?"

"His wife is a symptom. She's not the disease."

"You're narrow-minded."

The second screen came out easily. She flung it against the first and started out of the kitchen. "Your brother's a baby," she said as she left.

"He is not!" I followed her into the bedroom. "You'd like to believe that. You'd like us both to stay babies."

"I'd like for at least one of you to grow up."

"He's going to be a big success," I said.

"He can be the biggest success in the whole world. Right now he's a baby." She turned to me with the screen hanging half off its hooks. "And I only hope when he's a success he's not still a baby."

"That's impossible."

"That's what you think. And you know why you think that? Because you're a baby, too. And you know what a baby is? It's someone who makes things up. You make up your brother. He makes up his wife. You both make up the world the way you want it to be. That's what a baby does."

"And you're grown up, I suppose."

"Believe me, Jackie. Believe me."

She was working fast now. "And don't tell me I don't love your brother. You think I don't know what agony he's going through now? I understand him." She slammed down the window. "I know him longer than you, Jackie. I know him better. And I love him. You think I don't want to jump right this minute and help him?" She flung up another window. "If I didn't love him I'd meddle." She clenched her teeth. "What I wouldn't do to meddle."

"Margaret is a wonderful person."

"Stop defending people you don't know."

"I've seen them more than you."

"You've been with them, Jackie. You haven't seen them. If you did you'd know they don't want you around."

"That's not true!"

"She's a bitch. And your brother is a *schlemiel*." Her voice broke. She had all three screens out now and she took them quickly into the kitchen. I started after her. "Don't follow me."

When she came back she jerked her head toward my room and I followed. She waited for me to move my music stand so she could get to the window.

"You know my sister Sarah?"

I grunted.

"All my life I wanted to be her." She turned to look at me, then went back to work. "You think that's stupid, huh? Good. You want to hear something else? For fifteen years I was ashamed that I loved your father. You know why? Because Sarah's Meyer owns a business and your father is just a worker. How do you like that?"

"It's not the same thing."

"Why not?"

"You and Poppa are better than Sarah and Meyer."

"What's better? We're different. That's all."

"You're just making that up, anyway."

"I don't lie," she said sharply. "It took me forty years to be my own person."

"I love Lenny."

"You love Lenny or you love a hero? Heroes are for babies." She started for the kitchen again. "This time you can follow me."

I stared after her a moment, then I followed cautiously.

She started on the living-room window. I stopped at the archway.

"I don't care how many mistakes you make in your life, Jackie. They should just be your mistakes and not your brother's. *Versteh?*"

I didn't answer.

"What are you doing? Sulking?"

It probably looked like that. I was just afraid if I said anything she would use it to convince me. So I turned angry and resentful.

"I'm going out," I said.

"Don't go to Bank Street."

"I'm going out."

"They don't want you around."

"You don't know anything about it. You don't know anything about anything."

I took the subway uptown, feeling positively liberated. I hadn't realized how torn I'd been between my loyalty to Momma and Poppa and my loyalty to you and Margaret over the past months. Leaving the house that way and purposely disobeying Momma, I'd taken my first decisive step. Later I would storm back to the apartment in Brooklyn, pack my suitcase under Momma's eyes, and move in with you permanently. Once you both heard my version of what had happened, how I had defended you and risked my own position in the household, you'd recognize my love for you both and welcome me. I was going up to the Village now to make my report.

Your mail was still on the table in the hallway. It was like a sign. I would deliver your mail as my first useful act. I knocked at your door and waited. I knocked again. No answer. It was a weekday. I could feel the righteous anger drain as I stood there. I backed off from the closed door, feeling a little foolish. I replaced the mail on the table and headed for the jewelry store, trying to hang on to the energy that had propelled me uptown.

Margaret was helping a man try on rings. She glanced up briefly when I came in. I couldn't miss the irritation that flickered in her eyes. I said "Hi," as casually as I could. She nodded and threw me a tight smile. I went to the coffee urn and poured myself a cup, then wandered to the counter near the customer.

Margaret said, "Can I help you, Jackie?" but she kept her attention on the customer.

"Have you seen Lenny?"

She gave me a puzzled look. "He's at work."

"Oh, yeah. I forgot. I'm on vacation." I fell silent. Margaret's shoulders got tighter as I fiddled morosely with the bracelet display.

"Is something wrong?" she said finally.

"I had a fight with Momma." I knew it was stupid even as I said it. We both glanced at the customer. I looked at him, challenging Margaret to choose between us. She looked at him, letting me know she'd chosen.

I shrugged, dropped a bracelet on the counter, and wandered out. I knew she was watching me, so I tried to amble.

I walked down to Wall Street, still determined to prove Momma wrong.

The argument had done its work though. My walk lost its determination. I went over the scene in Brooklyn, struggling to stay convinced of my side. I had to fight not to think of the times I'd stood in front of your door on Saturday mornings and heard angry voices turn to whispers as soon as I knocked. I'd already seen the momentary desperation in your eyes when you glanced at Margaret, the confusion that suggested betrayal and unkept promises. I knew, really, that you both had already been unfaithful. I had to fight to believe you were proud of your junior job at Holtzman, that you believed in your future there, and that it was worthy of your education and your honors.

I needed your certainty. I depended on that. If you turned out to be as unsure as I, where would that leave me?

It was early afternoon. I waited around for three hours, drinking coffee at a drugstore across the street from Holtzman. I paced the block in the cold. At five o'clock the clerks, secretaries, and junior executives poured out of the office buildings. I scanned the faces of the young men wearing overcoats, gray hats, and rubbers. They streamed out the doors and into the subway. They all looked as confident, clearheaded, sure of their futures as you, but they hunched against the wind when they hit the street. They held their hats with one hand, their attaché cases with the other, and suddenly looked tired and vulnerable. And there were so many of them.

I went back to Brooklyn before you came out.

It's two o'clock in the morning. My wrist hasn't felt this way since one of my marathon sessions at Juilliard. I don't even want to stop now, but I haven't lost my reason completely. There's a committee meeting at noon and the big one right after. I have to get some sleep.

Now I'm in bed with you propped on my lap. Before I turn out the light I just have to tell you what a crazy business this whole thing is. My mind is racing. I want to keep going for another six hours. It's a good thing I'm exhausted. And it's hard to believe I saw Arthur Quasnosky just this morning. I can't figure out whether I'm so excited because I'm getting to the bottom of things, or because I'm finding out things have no bottom.

In the car after the committee meeting. About to drive over to the hall for the meeting of the full orchestra. No more fun and games. Everyone's tensing up. Seams are showing. I'm not the synthesizer anymore. I'll report it all when I get a stretch of time.

Later

I'm in my dressing room now. The meeting was all over the place. Tony is disassociating himself from the action. Now it's only Dudley, Phil, Eileen, and me.

Tonight I'll catch you up on everything.

Later

Back home. Now I can tell you what went on. The committee meeting was at Tony's place. I got there about ten minutes late. Everyone sat hunched around the dining-room table as though they were diagnosing the centerpiece. I slipped beside Tony and hunched right in there with them.

Eileen asked how Quasnosky was.

I said, "Terrible. The strike's made him worse."

"How worse?"

"Nastier."

Dudley made an impressed face.

"And sicker. He should be in the hospital now."

"Then why . . . ?" Laurence Gwynne looked puzzled.

"He wants to stay with the music."

"This is crazy, you know," Gwynne said. "I mean . . ." He hesitated. "I don't want to sound crass, but you're making an issue of a man who may be dead in a week."

"We're making an issue of a man who's alive now," I said.

"Don't you think that's a little sentimental?"

I said, "No, I don't." Then Gwynne made a terrible mistake. He smiled at me. "Don't patronize me, Gwynne. Talking about someone who may be dead in a week as if he was dead now. That's sentimental. And stupid. And unrealistic—which I'm sure is another word on the tip of your tongue. I've heard all that before."

Tony said, "All right, Jack," and threw an apologetic look at Gwynne. "Let's talk about how we're going to run the meeting."

That's when the real trouble started. Dowd and Gwynne talked like conspirators, giving us instructions on how to push the compromise package through. They took it for granted we'd already agreed to it. Tony seemed to think so, too. Eileen realized what was going on. She sat straight up.

"No, sir," she said. "None of us ever said we'd endorse the package. We only agreed to present it."

"That won't get us anywhere," Gwynne said.

"The membership has to decide."

"They want us to decide for them," Tony said. "You know that, Jack. You know the orchestra. They're children."

"Everyone decided to strike," I said. "Not just the five of us."

"There's nothing wrong with the committee making a recommendation," Gwynne said. "It's done all the time."

"Then let's recommend we turn it down," Phil said.

I cut in. "We can't manipulate the membership. One way or the other."

Tony said, "You used to be so reasonable, Jack."

That's when I flared. "When was that?" I said. "When I let a management take over the People's Symphony, change the name, and pull the whole thing out from under us? Or when we moved from the Orange Street Baptist Church, where everyone could come and hear us, to the big new Arts Center, where it costs fifteen dollars to sit inside and the people who first believed in us have to sit on the grass? Or when we took all that money from the Ford Foundation on the condition we get rid of ten of our original members and bring in solo musicians with a 'national reputation'?" I turned to Gwynne. "That's another thing this strike is all about, Gwynne. Quasnosky is all ten of those musicians we sold out because suddenly we had stars in our eyes." I turned back to Tony. "So don't tell me about when I was reasonable. When I wasn't reasonable I left a concert career to come down here with Lewis and Cross to start a people's symphony and you were playing in a strip joint on Division Street. When I was unreasonable we were all playing what we wanted for who we wanted."

"The membership went out for more pay," Tony said. "They're not all idealists like you. They'll listen to the union men."

"It's a real world out there," Dowd said.

((131))

I said, "It's a real world right here."

Gwynne said, "The meeting's in half an hour. We've got to have some kind of recommendation."

"Turn it down," Phil said.

"No!" Eileen and Dudley shouted it together, then Eileen took over. "You just tell the membership what you've got to tell them," she said to Dowd and Gwynne. "The membership will decide."

And they did.

Quasnosky was there. He arrived in the middle of one of Tony's famous speeches about lifting the hearts of the people of Georgia.

"I look around me at all of you," Tony was saying, "and I realize that only a handful of you were there at the beginning. Many of you weren't here when we were just the People's Ensemble, playing in the Orange Street Baptist Church. You weren't here when the best, the most influential members of the community, people who had looked on us with disdain and suspicion, built us this beautiful house, and made us what we are today . . ."

Somebody in the back of the house yelled, "What we are today is on strike!"

It was about then that Quasnosky arrived. He came right down to the front row, pushing out of the way anybody who tried to help him. He sat there, glaring and wheezing at us, through the whole meeting.

Dowd laid out the package. I underestimated him. He's a shrewd man. "Larry Gwynne and I have gone over the books," he said. "And we're prepared to ask for a fourteen-percent increment." Sensation. He made a calming gesture. "Don't get excited. That's only a bargaining tactic. It means we think we can get you ten percent across the board, twelve for solo players." That made everyone feel naive, so he slipped through the business of artistic control. He talked about legalities, the board, the charter, then promised an advisory committee. He made it sound like a triumph.

There was a lot of shifting and whispering. Before it stopped, Dowd said, "Let me get on to the third point." Quasnosky sat impassive. You could feel everyone avoiding him. "I suppose . . . this . . . I guess you all know it's the most . . . unorthodox . . ."

And Quasnosky said, "Get on with it, mister!"

"You're asking for no mandatory retirement," Dowd said. "Right now you've got a clause that stipulates sixty-five as retirement age, sixty-two for early retirement. That's pretty standard." He turned benign and wise. "Most people want it that way. It opens up jobs for new blood. Besides, by sixty-five people want to relax, live off a pension, Social Security. They've earned it. They're tired . . ."

Somebody in the back yelled, "Tell that to Pablo Casals."

"I'm not saying what you're after is wrong," Dowd said quickly. "It's just unusual." Dramatic pause. "But we can get it."

He rode out a burst of applause. Then he explained about the feasibility study. He clapped his hands. "That's the package . . . it's pretty much everything you want. A little give-and-take here and there . . ." and he asked for questions.

Jerry Frank, the first horn, wanted to know about pay phones backstage.

Somebody yelled, "For chrissake, Jerry. Stay with the big issues."

Fred Holland came through with the biggest one. Where did the feasibility study leave Quasnosky?

Dowd did his casualty-of-the-war *schtick*. Before it could really sink in, Laurence Gwynne was explaining about the temporary restraining order. Dowd and Gwynne were quite a team.

Reinhold Blesser said, "Please, I have a question," from way back in the auditorium. Reinhold is sixty-three, another violinist. He came over from Hungary in 1956. "Where I come from," he said, "I have learned that when you play the right notes one thing happens and when you play the wrong ones something else. You are sure which is right and wrong only after you make the sound. I would like to know, if you please, exactly what happens if we make the sound 'No.'"

Gwynne explained about show-cause procedures.

"Then it is very serious," Reinhold said. "Like an injunction."

"Yes."

"So that if we say yes, we go back to work, and if we say no, we go back to work. So that, if we play the wrong notes or the right notes, the same sound comes out."

Gwynne smiled. "I guess you could put it that way."

"That is very unusual," Reinhold said.

"Not really . . ."

"I meant for this country." He started to sit down. He thought again. "Please, I have one more question. What happens if we say no again?"

"To the restraining order?"

"Yes."

"You're cited for contempt of court and they arrest the strike committee."

All hell broke loose. In the middle of it, Phil Carnovsky grabbed the microphone. "I move we turn down the package!"

Somebody seconded.

Over the uproar I said, "You shouldn't have done that, Phil."

((134   ))

He said, "Fuck it."

Tony looked at me. "I told you this would happen."

Somebody from the house yelled, "Repeat the motion!"

Phil said, "That we turn down the fucking package!"

Eileen was shaking with rage. "Sit down, Phil. Let Tony run the meeting."

I glanced down at Quasnosky. His eyes burned back at me, and he was breathing hard.

Tony got everyone quiet again. Phyllis Lester, second cello, asked to hear from the rest of the committee.

Dudley took the podium. He was quiet and cool. He talked mainly about artistic control. "We've heard a lot of legal jiving about this particular issue from the union and the management," he said.

Gwynne interrupted. "It's not jive, Dudley. It's the law."

"I know that. I also know it was once the law that I couldn't sit anyplace I wanted in certain buses. But, you see, laws are made by people. So they can be changed by people if they don't make no sense. Now, a law that says a community of musicians can't decide for themselves what they want to play and who they want to play for don't make much sense to me. And it seems to me it don't make much sense to the management either, because they tell us they'd like an advisory committee. Well, I don't think an advisory committee makes a whole lot of sense either. I mean, there we'd be 'advising' them about what we want to play. That'd be like telling them we weren't sure about it. Man, we *know* what we want to play and we know who we want to play for. So it don't make no sense to 'advise' anybody else about it. We just got to *do* it. So unless our union brothers can find a way to get us a package with artistic control, I'm going to turn it down."

The applause was scattered. Quasnosky squirmed.

Lou Cianelli, cornet, stood up. "I think that's very inspiring. But right now there *is* a charter and there *is* a management and there *is* a state of Georgia, and I think it's a little too easy to be so cavalier about it. I'm not so sure I want to depend on Dudley Rogers and his ideals for my next paycheck. And I know my family doesn't. Management isn't going to see these issues our way," he said.

And Dudley said, "Then we'll just have to discharge the management."

There was scattered laughter in the house. Someone said, "Come on, Dudley. Get serious."

"Man, I am dead serious," Dudley said quietly. "This symphony began without management, didn't it?"

Lou said, "You can't have an organization as big as this without one."

"There was a time when *we* were the management," Dudley said. "When Jack Fleischman and Bob Cross and Fred Holland did all the work along with everybody else—including Ed Lewis, who also happened to be third chair. That means that somewhere along the line we must have agreed to the situation we've got now. Well, if the present management just can't seem to operate reasonably, we just have to admit we've made a mistake and go back to the old way of doing things. And if the organization is just too big for that—we'll have to get small again."

"All right!" Arthur Quasnosky's voice broke through like a thunderclap. "I've had enough of this bullshit." He struggled to his feet.

Tony said, "You can stay seated if you—"

"I want to stand, goddamn it!" He made it up and turned to face the rest of the house. He had to brace himself against the back of his seat to stay up. He was trembling. "What do all you guys think you're doing here today? Everybody getting up and dropping their pants and making sentimental speeches about the People's Symphony and the Gainesville Symphony.

Why don't you stop thinking so much about the goddamned symphony and start thinking about the music? That's the only thing that's important. You're all so worried about people and loyalties and your precious dignity you don't have time for the music. Dudley Rogers thinks we should play more nigger tunes? Well, I tell you what, Rogers. You get your boys to write us music as good as the white music we've been playing and we'll play that, too. And you know it. And Jack Fleischman and Eileen Simpson want to get their kicks from finding out they can keep me playing when Lewis laid me off? And all Lou Cianelli's worried about is where his next paycheck is going to come from. Nobody's thinking about the music. And the music is the only thing that's important. You're just a bunch of hacks." He swiveled his head toward me. "I told you where I stood yesterday, Fleischman, and I'll tell the rest of you today. Any bunch of musicians who decide to stop playing because of an incompetent old man who can't even control his instrument anymore stinks. And any bunch of musicians who stay out because of him stinks. I wouldn't stay out half a bar for any one of you if you couldn't keep up with me. Lewis is right to lay me off. And anybody who wants to make a northern-liberal charity case out of me doesn't *deserve* the music. So why don't you all stop whacking each other off here in the auditorium and get the hell back on the stage with your instruments. If you belong there."

He worked his way back into his seat. Nobody wanted to look at him. They looked at me instead.

Tony said, "Jack? Do you . . ."

I said, "Yeah. I've got a couple of things." Now I knew what Poppa meant yesterday, when I told him about my visit with Quasnosky. I took the podium and looked down at him. "You got your wind back?" I said.

He nodded.

"O.K.," I said. "Because I want you to answer just one question. Do you want to stay with us?"

His eyes got smaller. "You son of a bitch."

"Answer my question."

"What are you trying to do?"

"Do you want to stay with us?"

"The music is the most . . ."

"I know where you stand on the music," I said. "That's not what I'm asking."

"You cocksucker."

"Do you want to stay with us?"

". . . Yes." He tried to cover it with a wheeze.

"O.K.," I said. "Because you didn't happen to mention that in your solo just now. And it's kind of important."

It was very quiet in the hall. "You know what, Arthur?" I said. "This particular northern-liberal, Jew-boy kike happens to think the music's pretty important, too. So do a couple of the wops and niggers and krauts around you. So don't get off on the idea that you're the only one here who cares about the music. It's just that some of us care enough about the music to be bugged. I don't like the idea that the music I'm playing is unimportant, that I can get up here and play it and not give a damn about the human beings I'm playing with. That really scares me, Arthur. It scares me that a man can play like you've played with us and still feel humiliated and ashamed to say he wants to stay with us. That's wrong. And I don't like the idea that I'm standing up here right now with a choice to make between playing the music and doing something for another human being— even one like you. And I'll tell you something. If I really believed that I had to make that kind of choice forever, instead of for the two or three weeks I'm making it now,

I'd have to make the same choice I'm making now. Because even without the music, human beings would still be important, but without you and me and this whole crowd and those others who fill this place every night, without us there wouldn't be any reason for the music at all. But I don't think what I do is wrong. I still believe in the music, and if something's gone so wrong that it's finally come to a choice like this, it's not the fault of the music. *We've* made a mistake somewhere. I hate this silence. But I'm not going to be sentimental about it and say, 'The music's the only thing.' I have to be realistic and pay the price of silence while we work to make the connection between people and music real again. And we can only do that by fighting for control of what's ours."

He never took his eyes off me, didn't even flinch—until someone behind him called for a vote.

Dowd and Gwynne warned us that the union couldn't support a contempt action if we turned down the package. Tony said that, as union representative, he'd disassociate himself from the strike committee. Lou Cianelli called for a secret ballot.

The vote was close: 34 no, 30 yes, 6 abstentions.

We're staying out.

We're also calling Vic Jenkins up from Atlanta. We want him representing us.

After the meeting I went straight to Poppa. I knew he'd want a blow-by-blow, so I made a tape of the whole meeting. He was at dinner so I dropped the tape off with a short note and came home.

I'm sort of glad I didn't get to see him. He would have wanted to listen to the tape with me and I'm in no shape to go through that whole meeting twice in one day. Besides, I wanted to get back here to report to you.

I don't know how it works, but no matter how tired I am, or how jittery, it all disappears once I'm back into this letter. So you see that? You're still good for me.

It's eight o'clock now. My stomach is grumbling. I haven't had anything to eat since a Clark bar at five. I'm going to slap together a sandwich and put up a pot of coffee.

I'm planning to stay up with you again all night. I want to tell you about me and Molly, and you and your wives. So I'll stop here and get back in an hour or so for another marathon.

I didn't make it back to you. Just barely back with you now. I think I wrote yesterday that you're good for me when I'm tired and nervous. Now we'll see how you do on a hangover.

Ed Lewis came over last night. No phone call. No warning. I was deciding whether to run the dishwasher with only two nights of my dishes in it when the doorbell rang and there he was.

You've met Ed. He was the only person besides Molly I used to bring home while I was at Juilliard. There were at least three times you were there, too. He was the lanky kid with black unruly hair who had a terrible time with his glasses. They were always slipping down from the bridge of his nose and steaming up from Momma's soup—which was really just as well, because his eyes had a wild look that could get on your nerves. When the glasses steamed it was

((141))

like intermission. He went around in open-collared work shirts with the sleeves rolled over the forearm. That was Poppa's influence. Poppa was always giving him books to read. Marx. Lenin. Engels. The same ones he used to leave in my room—on top of my pile of *New Yorkers*. Ed really read them. In fact, there was a time in our college days when Ed was a little to the left of Phil Carnovsky. He was a compulsive bather, but his clothes and his swarthy complexion and the funny sprinkle of hair on his chest made him look as if he'd just finished sweating—or was just about to. We found each other our first day at Juilliard and stayed together all four years.

You wouldn't recognize him now. He's got contact lenses for one thing. He's fleshed out. His body is still hard, but his arms and legs don't look as if they're about to fly off in different directions. His hair is shot with gray, which is terrific for getting foundation grants, and his eyes are softer. He still looks intelligent, but not demonic anymore.

I haven't seen him in anything but business suits for the past ten years. Last night he wore a work shirt with the sleeves rolled up. He was smiling with his lips closed when I opened the door. That meant he was nervous. Ed has these spaces between his front teeth. When he's relaxed and laughing he looks like a happy hippopotamus. He only gets self-conscious when he's nervous. He was carrying a paper bag.

He said, "Hello, Jack."

I said, "Hello," but I couldn't decide whether I was talking to him or his shirt. Then I said, "I've got five sandwich plates, three coffee cups, and two highball glasses in the dishwasher. Do you think that gives me the right to run it?"

He said, "It doesn't sound very full."

I said, "If I let it go, all the food will get crusted."

"You could wash them by hand."

"Why have a dishwasher then?"

"That's a problem," Ed said.

"A dilemma," I said. "But not a paradox."

There was a short silence. Then Ed said, "Have you got any other things on your mind?"

"A couple."

"How about you invite me in and we can talk."

"You think it will help?"

"I want to talk, Jack."

So I let him in. "Where's Molly?" he asked.

"Right now? Probably watching some fringe theater group make a political statement by running around the stage naked. She's in Edinburgh for the festival."

"I didn't know she was away."

"So are Marty and Anna," I said. "I am solo during these difficult times. For chrissake, Ed. Sit down. You know where the chairs are."

He sat, still holding the paper bag. "I hate this," he said. "Feeling like a stranger in your house."

I realized things were pretty bad between us. Not because of what he said, but because I didn't believe him.

"I was just about to make myself a drink."

"Oh. I brought a little something . . ." He pulled a fifth of Dewar's out of the bag.

I said, "Is that legal? I mean, it might be construed as a bribe. I could report you to the N.L.R.B."

"You got a couple of glasses and some ice?"

"Right," I said. "And a nosh. You can help me fill the dishwasher." I left him and bustled around the kitchen. "I can't tell you what being alone does for my sense of self-reliance," I called in to him. "I am actually slicing this cheese and opening a box of crackers on my own initiative."

"Molly was a brave woman to leave you alone."

Calling between rooms like that, it felt as if we were back in our apartment at Juilliard. Ed was the first real friend I ever had. I stood there puttering with Wheat Thins and Velveeta and remembered that first day at Juilliard when we met. I had no idea who Ed was then. He claims that was the first thing that attracted him to me.

Ed's family was already a legend. I knew about Daniel Lewis, the cellist, and I knew about Ella Vlady, the harpsichordist. I didn't know Ed was their son. And I didn't know about his older sister and brother, who had been with the String Quartet of Turin for ten years.

We brought each other home for vacations and weekends. I would wake up in the guest room of the house in Westhampton and lie there trying to make myself believe it was really Ella Vlady I heard running through *The Well-Tempered Clavier* in the room just below me. At the dinner table the talk of music and musicians, conductors and composers, tours and recording sessions was as offhand and intimate as Momma's talk about Lorraine's pregnancy or the new rabbi's wife.

By the end of the first year I was as much a part of the Lewises as Ed. The family had embraced me as one of them.

At the same time, Ed discovered Poppa. Before then it had never occurred to Ed there was anything else of importance but music. He told me once that until he met the Fleischmans he thought the world was divided into artists and others. "Now look at me," he said. "I'm learning politics! Economy! I always thought workers were just people who failed their auditions." He would sit with Poppa for hours, long after I had gone to bed. Poppa would tell him stories I had heard for seventeen years. And Momma, as often as necessary, would retell the story. "Just so he shouldn't go off half-cocked," she said.

When he stayed in Brooklyn, he slept in your bed.

By our third year he wanted to drop out of Juilliard. Ed had known from the time he was born the kinds of risks that solo artists had to take. He was prepared for all of them, yet he couldn't stop himself from backing off. At the very times he could have let go, when he could have taken off and soared, his work would turn cold—technical and cautious.

He didn't drop out.

We were rooming together in a small apartment on Riverside Drive. I watched him struggle to wake up every morning for his lessons and develop headaches to keep from ensemble rehearsals. I rode out rages with him—against teachers, against "the system," against his parents. I couldn't help him. All I could do was to be there and to understand without judging. I was learning a lot about friendship.

The Lewises never judged him either. But they didn't understand. That kind of failure, the loss of nerve they could hear in Ed's work, was beyond their comprehension.

After a while they gave up. They turned their attention to me. If I had realized sooner I would have stopped it, mainly because it might have hurt my friendship with Ed. Ed told me he was grateful though. It took the pressure off him.

So while he read and joined study groups with Poppa and rolled up his sleeves, I took his place as the hope of the Lewis family.

Daniel Lewis and Ella Vlady started me thinking about myself in a way only one other person had ever thought about me. Momma. She had always said things like "When you are a great violinist, then you'll know how important clean fingernails are."

When we finished Juilliard the Lewises had my career and my reputation well in hand. Ed went straight to a job with the St. Louis Symphony.

I didn't see him for six years.

We met again in 1961, when I played with the St. Louis Symphony.

I was twenty-eight, well on my way to turning into a permanent prima donna. I was high-strung, prone to tantrums. I was learning how to preen and how to make irrational demands. It turned out Ed was on the verge of permanence, too. He carried himself like a disappointed man. There was a bitter tone in his voice, just the hint of a stoop in his shoulders, as if he was asking to be victimized. He was settling in, turning soft.

It took dinner, the concert, and a couple of drinks to find each other again.

We admitted how disappointed we were, with ourselves and each other. A sense of self-betrayal floated around the edges of everything we were doing.

We were both in trouble.

Neither of us had been able to talk to anyone else. Admitting it helped, but it wasn't enough. We had to do something.

A couple of weeks later he phoned to tell me he was doing something. It was new. It was a risk. Actually, it was crazy. He and Reinhold Blesser and Fred Holland were in contact with some people from the Atlanta Symphony. They had an idea for a new kind of organization. They were flying down to Atlanta to meet with them. Did I want to come?

In Atlanta we met with Bob Cross and Eileen Simpson to talk about the People's Ensemble.

((146))

Now here we were, fifteen years later, calling to each other between rooms again.

"I spoke to my mother a couple of days ago," Ed said.

"Where is she?"

"Turin. She's playing at a Bach festival."

"Is she with Anita and Danny?" I asked.

"They all send their love. They're planning a big affair for her seventy-fifth birthday in Paris next spring."

"She must be furious."

"How did you know?"

"I know how she feels about birthdays." I imitated her. " 'If my fingers vork, vat matters how old they are.' "

He gave a surprised laugh. "You remember that? Jesus Christ, it must have been twenty years ago."

"Twenty-four," I said. "I've got a freaky memory."

I brought in the cheese and the glasses. As soon as I was back in the living room we tensed up again. Ed almost dove at the bottle.

"When's the last time we had drinks together?" he asked.

"April. At the benefit party for the symphony."

"We were on opposite sides of the room then," he said.

"We still are."

He handed me a glass. "Should we drink to the end of the strike?"

"We both want it over." We took a slug. "Are you planning to get drunk?" I asked.

He said, "I think so."

"Then maybe we ought to get business out of the way first. I'm not going to tell you what happened at the meeting."

"You turned down the package. I know."

"How?" He didn't answer. "Dowd and Gwynne?"

He shook his head.

"Tony."

"I want you to call off the strike, Jack."

"We voted on it."

"But you swung the vote."

"That's not true," I said. "And Tony Querault is a *putz*."

"A what?"

"*Putz*. That's Yiddish for *schmuck*. Have we finished talking business?"

"At least hear me out. O.K.?"

I took another drink. "Are you really going to get a court order out on us?"

"I'm trying to hold this thing together with my bare hands."

"Do you know how pissed that makes me? That Tony's been running back and forth like that?" I said.

"He cares about the symphony."

"We all care about the fucking symphony."

"Then call off the strike."

"You call it off. Meet the demands."

"I want to give the artistic control back to you," he said. "I swear it. I want to keep Quasnosky. But the board . . ."

I made an impatient gesture.

"The symphony's in trouble." He took a drink and put his glass down.

"You going to tell me how poor we are?"

"No." Ed sat on the edge of his chair. His hands were clasped and he looked down at them for a long time. "I haven't had a good night's sleep since I told Quasnosky . . ." He gave a little laugh. "It's funny. I knew the strike would happen. I could see it coming. I was hoping for it." He glanced up at me. "I was afraid the membership would just let it go by. Then I really would have known it was all over. But you fought back." He gave me his funny tight smile and nodded. "Everybody thinks I've forgotten where we came from. Would I be tearing myself apart like this if I didn't remember?"

"What kind of trouble?" I said.

"The board's trying to squeeze us out."

"Us?"

"The symphony. They're looking for ways to kill it. Not all of them," he said quickly. "Just a couple."

"How?"

"Extend all the seasons, but limit the services to midweek. Two concerts, three rehearsals. Also want to limit the voices. They figure in five years they'll have financial reasons to cut the symphony in half." Ed paused. "They like the strike. It's giving them ammunition." He put up a hand. "And don't say it."

"I wasn't going to."

"Then how do you know what I meant?"

I told Ed eight years ago he was making a mistake when he stopped playing to manage the symphony full time. He said we needed him to survive. I told Ed it was a mistake to organize under a charter and create a board. By then he was able to tell me there were administrative problems I couldn't understand. And every year after that I told him we were losing the impulse that started the symphony; we were losing touch with our own community, with the people's music.

"Everything I've done was for the good of the symphony," Ed said. "We never would have made it another year without those foundation grants and without the board."

"Maybe we shouldn't have." He looked up, surprised. "It might have forced us to figure out what we were doing wrong."

"We weren't doing anything wrong."

"Then we would have survived."

He shook his head. "You've never learned how to compromise. That's your problem."

"And you did," I said. "That seems to be your problem right now."

"The union package is not unreasonable, Jack."

"It's beside the point."

"You mean Quasnosky." He gave a little rueful laugh. "That son of a bitch has been nothing but trouble since we started. The board . . . that's the one thing they won't move on. He looks like a cadaver already. You can see his hand shake from the back row. They don't want a dying man up there. They say it makes the audience nervous."

I laughed. It had struck me yesterday, after I saw Quasnosky, that maybe every symphony needed a dying man up there, somewhere in the middle of the music, just to remind us what it was all about.

"I'm pleading with you, Jack."

The Scotch was starting to buzz. "Did the union send what's-his-name, those two clowns down?" I said. "Or did you call them in?"

"I called the union."

I shook my head. "My father is a genius."

"What does Sy have to do with it?"

"He smelled it," I said. "You ought to talk to him. He knows better than anybody what's going on."

He made an impatient gesture.

"You used to be able to talk to him," I said. "Better than me."

"I was very young then. I didn't have the responsibilities."

I said, "Ah. Responsibilities."

He nodded. It took him a second to pick up my tone.

"I think we should drink to responsibilities," I said. "And all the damage we do in their name."

"I'm responsible for the symphony."

"Which one?" I said. "You started out responsible for the People's Symphony. Now you're responsible for the Gainesville Symphony. In a couple of years you'll be responsible for the Georgia Pops. Maybe after that they'll put us in spangles and sequins, throw in an electric guitar. Then you'll be responsible for Country Ed and the Fish. You'll just keep selling us out in the name of responsibility."

Ed's face got tight. "You're suddenly very proud of yourself because you're fighting back. You sat by and watched me do all the work to hold this organization together and build it. And now you're telling me I sold us out. Where were you before? On the sidelines, clicking your tongue. You should have done something then."

"We're doing something now."

"Now it's too late," he said. "You can't have the People's Symphony back."

"Why not?"

"Because it's over."

"It doesn't have to be," I said.

"We had it for a while, Jack. Be satisfied with that."

"No."

"It couldn't last," he said. "The kind of community we made, the kind of music we made. We could only do it because we were young. It lasted seven years. Seven years. That's a triumph. And the only reason you've been able to hold on to your ideals so long is that I've been protecting them. At least we can hold the line."

"As long as we learn to compromise."

He threw his hands up.

"I think you ought to give up managing and go back to the fiddle," I said.

"You need me where I am, whether you know it or not."

"You once told me I didn't need anybody." He looked away. "You weren't the first person to tell me that, but you were the first person I listened to. You remember that, Ed?"

He didn't say anything.

"It was when you convinced me to come down here. With you and Bob and Reinhold. And I don't believe you don't remember."

"This is different."

I said, "No. It's not."

"You were unhappy then."

"I'm not exactly dancing down Broadway now."

"Your brother . . ."

"My brother was sure I needed him. He felt responsible for me."

"You were one person," he said. "One career. This is a whole symphony. You can't afford to be so goddamned selfish."

"You are not being honest with me," I said.

The top of his work shirt was unbuttoned. The funny dark sprinkle of hair on his chest is gray now. It foamed out through the opening. "You should know better than anybody what this organization means to me." He looked up. "You should know why I put down the fiddle eight years ago."

"You were good."

"I was competent," he said.

"You were good enough to make music with us."

"Third chair of the first strings," he said.

"Wasn't that enough?" I asked.

"Not for a Lewis."

"You're a big boy now."

Ed said, "How old do you have to be to stop carrying your family around?"

There was a pause.

"Managing this symphony is the first thing I've been good at. Really good at." He studied me, then looked away. "You wouldn't understand that."

"Don't sell me short."

"You were used to making miracles. Before we came down here you were on your way up there to join Daniel Lewis and Ella Vlady. That's why they loved you. And that's why you could throw it away. You remember the first time you played with the St. Louis Symphony?"

"The Tchaikovsky."

"You made a miracle that night," he said. "You made that fiddle sing and I thought, Just once in my life I want to make that happen. Everybody I loved was a miracle maker." He closed his eyes for a second and held his lips very tight. "I spent twenty-eight years of my life trying to make miracles like everybody else. Then I gave up and came down here. And I found out I could do it, too. My way. This symphony is mine, Jack. I don't want to go back to the third chair."

"And you're not even drunk yet," I said.

He smiled wryly. "It doesn't show. That's part of my art. I need more ice."

"You're walking well."

"Carefully," he said. "Very carefully."

I watched him leave, then I watched the empty archway while this sadness spread through my whole body. I listened to Ed stumble around the kitchen. He had found the ice bucket and was filling it.

It's because Molly is away, I said to myself. Some big shot. Your wife goes away for a couple of weeks and you turn into a maudlin drunk. I shook my head, which was a mistake. It's because you're on strike, I said, and Arthur Quasnosky is dying and Tony Querault is an informer and Ed Lewis is right because the orchestra can't hold itself together without him and this has not been the most memorable day in your career as a musician. But it wasn't any of that.

I missed Ed. That's what it was. He was in the kitchen and he had left me in the living room and I missed him. And that reminded me how much I'd been missing him for the last ten years, because we'd started drifting apart even before he left the ensemble. I didn't want our friendship to be over.

He came back with the ice bucket.

I said, "I can't decide if that shirt makes you look younger or older."

He said, "I had the same trouble."

I watched him work with the ice and wondered what he'd been thinking in the kitchen, if he was looking for a way to find our friendship again, too.

"Jack?" His voice was cautious. "There must be something we can do."

"Let Quasnosky stay."

He closed his eyes. "It's my life, Jack."

There was a long silence.

"Are you very disappointed in me?" he said.

"I don't know."

He gave a soft laugh and nodded. "Remember St. Louis?"

"Long time ago."

"I couldn't decide how I felt about you then either. Such a prima donna. I hadn't seen you in six years. First thing you did was throw a tantrum."

"I was twenty-eight."

He chuckled. "Boy, did I let you have it. After the concert. You remember that?"

"You were disappointed."

"A couple of hours before, you'd made a miracle. I didn't know if I was disappointed." He smiled at me. "So I know how you feel."

"The People's Symphony came out of that one," I said.

"So who knows what'll come out of this? Right?"

We grinned at each other. It wasn't exactly a reunion grin. More like we were reassuring each other we were still there. "You have any idea of how tired I am?" he said.

"It's hard work."

I don't know how late it was when he said it was time to go. It felt too early. All we'd done was to signal each other that our friendship was still there. We still had a lot of groping to do before we touched. I wanted more time. I got it into my head that if Ed and I could find that old unused nerve of love between us and touch it back to life we could do the same thing with the People's Symphony.

"We don't see enough of each other," he said.

"Don't go yet."

"I've got a meeting tomorrow. Got to be on my toes."

"You going to be able to drive?"

He nodded to reassure me, one of those serious, drunken nods that isn't reassuring at all, and started toward the door. I followed him.

"I wish you'd trust me," he said.

"I can't."

"I love the symphony, Jack."

"But you think it's yours."

"I'll do anything to save it."

"Put us in jail?"

"It's my life." He leaned against the doorjamb and looked down at his shoes. "The t.r.o.'s in the works. I took it out as soon as Tony told me."

I laughed. "What's the timetable?"

"Show-cause hearing on Monday. You could be arrested on Tuesday."

"We really are something, huh?"

"Once this thing is over, Jack . . ."

"What?"

He shrugged. "Maybe we can see more of each other."

So that's where we stand. I'm sitting here on a Friday afternoon and by Tuesday I may be in jail. It's one-thirty in the afternoon. The meeting with the board is in half an hour. Then I'm going to see Poppa. We watch the six-thirty news together when we can. He likes to explain it to me. Especially the strike coverage. After that I've got a whole, empty weekend until Vic Jenkins arrives. I'll spend it with you.

July 31, 1975
Very early morning

It's not even light out. I had trouble getting to sleep after I left Poppa. Once I did, I kept waking up to check if it was morning. We saw you on television last night. It made me impatient to get back to this letter, to get it all said and in your hands. I wanted to write through the night, but I knew I'd screw things up if I rushed. I have to go slow if I'm going to say it all and have it make any sense. So I lay there as I did on the night before the concert with the Brooklyn Symphony, forcing myself to sleep, reminding myself I needed rest to play well, and that it made no sense at all to leap out of bed and try to fiddle through the night. My head was swimming with memories. They kept turning into dreams, then back to memories each time I woke.

So now I'm up, maybe for the whole, long weekend. I can see myself getting gaunter and gaunter. Molly will come home in two weeks and find me in a jail cell buried in reams of yellow paper, still writing, with the eyes of a madman. But that's all right. She tells me I dramatize.

Poppa listened to the tape. He didn't have much to say, except that he was glad Quasnosky came and that I waved my hands around too much—which was odd, since it was a tape.

I told him about Ed's visit. He smiled and nodded kind of sadly. "Eddie's a good boy," he said. "He thinks. He reads. He pays attention. He never gets the point. It happens."

We were alone in the recreation room for the six-thirty news. I helped him out of the wheelchair onto the sofa. He doesn't mind being wheeled around but he hates to stay in it once he gets where he's going.

Kissinger was answering questions about the Sinai agreement. Poppa heard him out, then he explained to me about the oil companies and the medieval church, how they're historically the same. Both transcend national boundaries; both are rich and corrupt; both bleed the workers and keep them in their place with promises of future reward. The church called it salvation, the oil companies call it energy independence. "That's why Henry the Eighth was so interesting," Poppa said. "He nationalized the church. He was smarter than our Henry."

He was still expanding on it when the commercial ended and there you were. The news is public. Poppa stopped midsentence and watched. John Chancellor explained about economic advisors and why the reorganization was so important. "No one is sure of exactly what the appointments mean," he said. "As in all the President's recent economic decisions, he has taken action. As in all his recent decisions, the significance of the action remains unclear. Leonard Fleischman is the youngest of the new appointees. He has the most liberal orientation, but over the past five years his thinking has become increasingly conservative. Some now consider him the most hard-line of the three." Is that true?

They showed you going up the steps of the Treasury Building. I think you wore the same suit you had on a couple of weeks ago. I can't be sure. You could change twice a day and it wouldn't show up on a black-and-white set. The tie was new. You've put on some weight but, as Momma would say, "On you it looks good." And you've grown into your face. It's a strong, responsible face. Television does that to people. I've never seen a Senator or Congressman on television who didn't look incredibly responsible. Your tinted glasses gave you a touch of dash.

They had another shot of you at the top of the steps, being photographed. You looked grim and vaguely familiar. That was peculiar, to be watching you on television and thinking you looked vaguely familiar. Then I realized what it was. You were being photographed and your face was frozen just like Momma's whenever she knew she was being watched.

It was a short report. I glanced at Poppa. He was concentrating on the commercial and I knew you hadn't told him.

The sports came on. He took off his glasses and cleaned them with a handkerchief. "You knew about this, Jack?" he said.

I nodded. "I didn't know if he told you or not."

"It was probably top-secret. Your brother still thinks I'm a security risk."

"He wrote me about two weeks ago."

He said, "Ah. So now you're writing a letter. Now I understand." He put his glasses back and grinned at me. "You better hurry up. In this business he might be out of a job before you finish."

"I'm not writing because he got the job. I'm writing because he told me."

He closed his eyes for a second.

"I thought he might call you. Or write," I said.

"If you thought that," he said, "you don't understand him."

"Maybe he wanted to surprise you. Like this." I knew it was lame. "He knows you're not a security risk," I said.

"Not national. Personal." He smiled. "If your mother were alive I would have known. He would have told her, she would have told me. I would have known and tonight I would have acted surprised. He can't tell me those things."

"Why not?"

"Because he wants too much for me to be proud of him."

"Aren't you?"

"Yes . . ."

"So?"

". . . and no."

"Oh."

"See? You like contradictions, Jack. Everybody thinks you're an idealist, but you like contradictions. Leonard's supposed to be a realist. That's why"—he nodded toward the set—"that's why that. But he doesn't like contradictions. I don't blame him. It's my fault." He sighed. "All he ever wanted was for me to be proud—without qualifications. You understand me? He goes to the Wharton School. He becomes an officer in the Navy. He manages you and makes you an international celebrity. He gets degrees in economics and becomes a man they listen to on Wall Street. He's got such *energy*. And I'm his father. Right? So I'm proud. And he knows that. Because those are all things a father should be proud of. But what can I do, Jackie? I'm proud—but I don't approve. Sometimes I don't even understand what he's up to. Sometimes I understand too much. And he knows that, too. It's hard for him." He considered that for a moment. "You should understand how hard it is for him."

He looked over at the baseball scores. "He gave us that set," he said. Then he shrugged. "I was the same way. I didn't start telling my father things until he was going deaf. I didn't show him things until he was going blind. Maybe that's how it is with fathers."

"I tell you things," I said.

He nodded. "So maybe Lenny is your father."

The local news came on. They had the latest on the strike. The t.r.o. is out. We go to court on Monday. They didn't mention that Vic Jenkins is flying in tonight. We meet with him tomorrow to work up our case. No one's sure we have one.

They flashed pictures of the strike committee—Dudley, Phil, Eileen, and me—and explained we would be the ones to go to jail. They used the symphony files, so there we were, in our formal wear. In fact, they used the Bachrach publicity still you had made in 1959. For ten seconds I was twenty-six and glossy again.

Poppa jumped when he saw it. "Two celebrities in one night," he said. "It's a good thing I like contradictions, too. You know what I mean, Jackie?"

It's starting to get light out. In a couple of minutes I'll get up and close the curtains. Then I'll tell you about us and our wives.

LOVE AND MARRIAGE

You've always said your divorces surprised you. I believe that. People who know their marriages are falling apart do everything they can to keep up appearances. That's why the end surprises everyone else. People who don't know squabble at parties as if it was the most natural thing in the world, denounce each other to casual acquaintances, draw blood in theater lobbies. Everyone else stands by and waits for the crash. When it happens, the couple asks their friends why they didn't warn them. The friends say, "I thought you knew."

That's how it was with you. Momma was the first to see it with Margaret. She must have known when we fought that Christmas vacation. I knew, too, but I wanted to be as much in the center of the marriage as you two. It took me longer to admit it. It took you longest of all.

I stopped dropping in on you after that Christmas vacation. You didn't notice. At least you never asked about it. You and Margaret still came to dinner every Friday night. That was the only time we saw you. At first I would look forward to it. All the magic I'd spun out about the two of you was a habit of mine that was hard to break. I treated each Friday as if the two of you were coming home from overseas. By mid-February I gave up. The dinners were too much of an ordeal. Momma would bark at me to set the table as soon as I got home from school. From the way she did it, I knew she'd been barking at the pots and glassware all day. She jumped if the phone rang, cried if the roast got overdone. Poppa would come home with a headache and go for the schnapps. I would shut myself in my room and practice, badly, until you arrived.

Nothing ever happened at dinner. That was hardest of all. Margaret would tell Momma what a good cook she was. Poppa would ask how things were going at Holtzman. Everyone was nice. But we never laughed. And if there was a silence we scrambled to fill it. When nobody made it in time I watched Momma wince at the clink of the silverware. Sometimes she let out a sigh that could break your heart. Everything stopped. The rest of us stared. "LaGuardia," she would say quickly. "He was a good mayor. I miss him."

Soon you started arriving alone. You were losing weight. Your neck seemed lost in your shirt collars. Your lips got thinner. Your whole face turned bony. Sometimes, during those long silences, I could watch you replay a whole scene in your head. Your lips tightened. You shook your head almost imperceptibly. Your jaws flexed defensively. Your eyes flashed in a counterattack. Then a flinch, a snarl, a jut of the chin. Poppa might say, "Lenny," and you'd snap to a closed, frozen smile.

Still, you had no idea what was happening. One night we were starting on the soup. You said to me, "Hey, Jackie. How are things going?" I told you about school, how I'd been asked to play at the senior honors ceremony, about Juilliard and how it looked as if my full scholarship was coming through. You said, "Terrific. That's great. That's really terrific." There was a silence. You took a couple of spoonfuls. Then you smiled at me and said, "Hey, Jackie. How are things going?"

Momma said, "Lenny!" She was tense and frightened.

You looked at her, bewildered.

"What's the matter, Lenny?"

You said, "Nothing, Momma," and you meant it. You were genuinely puzzled.

Momma's birthday was in March. No matter what kind of troubles she might be having, she enjoyed her birthdays like a kid. She would celebrate all day, humming to herself from the time she woke up, anticipating surprises from Poppa. Sometimes flowers arrived in the afternoon, sometimes funny telegrams. When Poppa came home he'd announce we were going out to dinner and the theater. Momma would shriek, "I'm in a housedress! It'll take me an hour."

Poppa would say, "Slip into something. You're gorgeous," and pretend not to notice that her hair was done and she already had her makeup on.

Once I told her how Ella Vlady felt about birthdays. Momma said, "She's crazy. You should celebrate. You should remember you were born. You know why? Because if you remember you were born, you remember anything is possible."

Poppa had tickets for *South Pacific*. It was Saturday night. He'd arranged for you and Margaret to meet us at China City. Momma wore an orchid corsage up on the strap of her evening gown. It tickled her cheek when she turned her head.

You were late. Momma was starting on her second whiskey sour. Poppa drank Scotch. I had just finished reading a life of Oscar Wilde, so I had asked for absinthe. I had to settle for a Tom Collins, which was very humiliating.

Nothing was going to spoil Momma's party. We had decided that, coming in on the subway. Momma had marched through the sliding car doors at Kings Highway, clutching her purse and holding her purple gown just above her ankles. She sat like a queen on the yellow woven seats. Poppa and I stood over her. As the train lurched forward she pulled Poppa down by his coat lapel. "Nothing but good tonight, Sy," she shouted in his ear. "You hear me?"

He nodded. When he straightened up I shouted in his ear. "What did she say?"

He told me in my ear. Then he grinned. "She thinks I got the tickets from a save-the-family benefit."

She pulled him down again. "No secrets, Sy."

"No secrets," he said.

Margaret was buoyant and smiling when you did arrive. She waved at us across the restaurant. She had on a new pair of hoop earrings. Her fingers and arms were covered with jewelry. Momma smiled at her as she threaded through the tables. Under her breath Momma said, "Sy? She looks like a street stand."

You were a little behind her, still wearing your topcoat. You kept your hands in your pockets. Your shoulders were sloped. Margaret surprised Momma with a kiss on the cheek. Poppa raised his eyebrows.

She said, "Happy birthday, Esther," and rumpled my hair as she slipped in beside me. "You all look wonderful." She squeezed my knee. It made my leg jerk. "I'm sorry we're late. Have you ordered? Is there time for a drink?"

You stood over the table. Margaret had left the chair opposite hers free for you, but she'd blocked off Momma.

You said, "Happy birthday, Momma," and she had to settle for a nod across Margaret and me.

Margaret said, "Darling, you forgot to check your coat."

You said, "No, I didn't."

She laughed. "You're wearing it, you idiot."

"I know I'm wearing it. I don't want to check my coat."

"Check your coat, honey."

"I want it with me."

"You'll be uncomfortable with it on the back of your chair."

"That's all right."

"Check your coat." Her eyes flashed. It was instantaneous and sharp. She covered it with a smile and a helpless shrug at Momma.

"At least take it off," Momma said cautiously.

You sat down and slipped it off.

Margaret shook her head. "He's such a baby sometimes."

She admired Momma's corsage and her dress, told Poppa and me how handsome we looked. Every time she smiled at me she touched my leg. Her smiles, her compliments, her concern for you—all of it had an edge of parody. She chatted and laughed through her drink. She pretended to have trouble with the menu. "You order for me, Sy," she said. "You know about these things."

You had been silent since you slipped off your coat, watching her closely over your drink. When she asked Poppa to order, you muttered something. She swung around. "What, honey?" Her voice was sweet, but the swing had happened too quickly.

"I said, 'Don't patronize them.' They've taken enough shit from you."

Momma said, "Lenny." It was half a warning, half a plea.

"The family can take care of itself," Margaret said. She squeezed my thigh, high enough so you could see it. "Right, Jackie?"

"I'm warning you."

She patted Momma's wrist. "Don't pay any attention. He's in one of his moods. You know how moody he is." She laughed. "You've lived with him longer than me."

"It's your mother's birthday," Poppa said steadily. "Should I order for all of us?"

When the waiter left, Margaret sighed. "If you want to know the truth, Lenny and I had a fight."

Momma said, "Tell us later."

"I just think we should clear the air. Otherwise we'll be tense all evening."

You straightened in your chair. "Don't."

"You see? You're making such a big thing about it." She leaned toward you. "Once it's out in the open you'll see how silly and trivial it was."

Momma said, "Sy?"

Poppa said, "Margaret," very gently. "It would be better for all of us . . ."

"It was about money," she said, as if she was confessing under pressure. "Lenny came home with a new investment tip. He wanted to borrow five thousand dollars from me. I said no. That's all it was." No one spoke. "I mean, it would have been one thing if this was the first time. But Lenny's already lost about ten or fifteen thousand dollars of mine. He just doesn't seem to have a head for business." She laughed.

You said, "You've made your point."

"So I told him no. Not this time. When he's saved up enough from his own work as a junior clerk at Holtzman's he can do anything he wants with it. Then he lost his temper. And you know Lenny's temper."

We must have looked like an ideal family. There was Momma in her corsage, her interesting-looking daughter-in-law patting her wrist, her husband and two sons in suits and slicked hair. But Momma and Poppa threw helpless glances at each other, as if they'd discovered they were having a picnic in the middle of a Roman arena. You sat silently, shredding a China City matchbook, and Margaret kept chatting at Momma with some of the words stabbing from the side of her mouth at you.

She was relentless. Her precision was dazzling. We could see every lunge, every penetration, even when we couldn't understand what weapon she was using.

The waiter had to brush away the pieces of shredded matchbook before he could put your plate down. Margaret ordered another drink.

You said, "You've had enough."

Margaret said, "No, I haven't."

You canceled the order but she caught the waiter by the

arm. "Bring the drink." The waiter looked at you. "It's for me. Not him," Margaret said.

Poppa said, "It's all right. I'll have one, too."

She turned back to Poppa. "Thank you, Sy. I mean, it really is the only way I'm going to get through *South Pacific* again. Do you know this is the fourth time I've had to sit and watch Mary Martin be a cute little bigot?"

"I didn't know you'd seen it," Poppa said.

"I told Lenny. But he said it was Esther's birthday . . ."

"You've seen it too, Lenny?"

"No. She told me all about it. She liked it the first time. When it was chic to get tickets."

"Lenny had to work late."

"Your faggot friends don't like me around."

"They're not charmed by your party jokes."

"I don't tell party jokes."

"You talk about all the girls you've had. Those are jokes."

"And all they want to hear about is the boys."

Momma said, "Sy . . ."

Poppa said, "It looks like maybe tonight is not a night for you to be celebrating. Maybe you'd rather be alone. . . ." But it was too late.

"My friends don't care about anybody's bedroom habits. As long as they're not boors."

"They put up with your habits."

"And I don't fuck every girl I see just to prove I'm not a loser."

"Watch your mouth in front of my family."

"Hasn't your father ever heard the word 'loser'?"

It always happens smoothly in the movies. Whoever's doing the slapping swings, meets the cheek with a good, loud snap, and follows through. In real life it's clumsy. It was a mess that night. You sprang up and reached across the table as the waiter came with the drinks. You caught me on the side of the head with the back of your hand, turned over the drink, and barely grazed Margaret's neck. But your finger caught in her earring. She howled. Momma yelled, "Lenny!" You pulled free. Margaret massaged her ear and looked down at the Scotch dripping onto her lap. She glared up at you in triumph. Momma pulled back to protect her gown.

Poppa nodded to the waiter. "A little accident," he said softly. He was trembling.

The waiter went for a towel.

You sat down again. You had locked eyes with Margaret when she looked up from her lap. Neither of you would let go.

Momma said, "Margaret, use your napkin."

She blotted her lap. I stood the glass up.

The waiter came back and mopped up the table. He asked if he should bring another drink.

Margaret said, "No. I'm going home to change."

You said, "And then what?"

"Then I'm going to Mason's party."

She pushed her chair out.

Poppa had orchestra seats, close up, but it felt as if we were watching the show through a telescope. Even the music seemed muffled. Momma and Poppa tried to turn the night back into a celebration. At intermission he said, "How do you like it?" And Momma smiled and said, "Wonderful. Wonderful." She fingered her corsage. Then she studied me a second and smoothed down a cowlick.

You had wandered off, still in your topcoat. I went to the bathroom and found you smoking in the men's lounge. I had started to feel it was up to me to save the evening. I thought: Maybe if I said something witty like they did in the plays I'd been reading. Or if I put an understanding hand on your shoulder the way they did in war movies. Or if I made a speech about how life was still worth living and the important thing was to love one another. Then I could lead you back rehabilitated. Momma and Poppa would shower me with silent, grateful glances.

Instead you and I nodded at each other like cautious acquaintances and I went to the bathroom.

When I came out you stopped me and asked if I'd come home with you for the night. I didn't think Margaret would feature that. You assured me she wouldn't be there. Mason's parties lasted all weekend. I said O.K.

"Do you want to go now?" you said.

The intermission lights blinked. "I don't think that's a terrific idea. It's Momma's birthday."

You nodded. "I'll meet you back at the apartment."

"Don't you think you ought to stay with us?" I said carefully. You almost smiled at me. "Yeah. I guess you're right," I said.

I told Momma and Poppa you were going home.

Poppa smiled sadly. "That's style. Huh, Esther? To walk out on *South Pacific?*"

Then I told them I was going to spend the night.

We'd all given up on paying attention. The three of us kept our eyes fixed on the stage, but the laughter and the music happened somewhere over our heads and around our seats. Once, while Mary Martin was alone and quiet, Momma let out one of her sighs. Some heads turned, but Momma didn't notice.

I was somewhere else, too. You had asked me to come home with you. You needed someone to talk to and you'd chosen me. I knew you hadn't had much of a choice in the men's lounge of the Majestic, but that didn't matter. The very fact that you'd asked had transformed me into a man of affairs. I sat there shamelessly offering up prayers of gratitude to Margaret for giving me the opportunity. I was impatient to leave Momma and Poppa, and ride to your rescue. I planned out all the wise things I would say to you and how I'd smile at your astonishment when you saw how strong and mature I was. "Why didn't I ever come to you for help before?" you'd say. "What a fool I was not to notice." I would chide you gently for hurting Momma and Poppa and you would hang your head sheepishly. "You're right, Jackie. You've always been right," you would say. Then I'd understand and forgive. I thought the curtain would never come down.

When it did I controlled myself. I left the theater slowly with Momma and Poppa. I kissed Momma in the street and said, "Happy birthday," again. Then I ran to the IRT.

You were vacuuming the living room. You had the hi-fi turned up loud enough to hear over the motor. You didn't hear me buzz. I had to go back outside to bang at the window. You peeked through the curtain. From behind the glass you said, "Hey, Jackie," and came around to let me in.

You had changed into your shorts and basketball shirt. "Just trying to get the place in shape," you said. "Helps me think." You unplugged the cord and wrapped it around the machine. "So, how are things going?"

I said, "O.K."

"She left the place like a pigsty."

"Looks O.K. now."

You laughed. "Sure. Did you like the show?"

"It was O.K."

"Don't be a snob. It's a big hit. Did Momma have a good time? Margaret didn't spoil it for her, did she? She couldn't have. She never lets anything spoil her birthday. You're looking great, Jackie. I've been meaning to tell you that.

You're really looking great. Growing up." You threw the vacuum cleaner in the closet. "You want to turn down the hi-fi? I just had it on while I was cleaning. You can turn it off if you want. I don't know if you like that music. It's called bop."

"Yeah," I said. "I know bop."

"Good. I wouldn't want you to just get so involved with classical music you don't know what's going on. You know what I mean? Wouldn't want you to turn into a snob. You've got to be able to walk with kings and never lose the common touch. Who was it always used to say that?"

"Momma."

You nodded. "She's right."

I turned off the music.

"Why don't you just leave it on low?" you said. "It's good music."

I put it on again. Low. You were dusting the tables.

"Sit down. Sit down," you said. "I just want to take care of a couple of . . . Then I'll make up the couch for you to sleep on. You must be beat. It's late."

I said, "That's O.K."

You hadn't looked at me since you opened the door. You moved around the living room, flicking the dustrag at all the wood, but you weren't really cleaning. I wondered if you'd had second thoughts about me, if you were trying to get rid of me. I started feeling very young again. I looked for a way to let you know that I'd come to your rescue.

You didn't stop talking. All the time you dusted, while you put the rag away and brought out sheets and blankets for the couch, you kept a steady stream of words aimed at me. It was disconnected and urgent, like desperate humming.

"You know what I ought to do? We both ought to do it, because it's important. You know what I mean? I ought to work on my accent. We're never going to get anywhere until we get rid of our accents. I never even realized I had an accent before I went to the Wharton School. And it didn't matter so much then because I was always writing papers. Besides, a lot of people liked it. I mean, I ended up valedictorian. Right? But once you get out in the business world, that's another story. You'll see. Nobody trusts a Brooklyn accent. That's incredible, isn't it? But it's true. If I could just change the way I talk. I mean, you see some of these guys with no more brains than me. But they're smooth . . . and my clothes. That's another thing. . . . So, how are things going? Momma didn't say anything about me, did she? She shouldn't be sore, you know. Those things happen. Her life hasn't been any bed of roses. You know that, don't you? With Poppa, I mean. So she should know." You pulled yourself up and stood frozen for an instant. You were catching your finger in Margaret's earring again. You flinched, then forced yourself back to work. "Did you see how she maneuvered that whole thing? It was her fault. She wanted me to . . . she didn't have to tell them all that. . . . You want a drink? I've got Coke in the icebox." You went into the kitchen. "First time she heard me call it an icebox she fell on the floor. 'It's a refrigerator. Not an icebox.' So I still call it an icebox." You brought back a Coke, which I didn't want. "Why don't you sit down? We can relax now." You sprawled in an armchair. "You can sit on the couch if you want. I made it up for you. You can get undressed and get into it if you want." You leapt up. "You need pajamas? You can wear mine. They might be a little big . . ."

I said, "That's O.K. I sleep in my underwear."

"No shit. You really are growing up." I was still standing, holding the Coke. You came back and leaned over the back of the chair. "Well? Why don't you get undressed?"

I shrugged. "I don't know."

"Go ahead. Just hop in the sack. It'll be like old times."

I wanted to say, "That's why," but I didn't. I started undressing. You fell back into the armchair. You watched me fold up my shirt and pants and shook your head. "Really growing up. You been laid lately?" I shook my head noncommittally. You looked at me more closely. "You been laid at all?"

I can never lie at point-blank questions. I shrugged and whispered, "No," as casually as I could.

"You're not queer, are you?"

"No."

"Good. I've been worried about you, Jackie. I have to admit it."

"You haven't even seen me."

"You're still my kid brother. I'm supposed to worry about my kid brother."

It wasn't happening the way it was supposed to. I tried to keep my back to you until I could figure out what *was* happening. One thing was sure. You weren't going to end up hanging your head sheepishly. You weren't going to tell me I was right.

I slipped between the sheets on the couch. The cushions sank. I sat back against the pillow with my knees up but it felt as if I were in tufted quicksand.

You had your legs sprawled under the coffee table. I kept my eyes on your sweat socks.

"You ought to get laid," you said.

I said, "O.K. Tomorrow."

"I'm not kidding. You ought to know what it's all about. You go around with a lot of romantic ideas in your head you'll be in trouble. You go around with a hard-on for five, six years, you get married just to get it off. Any girl looks beautiful. You know what I mean? You've got to be realistic. What are you waiting for?"

I shrugged. "I guess I just haven't had the opportunity."

"You gotta hustle."

I said, "Could we talk about something else?"

"You mad at me?"

I shook my head. I wasn't. Maybe I should have been. I might not have felt so depressed. But I had a feeling the most important thing I could do just then was to like you.

"You're still upset about tonight, huh?"

I shrugged. "A little."

"That's what I mean about being romantic. Those things happen all the time. You can't expect it to be all hugs and kisses. That's what marriage is. Disappointment, I mean."

"Why don't you get a divorce?"

"There's love and there's marriage," you said. "That's different things. When you first get married you're in love. You're young. You think you have the world by the balls. But you grow up. I mean, how long do you think you can stay in love with somebody when they leave hairpins all over the bathroom sink? Or when you see them wax off their moustache? Like, I didn't even realize Margaret's teeth were crooked until after we got married. I thought she was beautiful. You know why? Because I loved her. The first time I met her in Bucks County, I said to myself, Boy, that's what I want. She had style." You paused. "See? That's what I mean. Before I met Margaret I would have said she had class." You gave a little laugh. "She would wander around the grounds while I was doing the lawns. She always looked like she was distracted. And she always wore this jewelry that I'd never seen before. The other girls I went out with always looked like insiders. You know what I mean? We'd go out and they'd be wearing all this taffeta and crinoline.

It was like they had their money tacked in their petticoats. They always had their hair done. After a couple of weeks I'd realize they were just like me, after all. Nothing special. So by the time I saw Margaret I knew the difference between them and a real insider. She had this long, loose hair and she'd be wearing jeans and a shirt, but she wore them as if she had better things to think about. Besides, they showed off this nice, round little ass. But not like they were trying. You know what I mean? Sometimes she'd nod at me and the way she did it showed she could even afford to be nice to the help. You know how some people nod and they let you know they're noticing, but not really? She had that down. So we got together. First time I laid her was at her father's swimming pool. She called me her little savage. Always making jokes about my accent . . . how I'd never been to Europe . . . how I smelled of the city." You paused. The coffee table had a glass top. You stared through it at your sweat socks.

I was glad I wasn't mad at you now. You were telling me things you'd never told me before. You were talking about yourself. Even the silence between us was something new. It was the kind of silence only friends can sustain. I imagined I was one of your friends. I had come over, not to save you, not to punish you for spoiling your mother's birthday, not even to give advice, but because you'd asked me. You needed an ear. I wrapped my arms around my knees and nodded understandingly. It was wonderful. I could have been anybody.

You shrugged and crossed your shins under the table. "Shit, I was in love. She told me I had a great future. All I needed was a little polish. So she taught me what to like. How to drink wine with dinner. How to knot my tie so I didn't look like a hood. I thought about her all the time.

But you get to know a person, you can't keep that kind of thing up. They disappoint you. You get married and it's not the same anymore. I figured you knot your tie in the morning, go off to work, come home to wine with dinner, go out to parties with interesting people, then come home and fuck." You shook your head. "But it's not like the movies. Everything changes. So now you're married. But a man can't live without love. Right?" You fell silent again. I liked the silences best. "I'll tell you this," you said. "I'm learning." You looked up at me and remembered who you were talking to. "That's why I'm telling you. So you can learn, too. Right? It's for your benefit. So I'll tell you this. You've got to be realistic. Never commit yourself to something you can't get out of. You know what I mean?"

I didn't, but I nodded.

You studied me awhile, then clicked your tongue. "Really fucking growing up."

My face flamed.

"Hey, Jackie?"

"Yeah."

"Don't tell anybody about this yet. O.K.?"

"About what?"

"I'm quitting Holtzman."

"What are you going to do?"

"Can't have any self-respect at a place like Holtzman. They treat you like you should be grateful for every crumb. Like you're nothing and just being there is a big favor. Shit, I was valedictorian of my class at the Wharton School. Right? I don't have to take that from anybody."

"What are you going to do?"

"I decided about a week ago. I was in the office, see? And Holtzman walks in. He says, 'Good morning, Lenny,' and walks by my desk. I say, 'Good morning, Mr. Holtzman.'

((177))

Then I think, How come he calls me Lenny and I have to call him Mr. Holtzman? And how come whenever he walks in I watch him all the time, but he looks at me once and forgets about it? I deserve better than that. I've earned it. Shit, I'm twenty-three years old already and I broke my ass to be valedictorian. I'm married. I'm stable. I live in the right kind of place. It's about time I got the respect I deserve. Right?"

"What are you going to do, Lenny? You got another job?"

"I'm joining the Navy." My eyes must have popped. "Officer Candidate School," you said quickly. "I'm not just enlisting. I'll be an officer. I should have done it a long time ago. I'm tired of people looking funny at me when they find out I've never been in the service. Especially now. With Korea and all. You know what I mean? Besides, I think maybe my real problem is that I don't carry myself right. I don't look like anybody's ever called me 'sir.' So they've got this thing now where if you've got a college degree you go to school for three, four months and you come out with a —whaddayacallit—a commission. Then you serve for three years. I applied for May. What's wrong?"

I was trying to imagine a Fleischman in uniform. I tried to imagine myself, but I couldn't get higher than Eagle Scout. "What about Margaret?"

You shook your head. "She doesn't know about it yet. She won't care, anyway. Don't say anything about it, though. In case . . ." You looked away from me.

"What do you mean?"

You shrugged. "I might change my mind. Or they might not . . . security clearance . . . a lot of things . . . Poppa . . . I don't know what kind of files they have. Things could happen. If I don't get in I wouldn't want her to know I tried."

"You'll get in," I said.

You glanced around the room. "You didn't finish your Coke." I had left it near the stereo.

"I didn't really want it."

You got up and emptied it in one swig. You could have been standing in the kitchen in Brooklyn after a game.

"What's going to happen when you tell Margaret?"

"I don't know."

"She'll be mad, Lenny."

"She's done plenty of stuff without telling me."

"You want her to get mad?"

You shrugged.

"What if she . . . ?" I stopped myself.

"What?"

"Nothing."

"I don't have to ask her permission," you said.

"I know."

"I'm my own person. You know what I mean?"

I nodded.

"Don't get the idea she leads me around by the nose."

"O.K."

"If she doesn't like what I do, she can get the hell out. Right?"

"I guess so," I said.

"I mean, that's always been her problem, anyway. She can't stick anything out. The minute things don't go her way she walks out. So if she wants to walk out for good that's her responsibility. She can be the one . . ." You stopped yourself. "Just don't say anything to anybody." You looked at the empty Coke bottle. "You want any more of this?"

I shook my head. "Poppa says it's a thinly disguised imperialistic war. Did you know that?"

"Poppa says a lot of things."

"He says if we win there's going to be others. Worse ones. In India, maybe."

"Poppa's got problems."

You put the Coke bottle in the garbage and said it was time to hit the sack.

You went into the bedroom. I lay alone in the dark and listened to you get undressed. You made a lot of noise, as if you were getting out of armor.

I stayed awake a good long time that night. I was worried. About you. About me. Love had been on my mind a lot lately. I'd figured I'd learn about it from you the way I'd learned about everything else. That was why I had wanted so much to find a place for myself in your life with Margaret. Now, here I was, lying smack in the center. And the prospects weren't too hot. If it wasn't working for you, how the hell was it going to work for me? Up until that night I'd wondered about how it would happen for me. Now I wondered whether I wanted it to happen at all. I started to understand about monks. Maybe a celibate life wouldn't be so bad after all. If I worked hard I could become a saint. That might piss Poppa off, but it probably wouldn't be any worse than your going into the Navy. Then I remembered that saints had to go through a whole tortured youth before they reformed and became saints. That meant falling in love, so I was back where I started.

My eyes were getting used to the dark. I looked around the living room at the paneled walls, the fireplace, the heavy furniture I'd helped you and Margaret shift around when you first moved in. I knew it was the last time I'd see it. The two of you were circling each other as I'd seen you circle kids on Twenty-seventh Street, daring each other to make the first move, jockeying for the right to say, "He started it."

I fell asleep thinking of all the girls I'd never marry. Seventeen years old. Who knew there were people like Molly?

You stopped coming to Brooklyn after that night. A couple of weeks later you called to tell us you had gotten into Officer Candidate School, and that you and Margaret were separated. You couldn't understand why we weren't surprised.

I didn't see much of you for the next three years. I started at Juilliard in the fall. My time was split between school, weekends with the Lewises in Westhampton, and Momma and Poppa in Brooklyn. Sometimes I would get to my room on a Sunday night, call home to say hello, and find out I'd missed you. You still had that habit of popping in without warning.

A couple of times Ed and I were in Brooklyn for Friday night when you surprised us. Each visit you looked better. You liked your uniform. You wore it like Thelma Moskowitz had worn her cast, as if it was helping all the pieces inside knit back together. You held yourself taller. Your face was tan from stopovers in Guantánamo Bay. You were losing your accent, too. With each visit your *a*'s were a little less flat, your *r*'s more distinct. And you always brought gifts, silk from Hong Kong for Momma, a Swedish pipe for Poppa, temple rubbings on rice paper from Singapore for me.

I was thrilled. You were turning back into the hero I'd given up for lost. Once you sent me twenty dollars from Oslo with a short note.

> *Dear Jackie,*
> This is for drill.
>
> *Lenny*

There was no reason for it. You never did it again. The bill stayed in my wallet for months. It meant that sometime, while you were halfway across the world and involved in doing whatever lieutenants did, you had thought about me. I finally had to break it one night in March to get a bus. The driver wasn't too happy about it. Neither was I. But it was freezing out—and it was all I had.

It wasn't until my last year at Juilliard that I was able to really see you again. You were out of the Navy. Molly and I were together by then. The two of us drove down to Philadelphia to spend the weekend with you and your new wife. I think I was more excited about seeing you that weekend than I'd ever been in my life. You'd been traveling to new worlds for three years. So had I.

There was Molly, for one thing. And Juilliard. And a career as a soloist that was already taking off. And my friendship with Ed. I wanted to share it all with you at once.

Molly happened when I was a junior.

I had played in a program of student work at the Recital Hall. Arthur Birnbaum had asked me to do a violin sonata of his. Molly was at the reception.

Those receptions were the only athletic activities Juilliard offered. The room would divide into two teams, offense and defense. The defense were the performers. They would stand in corners, half hiding, but alert, on the balls of their feet, ready to receive. The offense was the audience. They would start at the door, scout the room for soloists, then sprint around the punch bowl and fling themselves into the arms of the defense, usually weeping. I wasn't very good at either position, but I'd become a pretty competent miller. Milling happened about a half hour into the reception. You didn't need coordination to become a good miller, just cunning. It consisted of circulating slowly around the room with a drink, looking as if you had just finished a conversation. I have been known to mill nonstop for two hours.

That night I milled smack into Molly.

She was standing right in front of me, but I was so busy looking comfortable I didn't notice. You know how short Molly is. And my own body had decided to break six feet only recently, so I hadn't yet adjusted to it. I still thought the rest of the world ended a little above eye level. I didn't even realize she was there until her nose touched one of my shirt studs. I almost spilled my drink on her.

She said, "Why are you avoiding me?"

I said, "I'm not."

She said, "You've circulated past me eight times."

I said, "I didn't notice."

She said, "That's what I mean. When a person passes another person eight times without even noticing, they're avoiding them. My name is Molly Reisdorf."

She had both hands in the pockets of this green cloth coat. She took one out and extended it. I shook hands from the hip.

Whenever I met a girl I had a habit of thinking of you, wondering if you would approve. If I figured you would, I turned tongue-tied and foolish. If you wouldn't, I got angry at myself for being interested in the first place. Molly didn't stand a chance. But it was all right because I wasn't interested in the first place.

My first good look at her was mostly the top of her head. Her hair was windblown, which was odd since it was a calm night outside and we'd been indoors for at least three hours. It was that curly kind of hair that looks like an afro the morning after it's cut. She's always said she was born twenty years too soon.

She tilted her head up. She was still standing in close to me and the angle made her look like a Picasso, square chin with round cheeks and rectangular forehead. She took one step backward, smiled. Molly has this dimple in her left cheek when she smiles that has been knocking me out for twenty-three years. That was the first time I saw it.

I smiled back at her and thought, I could never marry her. It didn't occur to me that I'd never thought anything as specific as that in my whole life and that it was a little peculiar to think it about a girl I'd just shaken hands with.

I told Molly about that a couple of weeks before we were married. I wondered if it was my version of a mystic experience and if I should send it in to some Sunday supplement as an ESP thing. Molly said no, I was just picking up on her signals. Then she explained that she had wandered into the concert that night because she was depressed about a statistics assignment. She had decided to give herself two hours of numbness, then go home and tear into it. It seemed to be working until I came on the program. She said it had something to do with the way I carried myself, erect, self-assured, as if my bow tie wasn't tilted. The way she tells it, when I reached my position on the stage, she decided, "You're it, mister." That was why she was wearing loafers at the reception, and her green cloth coat over slacks and a wrinkled blouse. She hadn't expected to come.

So I wasn't psychic at all about our getting married, Molly said. Just observant.

I waited for her to say something about the concert. It was standard for the offense to begin. The worst move for a performer was to start, especially with something like "How did you like the concert?"

I said, "How did you like the concert?"

She said, "I don't like it when they put tacks on the piano hammers."

I said, "I played the violin."

She said, "You asked how I liked the concert. I mean,

when Hanns Eisler puts tacks on the hammers, that's political. When some eighteen-year-old schmendrick does it,
it's just arty."

That didn't sound as if she was from Juilliard. I asked if
she was a musician.

She laughed. "My mother wanted me to be a cellist. But
I never got tall enough for it to fit. I'm in graduate school."

I thought, She's even too old for me.

"Psychology," she said.

"You're going to be a psychiatrist?"

"Psychologist."

"What's the difference?"

"They subscribe to different journals." She glanced around
the room. "I've never been to one of these before. Are they
fun?"

I shook my head. "Mainly we stand around asking how
people liked the concert and waiting to hear how they liked
us."

She grinned. "I thought you were terrific."

"It's too late."

"Why?"

"It's no good if you have to explain it," I said.

"You want to get some coffee and Danish?"

"Riker's?"

"My apartment."

I said, "Sure."

That's the way it's been with Molly ever since. She's the
only thoroughly sane human being I've ever met. When I'm
mad at her, I remind her of how she picked me up that night,
how cool and detached she was. I tell her how she tricked
me into a sense of safety. "Not one sign," I shout at her.
"Not one sign you were already in love with me." She shouts,
"Like what?" I yell, "Dewy eyes would have helped!" and

she says, "Terrific. I have enough trouble looking like a statuesque midget. I'm supposed to look like I have a cold, too. For the man I want to marry." Then I tell her she has no soul, not an ounce of romance in her whole body. "Romance turns to fat after forty," she says. "Besides, I was already in love with you. I couldn't afford to indulge myself." "Are you telling me it was love at first sight?" "Yes!" "You see? You *were* romantic!" Then she waits for me to realize I was the one who accused her of not being romantic in the first place. I still haven't figured out how she does that. Every time.

She lived on the same block as Ed and me, four doors down. She had a roommate who was never there, a graduate student in English who was having an affair with her dissertation director and used the apartment only as an address for her parents. Which was just as well. The place was tiny, one central room, a curtained-off section with two beds, one unmade, the other covered with notebooks. There was a white card table and two folding chairs near the kitchen area. Her dinner dishes were still on the table that night and a textbook was propped open against the sugar bowl.

Molly cleared the plates into the sink before she took off her coat. She flung the book on a desk.

I took off my coat and sat at the table.

I was already talking. Molly has a genius for getting people to talk about themselves. Some people think it's her professional training. It's not. It's something she was born with, and it's magic. I've seen it work at parties, on airplanes, even in traffic jams. At a restaurant she will come back from the bathroom and tell me, "I just met a woman whose husband is a compulsive gambler. She wants to leave him but she feels guilty because she's been having an affair with a lesbian neighbor." I say, "How did you figure that out?"

She looks at me as if I'm crazy. "She told me," she says.

That's how it happened with me that night. I told her about you, about Momma and Poppa, about Mr. Resnick. I even told her about Super-Fiddle and about Ed and the Lewises. She had made an eight-cup pot of coffee and put out a half-dozen Danish. When it started getting light out we finished it off for breakfast.

I thought I had been talking nonstop, but when I got back to my apartment I realized I knew as much about her as she did about me. It was as if we had spent the night catching up.

She was from the Bronx. Her father had left Germany in 1930, when her mother was already pregnant with her. She didn't like her father very much. He was a man with no imagination who made up for it with arrogance and tyranny. He called himself a jeweler, but he mainly fixed watches in a little store off Sixth Avenue. Her mother had married when she was sixteen. Molly adored her and used to dream of becoming rich and famous so that one day she could rescue her from her father. He had been in his late forties when Molly was born. He died in 1948. Her mother went to live with a sister in Israel.

From as far back as she could remember Molly had always been a threat to her father and a bafflement to her mother. At about eight she decided that when she grew up she would work out a system for licensing parents. When she was twelve she realized that someone like her father might end up issuing the licenses, and she dropped the idea. She decided to become a psychologist instead and work with children. She was at Columbia now, where they mainly had her working with rats, gerbils, and pigeons. It wasn't easy to learn about breast-feeding and toilet training from rats, gerbils, and pigeons, but she was on a full teaching fellowship and would have her Ph.D. in two years. Then she could study what she wanted.

I fell asleep that morning trying to figure out how she had laid all that information in, and feeling very pleased with myself for remembering it, even though I had done most of the talking.

If you had been around during the next couple of weeks you probably would have been able to spot what was going on as clearly as I had been able to see what was happening between you and Margaret. You might even have said something. I wouldn't have believed you. I had never fallen in love before, but I had some ideas about how it was supposed to happen. I'd seen the Coming Attractions in my head. "Coming Tuesday," it said, in big, sparkling letters. "John Garfield as Jack Fleischman, Joan Leslie as 'The Woman,' in *It's About Time!*" It opened with a shot of a lonely, windswept beach. "They met on a lonely, windswept beach," the narrator said. We chased each other around the beach for a while, then fell into a sand dune. "Don't you understand?" I said. "I'm crazy about you. Crazy about you." Shot of me playing with the New York Philharmonic. "He had to make the decision of his life. His violin—or 'The Woman.'" Close-up of me. "He knew it the moment their eyes met." Close-up of her. "See young love. See Jack Fleischman and 'The Woman' dance down windswept Riverside Drive. See Jack Fleischman distracted from his practicing! See Jack Fleischman make love like John Garfield! Also selected short subjects."

None of that happened with Molly. She never distracted me. I never even fell in love with her. I just relaxed into it. We ate together every night. Sometimes at her place, sometimes at mine when we felt like spaghetti. She and Ed would fight through the meal. He claimed psychology was all political. She said politics was all psychological. Then we'd play hearts until it was time for one of us to go to a rehearsal or a lecture or a meeting.

Molly claims she worked very hard to make it easy for me those first couple of months. "I'm not what you call natural material for a magnificent obsession," she says. "I realized that about third grade. Neither are you, by the way." That always stings. "So I had to use my head. I had to make you see I was the only logical person to spend the rest of your life with. You do that with comfort, not passion. It's just as well. Who wants to spend their life pulsating with lust? You never get anything done." I ask, "Why?" "Passion is exhausting," she says. "At least if you start relaxed you have some stamina." Then she giggles. "God knows, you were relaxed enough." She's referring to the fact that we were together three months before we went to bed.

It took me that long to realize I was in love. It was on a Friday afternoon in early March. Ed and I were supposed to go to Brooklyn, but Mme. Vlady had called. Anita and Danny were arriving early from Turin. Ed had agreed to meet their plane. I called Momma to tell her Ed couldn't make it.

She said, "So bring Molly."

I was baffled. "How do you know about Molly?"

There was a long pause that made me very nervous. "You don't know how I know about Molly?" Momma said.

"Have I mentioned her?"

"You've mentioned her."

"She works late at the lab on Fridays."

"The BMT runs all night. Bring her late."

It was the way Momma said, "Bring her late." My hand on the receiver trembled. I looked around the apartment. Her notebooks were mixed in with my music. Her Fritz Kreisler records lay next to the phonograph. The old sweater she put on when the apartment got too cold hung on the bedroom door. She was everywhere. I started sweating. "Figure nine o'clock," I said, and hung up.

It was after four. Molly was already at the lab. I left the apartment and walked down Broadway to Columbia. The whole thing was impossible. I knew I loved her. I'd known that for weeks, but it didn't mean anything. There hadn't been any big revelation about that. Somewhere along the line we had both taken it for granted that we'd know each other for the rest of our lives. She was even a part of my fantasies. Whenever I saw 'The Woman,' Molly was always there, too. Just the three of us, having a terrific time. I tried to think about 'The Woman' as I walked, but she kept turning into Molly. Every time I tried to look deep in her eyes I had to look down. I panicked, then I realized I was safe after all. I had proof I wasn't in love.

First of all, there was you. Lenny would never approve, I told myself. She's short and funny-looking. There's nothing special about her, except maybe her dimple. I knew you would kill me if I ever announced I was serious about someone like Molly. All your training would go down the drain. Besides, I was nineteen. I didn't have to start thinking about love and marriage till I was twenty. And I had already decided I could never marry Molly. I remembered that from the reception. It had been the basis of our whole relationship. Take that away and what would we have?

And there were none of the signs of passion. My concentration was better than ever when I played. I never thought about her when we weren't together. I didn't have to. I always knew where she was. Most important of all, I was thinking rationally. Anyone who could review all the evidence as coolly and logically as I was doing couldn't be in love. I was relaxed. My appetite was fine. I was starving, in fact. I was in control of myself and undistracted, maybe a little chilly because there was still snow on the ground and I'd left the apartment wearing only my T-shirt. It wasn't anything like The Real Thing.

Besides, it was happening to *me*.

I stopped outside Fayerweather Hall. I had started running at about 120th Street. The afternoon sky was dimming and the lights in the windows all over the campus were popping on. I was trembling. Just as I had reached the campus it occurred to me that Molly might be going through the same thing I was. Then a worse thought hit me. She might not be. I might ruin our whole relationship if I told her I was in love with her, even though I was sure I wasn't. I backed off from the steps. I needed to talk to somebody. Ed was gone. Besides, he'd been telling me I was in love for a couple of weeks. I couldn't trust him to be objective. The only other person was Molly.

She was feeding some gerbils with an eyedropper when I found her. She's trying to prove she'd make a good mother, I thought. But she was really surprised to see me. She couldn't have planned it for my sake. I grew sane again. Well, not really. She smiled at me.

I said, "Look here . . ."

Her eyes got wide. "Look here?" she asked.

"What's wrong with that?"

"You never say, 'Look here.' I don't think anybody does."

I said, "Oh."

"You're supposed to be in Brooklyn."

"How did you know that?"

She started to answer, then she just shrugged. I was trying to find signs of hidden passion in her face, but she was just the same old Molly. And I knew I was in love with her.

((191))

"Do you want to come with me?"

"To Brooklyn? I don't finish here until—"

"My mother says to come late."

"Your mother?" If I'd been on my toes I would have noticed she was overfeeding the same gerbil while we talked.

I've got to handle this smoothly, I told myself. Suavely. I said, "I think I'm in love with you."

She glanced up at me.

I said, "Well?"

She said, "Well what?"

"What do you think? Do you think I am?"

She lay down the eyedropper and put her hands on her hips. I was afraid she was going to laugh, but she shook her head. "It's a damned good thing I gave up expecting things to happen like they do in my head a long time ago. You know what I mean?"

I said, "No."

She threw up her hands. "We'll talk on the subway."

"So you're coming?"

"I'm coming." She started feeding the gerbils again.

"I'll meet you at One Hundred and Sixteenth Street," I said.

"Meet me here."

"Why?"

She made this funny growling sound. "So I have somebody to walk with. O.K.? It's the least I can ask for."

"O.K." I started out.

"And, Jack. Put something warm on."

We didn't talk on the subway. We held hands. I had never held hands nonstop from 116th Street to Kings Highway with-no-time-out-for-the-change-at-Times-Square before. I had seen other people do it and always wondered how their palms didn't get sweaty. Now I knew. They did. But Molly had slipped her hand in mine as we crossed the campus and never let go. She told me later how terrified she was. She was worried about her height. All the way down she was trying to figure out a way to let Momma know she really had a normal, childbearing body.

Momma answered the doorbell. She didn't even look at me. Her eyes swooped down on Molly. She approved. I knew that because she smiled without twitching her lips first. "You're sooner than I thought."

Molly was practically standing on tiptoe. She wiped her hands on a Kleenex and reached out to Momma. Tears sprang into Momma's eyes. She shook hands and turned away quickly. "It'll be another ten, fifteen minutes." Then she yelled down the hall, "Sy!"

Molly said, "Can I help?"

Momma said, "This time? No."

Poppa came out of the bedroom. The only time I've ever seen him shy like that was the first time he met the Lewises. Then he kept saying, "All your records. I've got all your records." With Molly it was "Jack's a good boy. He really is."

Molly was spectacular. She managed to get them both talking. I learned things about Momma and Poppa I'd never known. Did you know Momma was a receptionist for a theatrical agency for three months before she married Poppa? She booked the first revival of *The Red Mill* all by herself. Poppa drew a diagram of the little house he grew up in on a paper napkin and told how they slept on the stove. Then he drew a diagram of the whole shtetl.

At midnight Momma said she would make up the couch for me. Molly could sleep in my bed. We hesitated together. Poppa said, "Esther . . ." and Momma dropped it, careful to make it clear to the world that she understood nothing.

If Molly was nervous on the trip down, it was nothing

compared to me on the uptown express. They were the two most silent train rides I've ever had. All I could think about was the Trojan in my wallet. I'd bought it three years before, at an uptown drugstore. I'd been carrying it around ever since. It had always given me a sense of security. Now I was worried that it might be too old. I tried to figure out a way to get alone for a couple of minutes, just so I could read the foil wrapper for special directions. I even thought about calling you ship-to-shore for advice. I could convince them it was an emergency.

Molly snuggled in under my arm. We were both wearing winter coats. I felt like some huge tame bear.

We walked back to 123rd Street. For a moment I thought, Maybe she doesn't know where we're headed. Maybe I still have some time to prepare. Nothing's really happened yet. I can treat it like any other night, kiss her on the cheek, pat her on the shoulder, go home, take a cold shower, and practice for ten hours. I said, "Gee, I wonder if Ed picked up his brother and sister all right. He'll be away all weekend."

Molly laughed nervously. "Your place or mine, huh?" There was a little silence. "That's an old joke," she explained, and I gave up thinking about treating it like any other night.

We went to her place. Molly had her back to me as she took off her coat. I put my arms around her from behind and she leaned back against me. It was a terrible position. I had to kiss the top of her head a lot. She seemed to like it though, so we stayed that way for a while. When she turned around she was a Molly I'd never seen. She'd been serious before—when she explained about psychology or when she argued with Ed—but never solemn. She was solemn now. I had never noticed that her eyes were brown and I never imagined they could be so tender about looking. She touched my face, then pulled my head down and kissed me. We had touched lips, touched cheeks, hugged each other a hundred times, but I never had a clue she could be so warm.

She whispered, "I love you, Jack. And I'm a virgin."

My heart sank. I'd been depending on one of us to know what we were doing. I wondered if it would make her more relaxed to know I was a virgin, too. But if her news had thrown me, what made me think my news wouldn't rattle her? Besides, she didn't seem very tense about it. I was the one who was shaky.

"Do you want some coffee or anything?" she said.

"What for?" I had wanted that to sound suave, but it came out like a real question. I was distracted by mechanics. I had to get my wallet out and onto her night table. Then I had to unwrap the Trojan. How was I going to do that in the middle of everything without feeling like a hospital orderly? And there was the problem of undressing. I didn't know whether I was supposed to undress her first—or myself. They never showed that in the movies. And I couldn't remember whether I was wearing my torn jockey shorts.

I kissed her again, mainly to stall.

Molly said, "I'll be right back." She disappeared into the bathroom.

I stood alone for a second, then ran into the bedroom, emptied my pockets on the night table, tore out of my clothes, and got under the covers.

Molly was a little surprised when she came back.

I lay on my side, trying to look natural. Molly tells me I looked like a magician's assistant about to be sawed in half.

She said, "Feel around under you and see if you're lying on my pajamas."

I was. She threw them on the other bed, then slipped out of her clothes. The light was on my side of the bed. I rolled over to turn it off.

Molly said, "Why are you doing that?"

I swung back, afraid I'd made a mistake. I hit my head on the headboard.

"Are you all right?" she said.

I nodded. It was about that time that I realized I couldn't talk. Molly says it was about that time that she realized it was the first time for me, too. That was why she started to smile. I thought she was just trying to look lascivious.

"Leave it on," she said. "We might want to look at each other."

I shrugged, which was the closest I could get to saying, "O.K." She slipped in beside me and suddenly we were thrashing.

We thrashed a long time. Then Molly said, very softly, "Jack? I think maybe we don't have to thrash so much." She was born with the wisdom of the ages. "Maybe if we relax. Just hold me."

I was worried afterward. Molly lay nestled in my arm, but she could tell I was worried. She asked what was wrong.

"Do you think it was all right?" I said.

She nodded on my chest.

There was a pause. I was still worried. Molly said, "What?"

I said, "How would you know? You've got nothing to compare it with."

The bed started shaking. She turned her head and laughed into my rib cage. "I said it was all right," she said. "I didn't say it was perfect. We still need practice."

So by the next autumn, when Molly and I drove down to Philadelphia, I had a lot to tell you. I was anxious to show you that your worries about me were over.

I had spent the summer at Tanglewood. The Lewises had gotten me on the teaching staff and arranged to have everybody in the world hear me. Molly had a research grant at the

Menninger Clinic. In September I came back to New York with promises for solo appearances and tours when I graduated. I was getting a reputation. Molly and I picked up where we'd left off. I was becoming someone I wanted you to meet.

You were married again. It had happened very fast, during your last year in the Navy. You were stationed in Norfolk and had taken a leave in Philadelphia. You ran into Cynthia Dicks at the Officers Club. Poppa told Molly and me about it. "Lenny says we met her."

"She plays the bagpipes," I reminded him.

"How come that one?"

I shrugged, but I told Molly what I thought. "Lenny's going to prove to her father he can amount to something."

Momma said, "Something's fishy."

Poppa said, "Why?"

"Her father's got a seat on the stock exchange."

"That's not fishy."

"How come he's not making a big wedding?"

Poppa shrugged. "It's a wartime marriage."

"They're not getting married on Iwo Jima."

Momma was right, but none of us knew the whole story for another five years. Both of you were on the rebound. Cynthia had eloped to Los Angeles with an actor. Irving Dicks had traced them, arranged for an annulment, and brought her back to Philadelphia. He was looking for a way to get Cynthia settled when you met them at the Officers Club. In your uniform, without your accent and with a couple of years' experience, you probably looked more promising than you did at the Wharton School. He gave you a job with Dicks, Martin and Golden and promised to pay your way through graduate work in economics.

You'd been married and out of the Navy for three months

when I borrowed Poppa's car and drove down with Molly. I talked about you all the way. I wasn't very good yet at reading Molly's silences. I figured she was nervous about meeting you the way she'd been with Momma. Ten years later I would have been able to tell the difference between when she was nervous for herself and when she was nervous for me. Momma and Poppa had gone down for the small ceremony in July. They had told us about it. I heard everything they said about how handsome you looked and how Mr. Dicks had taken you all out to dinner at his club afterward. Molly heard everything they didn't say.

"Wait till he hears about the Lewises," I said. "Lenny always used to worry about me because I wasn't realistic. He used to say, 'You're good, Jackie. But are you a star?' Wait till I tell him about Carnegie Hall."

Molly said, "Carnegie *Recital* Hall."

"Even so." Mme. Vlady had arranged to have my senior recital at Carnegie Recital Hall. She was also taking out an ad in the *Times* so it would get reviewed. I was more excited about having that to tell you than the opportunity itself. "Do you think he'll be able to come?" I said to Molly. "Wouldn't that be terrific? The four of us could go out afterward." I told her about how you had surprised me that night at the Brooklyn Symphony. She had heard it before.

Your house was outside Philadelphia, a big old stone carriage house just on the fringes of the Main Line.

"Watch this," I said as we drove up. "Watch how he says, 'Hey, Jackie' when he meets us. Like that. 'Hey, Jackie.' "

And you did. You bustled us into the living room and made drinks. On the way you pushed an intercom and said, "Honey? They're here."

You wore leather pants and a golf shirt. You looked happier than I'd seen you in years, mixing the drinks with a furious kind of domestic energy. There was a fire going. Molly settled in on the sofa near it. I sat on the edge of an armchair, impatient for the weekend to get started.

"How do you like the house?" you said. "Terrific, isn't it? Cyn will give you a tour later."

I had noticed a mezuzah on the front door.

"That's for Dad. Cyn says it makes him happy, so what the hell."

It gave me a funny little pang to hear you call Cynthia's father Dad. You settled into a chair opposite me and sprawled your sprawl.

We grinned at each other for a while. All the things I'd wanted to tell you jumbled in my head. It was too soon to start. So we just kept grinning.

"You look terrific," I said.

You nodded.

"It's been a long time."

"It sure has. You been keeping yourself busy?"

I sort of laughed and nodded. It still wasn't time.

"Did you have any trouble finding us?"

"No. The directions were terrific."

You looked over at Molly. "You're being kind of quiet. Everything all right?"

"I'm enjoying the fire," Molly said.

"It was a long trip. Molly's a little tired."

"No, I'm not." There was a funny edge to it.

You had already looked away, as if you'd made a decision about her. I wished she would smile once while you were looking at her, or come up with one of those sharp observations that always made my teeth rattle, anything to make you look again more closely. Molly caught me at it. Our eyes met. It was the first time I ever saw hers flash with anger.

Cynthia came downstairs. She swept into the room in a

gorgeous blue hostess gown. She had a small, heart-shaped face and she wore a heart-shaped locket around her neck.

You jumped up and kissed her and went to make her a drink. "You're Jackie," she said. "I remember you."

Molly smiled at her when I introduced them, but you were mixing a drink and didn't see it.

"Dad said he'd be here about four," Cynthia said. "What time is it?"

Cynthia's father had dinner with you once, twice a week. He lived in the big house that yours used to be part of.

"Wait till you see him," you said. "Sharpest man I ever met." You told Cynthia to show us the house.

I'd never seen Molly so quiet. She was nice enough to Cynthia. She smiled and nodded as Cynthia explained the furniture, pointed out views. But she said very little and when she did it was bland. For Molly, that was hostile. And I got the feeling it was me she was being hostile to.

We found ourselves alone in a connecting bath for a couple of seconds. I said, "You O.K.?"

She said, "Yes."

"You seem a little tense."

"I tell you what then. You relax."

Cynthia's father arrived while we were in the master bedroom. Your voice came from the wall to tell us.

Cynthia said, "We'll be right down." She stood uncertainly. "There's still the terrace and the dormer . . ."

"That's O.K.," Molly said quickly. "Maybe later."

Cynthia smiled at her gratefully and started downstairs. We'd hardly been there an hour, but Molly and Cynthia had already come to an understanding. That's a talent women have that's always amazed me. Men have to have secret societies where we make up handshakes and codes, but women don't need them. They're like bats; they pick up signals on a frequency our ears are never tuned to.

I followed Molly downstairs, trying to figure out what I was missing.

Irving Dicks must have been in his fifties, but he looked younger. He had the kindest face I'd ever seen. It was round and open without being soft. He didn't say much, but his lips seemed set in a permanent grin, as if he was enjoying what he was thinking. His eyes were blue and his hair pure white.

We shook hands. "You've got a violinist's grip."

"Dad's on the board of the Philadelphia Orchestra," you said.

Irving Dicks laughed. "Don't sound so meaningful, Lenny."

"I only meant . . ."

"It puts people on their guard."

He hugged you around the shoulder.

Cynthia put a bowl of water and a towel at the head of the dinner table. Before we sat down Irving Dicks put on a yarmulke and washed his hands. I shot you a puzzled look. You winked back at me and put on your own skullcap. Molly helped Cynthia serve. While the women were out, you and Irving Dicks talked business.

I watched you, fascinated. You were a whole new person with him, precise, knowledgeable. You talked accounts and investments, futures and options. Your mouth took on the same amused and confident set as his. You nodded a lot while you listened and held his eyes when you talked. That impressed me. His eyes were that penetrating blue it was hard to hold. The junior clerk at Holtzman was dead. You were in training for the big time. And Irving Dicks liked you. I remembered that first Thanksgiving you came home from college. Your father-in-law was giving you all the respect, all the approval you'd wanted from Poppa then. Irving Dicks's black yarmulke practically gleamed against his white hair. Yours was almost invisible, but the two of you sat there like a couple of rabbinical scholars.

When the women came back, Irving Dicks turned to me. "Lenny tells me you're very good. If I can be of any help . . . you're a member of the family now, too."

I thanked him.

"You're not one of those kids who's decided to do it on his own, are you? You're not too proud to take help."

I shook my head and told him I had all the help I seemed to need. It was my cue. I turned to you and the floodgates opened. Everything that had been happening for me came rushing out. I told you about the Lewises and Tanglewood and Carnegie Hall and the tours and appearances in the offing. The timing didn't feel right. I was uneasy at how suddenly it was all released, but there was no way to stop it. I took over the table. When I was finished, Irving Dicks nodded to you. "He's a hustler."

"No, I'm not. It's all just happened that way."

He grinned skeptically. I managed to smile back, but I was puzzled. You hadn't responded to any of my news. It was as if you'd turned away from it the way you'd turned away from Molly before. I felt as if I'd done something wrong, but I had no idea what it could be.

Cynthia served black coffee in the living room.

"Tomorrow night we'll have dinner at the club," Dicks said.

Molly had just settled back in her place near the fire. "I'm afraid we can't. Jack and I have to get back to the city."

You were surprised. "Tomorrow?"

So was I.

"I told you about it, Jack. I've got to be in the lab." She was smiling and apologetic, but her jaw was tight.

"I was going to invite a few people over," Irving Dicks said.

"I can take a train back if you want to stay," Molly said to me.

"No. No, that's all right." I was bewildered.

"We'll have to leave after breakfast." She turned to Cynthia. "I'm sorry."

Cynthia nodded. Some more signals passed between them.

I was angry. I hadn't even begun to show you who I was yet. I'd told you everything at dinner, but it hadn't taken the way I expected. And Molly was behaving strangely. I needed the whole weekend to get you to really see me, to know Molly. Now I had to cram it into one night and a breakfast. And I'd already lost so much time.

Irving Dicks finished his coffee and got up to leave. "It's already later than I usually stay."

"That means you're good company, Jack," you said.

Your father-in-law nodded. "He's your brother, isn't he?" He clapped you on the shoulder. "Take care of him."

You went to the door with him. Molly and I were alone again. I said, "Molly?"

She said, "Not a word, Jack." She smiled. "You see how I'm smiling? Don't say a word."

"You never told me about the lab. I could have come down myself . . ."

"Be smart, Jack."

"What the hell is wrong?"

She was still smiling. "There's too much expensive glass in the room. Be smart."

When you came back Molly disappeared into the kitchen with Cynthia. You poured some brandy and relaxed into a chair near the fire.

"I wish you could have seen the club," you said. "You'd like it. We've got a little theater we added on to the club-house. Some of the members like to fool around with it. For fund-raising and stuff like that. Maybe we could get you to play in it for us sometime. Dad would like that. And you can never tell . . . it might be . . ."

I was stung. Two hours before I'd told you I was going to play at Carnegie Hall and now you were suggesting it might be helpful if I fiddled in the rec hall of your father-in-law's country club. You hadn't heard anything I'd told you.

You sat back and beamed at me. "Well, what do you think?"

"About what?"

"All this."

I said, "It's nice."

"A little different from Bank Street, huh? I tell you, Jackie. I didn't know I could be so happy."

"I'm glad for you, Lenny."

"And it's not the money," you said. "I learned my lesson about that the last time. It's the whole thing. Settling down this way with someone like Cynthia. What do you think of her?"

"Really nice."

"She's terrific. And Dad." You were grinning at me, but your eyes were also defiant, and pleading for reassurance.

"Terrific," I said.

"It's all so easy, Jackie. That's what's so incredible. All I had to do was give up a lot of fantasies. Then it all just sliced right through." You showed me how with the side of your hand and popped your tongue. "It started with the Navy. I learned there. You go a step at a time. You do your job now, it leads to other things, but the important thing is to go a step at a time and everything else takes care of itself. Before, I was all over the place. I acted like I was Henry Morgenthau already when I was just a schmucky little clerk. That's why I got into so much trouble. Now I know who I am, what I have to learn. I can take it a step at a time. Dad's teaching me everything." You paused and lowered your voice. "I'll tell you something. Sometimes, after Cyn is asleep, I get out of bed and drive over to the club and just sit there in the den. A couple of nights ago I did it. I thought, Jesus, I was in the Wharton School for three years and I never had any idea this place existed. Now I'm a member. A *member*, for chrissake." You took a sip of your drink. "Can I give you a piece of advice?"

"Sure."

"Don't be too quick to turn down opportunities."

"O.K."

"Do you know what I mean?"

"No."

"You almost messed up an opportunity tonight. You've got to learn to recognize them. Dad said he could help you. You just can't afford to close doors like that."

"I told you why. I've got a career going as a soloist. Just like you always said . . ."

"You've got a lot of promises, Jackie." You tried to say it as gently as you could. "That's one of the things you learn in my business. You can't live on the way you hope things will be. Or on the way you want them to be. You have to see them the way they really are. That's why Dad's so successful."

"Daniel Lewis and Ella Vlady say I have a great future." You smiled sadly.

"I . . . I thought you'd be proud of me," I said.

"I am. You know that. I've always been proud of you. You

think I would have introduced you to Dad if I wasn't proud of you? If I didn't want to help?" You took a closer look at me. "You're not brooding, are you?"

"I don't know." I stared into the fire. "Nothing's working out like I thought it would . . ."

"You're growing up." You said it tenderly.

I shrugged. "That's not what it feels like."

"You're graduating this year. What's going to happen after that?"

"I'm good, Lenny." It came out as if *I* was pleading this time.

"What happens when you want to settle down?"

I froze. I had been planning to talk with you about Molly. Now I was afraid. "I may not do it the way you're doing it," I said.

"You know what I think you should do?"

"What?"

"Stay for the weekend. Get to know Dad better and let him know you're not as locked in as you seem to be. I'll take your friend to the train . . ."

"Her name's Molly."

"By tomorrow night Dad'll have everybody important knowing who you are."

"Her name's Molly and we're getting married." It was out before I could stop it, and it was out wrong. I'd been saving for this time alone with you for three years, collecting the best pieces of my life. I was going to throw them all in your lap so we could sort through them together. The astonishment, the delight on your face would be louder, more decisive than any applause I could imagine. Now, instead of dropping it all in your lap, I was holding each piece up defiantly, and you kept snatching them and throwing them carelessly over your shoulder.

You took a second on Molly. "When?" you said, finally.

"Right after I graduate."

"Do Momma and Poppa know?"

I shook my head. Molly and I had agreed to say nothing until spring. It was a betrayal to tell you. I had only done it because my supplies were running low. I would have given anything to be able to take it back.

"She's older than you."

I nodded.

"Margaret was older than me."

"It's not the same."

"What are you going to live on?"

"We've worked that all out." I wanted to sound reasonable and secure. The more I tried, the more defiant it came out.

"You think she's the right person for you?"

I wanted to say, "I love her." I couldn't. I was afraid of what your face would show. I nodded.

"Have you screwed her, Jackie?"

"Uh huh."

"Have you screwed anybody else?"

"Sure," I said loudly. "Plenty."

You blew some air out of your mouth. "The one thing I've always been afraid of was that you'd end up with somebody who didn't appreciate you."

"Molly appreciates me."

"She's so . . . quiet . . ."

That was when I made a mistake. I launched into a speech about Molly. I tried to make you see how wonderful she really was. I knew it was wrong even while the words were coming out and you sat there nodding, understanding. It felt like a betrayal of Molly, but I couldn't stop. I couldn't understand why I had to convince you of something I was

((207))

so sure of, how I could believe that the whole three years I'd just lived through weren't real, that all my sense of myself, my pride and confidence and joy could feel about to crumble just because you were looking at me with all the compassion, the understanding, the tenderness, and the contempt of an older brother.

It was humiliating, but I couldn't stop. And it was naked and embarrassing for you. I knew that, too. You didn't like Molly. You couldn't conceive of what I saw in her, no matter how urgently I tried to explain. Yet there I was, practically pleading with you to approve.

What made it worse was that all you had wanted the whole evening was for me to look at you, to really look around at your own life in wonder and approval. Since I'd arrived that afternoon the two of us just kept offering up our separate lives for scrutiny. We both were so busy offering, neither of us had time to scrutinize, only to wonder, you sadly and I with nineteen-year-old impatience, why we could never communicate.

Somewhere, way in the back of my head, I knew you were looking for my approval. You may not have been looking forward to it as long or as urgently as I was yours, but now that we were together, I knew you wanted it. I couldn't afford to admit that though.

So I just kept talking at you and you kept nodding until one of us said it was time to go to bed. My head ached. I was angry at your blindness to everything I was, but for the first time there was a bond between us I'd never felt before. I hadn't really looked at your wife or your father-in-law. I hadn't paid attention to your new maturity. I had no more admiration or belief in your future than you had in mine. I'd disappointed you as much as you had disappointed me.

Some deeper, closer relationships I knew had been built on less than that.

The next morning there was a rush of laughter and good-byes and thank-yous and come-again-soons at the car.

Then Molly and I were alone.

"Now would you mind telling me what the hell is going on?" I said as soon as we were out of the driveway. Molly sat rigid. "You don't have to be in any lab, do you?"

She shook her head.

"Then what was all that bullshit about?"

"Don't talk to me like that, Jack."

"Oh, that's terrific," I said. "That's really sensational. I take you to meet my brother and you practically turn into a deaf-mute. You ruin my whole weekend after I haven't seen him for a couple of years. And when I ask you what it's all about you tell me not to talk to you like that. That's really terrific."

"I'm sorry," she shouted. "I'm sorry if I spoiled your weekend."

"You don't sound it."

"I'm not." She was still staring straight ahead, but she shook her head as if she was looking at me. "I don't believe what I was seeing. I can't believe what happened to you."

"Nothing happened to me."

"You turned into a twelve-year-old. That's what happened to you."

"Well, you weren't exactly Eleanor Roosevelt."

"That doesn't give you the right to make excuses for me. Ever." She shifted in the seat so she could look at me directly. "Do you hear that, Jack? I'm telling you that now. Never, never make excuses for me again. To anyone."

"I don't know what you're talking about."

"That makes it worse."

"And I don't know what you mean by twelve-year-old. I didn't sit around like a sullen lump—"

"No, you sure didn't. You were so damned busy singing for your supper—"

"I had twice as much work to do. You weren't helping to keep things going."

"Is that what goes on with you and your brother? You have to keep things going? Bring offerings?"

"You don't know anything about it."

"I was one of the offerings."

"I love my brother," I shouted.

"And that means you have to prove yourself every move you make? For God's sake, Jack. Lenny's a kid."

"He's twenty-six."

"And you're nineteen. And I'm twenty-four. And Irving Dicks is two hundred and thirty-five. And you know that's not what I'm talking about. Your brother's a little boy looking for a daddy. And you're probably the only person in the world who treats him as if he was anything different."

I'd never heard anyone call you a kid before. It was impossible. I was the kid. You were older. If you were a kid, too, where did that leave me? One thing was sure, Molly was her old self again. Even in the middle of our fight, I was wishing you were there to see her. Which shows how much I was getting the point.

"Don't you say anything against my brother, Molly. You hear me? You don't know him like I do."

"All I said was that he's a kid."

"Don't say anything against him."

"That's nothing against him! Jack, Jack. You're a sane human being. What's making you crazy?"

"I love my brother."

"Say it one more time at the top of your lungs like that and I'll tell you what's really doing."

"I knew it," I said. "I knew it would get down to this. That's your analyst's voice. You want me for a subject."

"No, I don't."

"Ha."

"Analysts don't throw things at a subject's head. And that's what I'd do right now if you weren't driving."

"You don't like Lenny."

"I don't *know* Lenny. I only know what happened to you when you were with Lenny. And I don't like that."

There was silence in the car for a long time. It gave me the chance to figure out the feeling I'd had since we left. It was a familiar one and it hit even before Molly and I started fighting. It was a feeling I took away with me after every visit you and I ever had, a mixture of disappointment and anger, tenderness and guilt, as if the failure was my fault. And it suddenly struck me that every meeting we'd had since you left was some kind of failure, that somehow neither of us could live up to the other's expectations.

I knew what I expected of you. And I was beginning to figure out how unjust of me it was to expect it. You were to be my advance guard, cutting a path ahead for me and looking back every once in a while in pride and admiration at how well I was coming along. And in order for me to feel safe, you had to be a perfect guide. But what was it you expected of me? Why was it that I always left you feeling I'd made mistakes, that all my own choices, the very ones I most wanted to show you for approval, were the ones that caused you the most concern? The very things that made me a man made me feel like a kid when I was with you. You had a knack of finding the thing of the moment, whether it was Molly or my music or my friends, whatever

I was most sure of, whatever it was that might insure my release from childhood—you had a knack of zeroing in on it and then shriveling it with dismissal. I wondered why.

At Trenton I asked Molly.

"You want my theory?" she said.

"Whatever."

She shrugged. "He can't afford to let you grow up."

"Is that psychology?"

"Common sense. If you grow up, he grows old. Who needs that?"

August 3, 1975

Tuesday night already. Haven't had time to write since Saturday. Now I should have plenty.

I'm in jail. Sitting on my cot, propped against an institutional green wall, after my first institutional meal. No idea what it was, but I ate it from a metal tray with something different in each section. It was a little like flying Pan Am. Phil, Dudley, and I sat together in the mess hall. That was tricky, but the word's around about who we are. Except for some curious stares, the other inmates left us alone. That's what we're called. Inmates. I asked Dudley if he was edgy about sitting with us. He shrugged. "No more than the last six years."

Phil was very quiet. "It's not like Chicago," he said.

Dudley smiled. "There were more of you then."

I have no idea of how long we'll be in. Vic Jenkins figures a week to ten days. We asked if that was a conservative estimate, but he couldn't say.

Vic didn't get to Gainesville until late Saturday night. We spent all day Sunday with him. He was worried. At first he kept trying to get us to use Dowd and Gwynne again.

"We don't have a case, you know," he kept saying. "You'd be better off going with the union."

We said we wanted him. If we had to go to jail we'd rather do it because he couldn't make a case than because Dowd and Gwynne couldn't. He didn't quite know how to take that, but I think he was touched. He said we were crazy.

I went to see Poppa on Monday before the hearing. He was in the garden, reading *Sisterhood Is Powerful*. Anna had sent it to him.

"She's a good girl," he said.

I asked him what Momma would have said if she knew about all that.

He said, "What makes you think she didn't?" He closed the book and studied the fist on the cover. "That's the only thing that worries me. They talk as if nobody else thought of those things. We got married in 1924, the year Momma voted for the first time. She was twenty-one. You think she didn't know what was doing? I said to her, 'You don't have to be a housewife, Esther. It's a new world. You can do whatever you want.' She said, 'What are you doing, Sy? Giving me permission?' She knew what was doing."

"It looks like I'm going to jail," I said.

He asked how I felt. I shrugged.

"Where?" he asked.

"Right here. The county jail."

"I was in the Federal."

"Have you got any advice?" I asked.

"Learn as much as you can. How long?"

I told him.

"I'll miss your visits."

"So will I."

"First I have to give up the music. Now your visits. I feel like I'm a part of this thing, with all the sacrifices."

"You are."

He shook his head. "I'm too tired. When I was younger I'd do things first, then I'd find out what I had to give up. Now all I can do is give things up. That's what I hate. More than anything else. Being tired. I've got maybe an hour a day when I don't feel like I have to fight sleep. I look forward to it, I jump into it, then it's over so fast. *You* look tired," he said to me.

"It's been a hectic week." I paused.

"And?"

"And nothing."

"And something."

It had been in the back of my mind since the first week. Nobody cared about the strike, nobody that mattered. Sure, it was getting all kinds of coverage. Even national coverage. And I could be sure there'd be cameras and reporters to cover us when we went to jail. But the people that mattered were the people we played for. They'd been quiet. They'd been standing by, waiting to see how it turned out. No one was doing anything to help get the music going again.

"Where are they?" I asked.

"You want demonstrations?" Poppa said.

"Even a letter to the editor would be something. It's their symphony."

He shook his head. "It *was* theirs. That's why the strike in the first place. Watch out for contradictions, Jack."

"But some of them must remember . . ."

"Why? If it took *you* this long? You do what you have to. If it's right, they'll remember."

"What if they don't?" I asked.

"Then they'll learn all over. And they'll think it's the first time." Poppa wiggled the book at me. "Again. I just thought of another piece of advice. Don't get bored. That's the worst thing about jail. You get bored and you start to think like you're thinking."

"How?"

"Like a disappointed hero."

"You know what else I was thinking?" I said.

He nodded. "That maybe it was a mistake in the first place to strike."

"Worse. I was wondering what would have happened if I'd stayed with Lenny."

"What do you think?"

"I'd be richer, more famous. I'd have played for more people . . ."

"But you wouldn't have the chance to go to jail."

I left him and went straight to the courthouse. It was a private hearing. Ed was there with the management's lawyer.

I guess you know all about legal proceedings. It was new to me. I was fascinated. They never called us by name. We were always "the defendants." Vic and the other lawyer went through some kind of preliminaries with the judge that none of us understood. Just when I thought I was catching on they'd say something in Latin. I felt like I was waiting for the punch line in Yiddish theater. None of it seemed to have anything to do with the People's Symphony or Arthur Quasnosky or artistic control. We might have been able to talk about those things in the green room, but here in the judge's chamber there was something else going on. All our principles seemed pretty thin against the stack of folders and budget figures Ed had brought in with him. It was a familiar sensation, coming in with belief in myself and what I was doing, and banging my nose against a different world. Phil was subdued. Dudley sat back in the big leather chair, trying to look relaxed. Eileen sat on the edge of hers, leaning forward, as if she was a little hard of hearing. We were all intimidated.

The management lawyer was very convincing. But I figured anybody could be convincing when he had a case. Vic, on the other hand, was eloquent. He objected to everything. Including the decision, which was what we expected. We had to report for rehearsal Tuesday and play the evening concert. Failure to comply would place us in contempt of court.

When the hearing was adjourned, Vic led us into another room. I asked him what he thought was best. We all still felt we needed Vic to interpret the world for us. He said he didn't make a habit of advising his clients to go to jail. So, professionally, he thought we should comply. Then he pointed out that we were in a pretty weak bargaining position. All we had was the strike.

"How do they arrest us?" Eileen asked. "I mean, they don't go through the business with handcuffs and things like that, do they?"

Vic laughed this little reassuring laugh. "It's nothing like that. As soon as the judge issues the contempt citation, you'll probably get a phone call."

"A phone call?"

Vic nodded. "They'll ask you to come down to start serving your sentence."

"Just like that?" Eileen said.

"It's not very romantic, but . . ." Vic shrugged.

Eileen looked around at the rest of us. We shrugged, too. "Vic?" she said. "I hate to be such a pest, but I've got an awful lot of shopping and things to take care of before I go. I don't want to sit around all day waiting for the phone.

Do you think you could tell the judge now that we're not going to play? Then we could have our clothes all ready and we could just agree to meet tomorrow and get started."

That sounded reasonable to the rest of us. Vic left for a little while. When he came back he said we were to be at the jail at one this afternoon.

"Would it be all right if I brought my harp?" Eileen said.

Vic was stumped.

"There's always someone in the movies playing 'The Trail of the Lonesome Pine' on a harmonica," I said. "If they can bring harmonicas in . . ."

"It may be pretty damp in there," Dudley said.

"It would be a comfort though."

"I don't know. You could give it a try." Vic seemed fascinated with the whole idea.

"Well, I don't want to haul it down there if I can't be sure."

"I tell you what. I did such a lousy job for you this afternoon, the least I can do is check with Sheriff Howells."

Eileen gave a little start. "Buck Howells?" she said. "I know Buck Howells. He took me to the senior prom. Is he in charge there?"

Vic nodded.

"I think we'll be able to work something out," she said and sat back. She shook her head and clicked her tongue. "Buck Howells," she said.

Phil, Dudley, and I snuck looks at each other. I'd been wondering all along whether I could bring my fiddle in with me. They'd been thinking the same thing about their instruments. Only Eileen had been gutsy enough to ask.

Phil called Mel Sandler to let him know what happened. Mel and Phyllis Lester threw together a going-away party.

Practically all of the symphony wandered in sometime during the night. Even Tony Querault showed up. He was uncomfortable and didn't stay long, but while he was there he managed to find a reason to burst into tears and hug me. By two o'clock there was a core of about thirty. Fred Holland got the idea for everyone to go with us the next day. We would meet at the Arts Center and make it a caravan.

We were a hell of a crew. Dudley, Phil, and about fifteen others were already there when I arrived. Dudley's wife was with him and a few of the neighbors. Fred brought some of the picket signs and had put together a couple of new ones. "Music Hath Charm," "We Love the Gainesville Four," "Every Good Boy Does Fine," and a couple of bars from Beethoven's Fifth. Eileen pulled up in her husband's flatbed truck. Her two oldest sons stood on the back, taking care of her harp. Phil loaded his cello beside it and as many of us as could jumped on.

Vic Jenkins and Mel Sandler led the procession in Mel's Volkswagen. Then came Eileen with us, her harp, Phil's cello, and all the signs. Dudley's wife was right behind us with a loaded station wagon. Reinhold Blesser had brought his antique Ford. Sally Hartman had borrowed her son's exterminating truck with a big picture of a dying bug on the side.

We straggled from the Arts Center down Main Street to the jail. Vic had alerted Sheriff Howells. He had five or six officers waiting to help us unload and get booked. The television and newspaper reporters were there, too. They crowded around us as soon as we pulled up, but Sheriff Howells kept them back.

"Hold on. Now just hold on there," he said. "We've got some expensive equipment to take care of."

Eileen got out of the truck and greeted him.

He was very shy with her. He made a gesture to tip his hat but he wasn't wearing any.

"How've you been, Buck?" Eileen said.

"Fine. Just fine."

"Buck, I want you to meet my youngest, Julie. She's twelve now." She was holding Julie by the hand. "This is Buck Howells, honey. He's going to take care of me while I'm in jail."

Buck said, "How do?" and Julie made a little curtsey with all Eileen's old-South training in it.

"I want to thank you for letting us all bring our things like this."

He eyed the back of the pickup where Eileen's boys were starting to unload. "I didn't realize it was such a big instrument," he said. "You're not going to have much room . . ."

The harp tipped as they backed it off the truck. "Be careful with that!" She turned back to Buck, said "Excuse me," and ran to supervise the unloading.

The others had formed a small ragged group to one side. Maury Rice kept pumping Beethoven's Fifth up and down. Jerry Frank had cornered a reporter and was explaining the problem about the pay phones backstage. Dudley's kids played chase on the jail steps and counted the number of times flashbulbs went off. One of the reporters asked Fred Holland if this was a demonstration. He said he wasn't sure.

Sheriff Howells had to ask Vic who else he was supposed to be arresting. We introduced ourselves. He was as shy with us as he'd been with Eileen. He kept wiping his palms on his pants as if he was trying to decide whether to shake hands.

"I've been to the Arts Center many times," he said. "The missus really enjoys it. I do, too," he said quickly.

They were carrying the harp up the steps by now. Eileen was giving worried orders. Bob Cross and a couple of others followed behind with our valises and instrument cases.

Sheriff Howells stood uncertainly. "Well, I guess we better get on in," he said. "Unless there was something else you had to do out here . . ."

Dudley said good-bye to his wife and kids. Phil had a short conference with Mel Sandler. Reinhold Blesser and his wife came over and assured me they'd keep an eye on the house. I was missing Molly. I would have liked to hear what she had to say about it all. She'll have plenty to say when she gets back in a couple of weeks, but it would have been nice to have on-the-spot coverage. Besides, the Blessers hugged me, but it wasn't the same as Molly.

Eileen's family and a few of the others followed us inside. They watched the whole booking process. The Simpson boys were fascinated by the fingerprinting and everyone crowded around to see what we emptied from our pockets.

Sheriff Howells and his men tried to stay as official as they could. No one had ever been so interested in their routine. They smudged Eileen's prints and had to fill out a whole new booking sheet, and they kept dropping coins from the counter as we emptied our pockets.

Eileen gave her children last-minute instructions and told her oldest to drive home carefully. A matron led her through one door, while one of the Sheriff's men led us through another. We weren't allowed to carry anything in, so three other men followed with our instruments. The two who carried my fiddle and Dudley's oboe looked a little uncomfortable.

So here I am. I thought I'd have some time tonight to

((221))

write about when you were managing me. I don't think I will. Not yet. I'm still distracted. Dudley is playing his oboe. The three of us agreed to play at different times because of the way sound carries in the corridors. Even with the one instrument going it sounds like the hall outside the practice rooms at Juilliard. I'm wondering if this is the right place to be just now. It all made sense at the strike meetings and at the Arts Center. Now there's nothing to do. Arthur Quasnosky is still dying, there's still no music, and nobody seems to notice.

Poppa warned me about getting bored and thinking like this, and I haven't even been in a day. Dudley's hour should be up soon. Then it'll be my turn. Fiddling might help.

August 4, 1975

Vic was in to see us this morning. We met in the visitors' room. It was the first time we'd seen Eileen since she disappeared behind the door yesterday. When the matron led her in, she said, "Thanks, Ginny." It seems she went to school with half the staff here. She seems fine, except that she had trouble sleeping. She kept thinking of things she'd forgotten to tell the boys. Vic took them down and promised to take care of it for her.

He met with Ed this morning. The board wants to wait us out. They figure it won't be another week before the members get tired of the dramatics and want to get their paychecks again, at least enough of them to swing the vote to the union package. Dowd and Gwynne are hanging around, waiting for a break so they can take over again.

Vic told me Poppa had tried to reach him. He wasn't able to get back to him. He must be hungry for news.

Vic also brought in a stack of chamber music we could adapt for our instruments. Reinhold Blesser had pulled it out of his own library and sent it along in case we could get together. Buck Howells is making arrangements to set us up in some place he calls "the library."

Right now I'm tired. It's the most peculiar thing. I haven't had so much time on my hands since Molly and I went to Bermuda three years ago. All I have to do now is rest and write to you, but I go around feeling tired all the time. I thought I understood how Poppa felt the other day. I didn't. I keep wanting to write you about us, but every time I look at the pad all I want to do is sleep. I wonder if that's because of where I am, or because of what I have to write about. You see? I'm starting to edge toward it now. Instead I'm going to take a nap.

Later

Just back from our session in the library. It's this room that was set up by the Christian Women of Gainesville for use by the less fortunate. Nobody ever uses it. There are about a hundred books in there with brown cracked leather bindings, the kind you always see in antique stores, and they're all called *Not by Bread Alone*. The only furniture is these musty old wing chairs that make you feel very righteous if you sit in them. They scouted up some folding chairs and even some music stands and we played some Handel and Mozart, then some Ravel and Debussy for Eileen.

A guard came in and asked if we'd mind keeping the doors open. The people outside wanted to listen. About fifteen minutes later Buck Howells asked if we'd be distracted by an audience. Soon there were people wandering in and out. Some of them just peeked in, some stood at the door for a while. A couple sat on the floor and stayed. Buck let some guards bring in a couple of inmates. One of them came up to me just about the time we were winding down. A white man, about fifty years old. He'd been sitting on the floor, straining forward since he came in. He never took his eyes off my violin. He'd finally worked up the courage to ask if he could try it.

I tightened and asked if he knew how to handle it. It's my Guarnerius.

He said, "A little."

I offered it to him. He took it gently and I was relieved.

He gave me an awkward little grin. "I get a different kind of sound . . ." he said.

He took a couple of preliminary runs, made an adjustment or two, and jumped into a country fiddle tune with some of the most astonishing fingering I've ever seen. His face was absorbed but his eyes kept getting wider. He'd never heard that kind of resonance. He asked how they got that sound. I showed him the arching and pointed out the wood grain, then I told him I didn't know. I asked him to show me what he'd been doing with his fingering. He had a little trouble because he'd never thought about it. It was hard for him to slow down enough for me to see what he was up to. He kept stumbling until he found a way to race through a phrase at a time, then figure it out. He started at the beginning again for each run. He'd been playing since he was six, but only at fairs and amateur contests.

Phil said, "Man, do you know how good you are?"

He half-nodded and reddened. "Can't read music. Tried to learn once so's maybe I could get in the union but . . ." He shrugged. He asked us about the stuff we'd been playing. We didn't know what to tell him, except who wrote it and when. He said he liked it and asked if we'd be here tomorrow. We said we figured we would.

A guard took us back to our cells. Phil and Dudley did

everything but click their heels in the air, they were so excited. The traffic in the room had confused them at first. Eileen and I caught each other's eye as soon as it had started. Phil saw us grin and threw us a puzzled look. It took another couple of movements before he understood. Then he got excited. So did Dudley. Neither of them could have felt the way Eileen and I did though. They'd never played in the Orange Street Baptist Church. They couldn't know what it was like to be back. It was all there, the same musty smell, the terrible dead acoustics, the folding chairs with dried gum in every crack, and the people ambling in and out, hearing the music for the first time, curious, bored, surprised, but not afraid to listen, not afraid to tell each other about what they heard even while we played because we were playing in their own familiar territory, and nobody had told them they had to listen, or that it was a good thing to do.

Phil said, "We ought to get the whole fucking symphony in here. Then we wouldn't have to take strike votes."

Dudley said, "It might not be a high for everybody, baby."

"Did you hear what that guy made Jack's fiddle do?"

"When we get artistic control we'll bring him in to solo."

"Can you do what he did, Jack?"

I told him no. But I only started at eight.

At dinner Dudley admitted he'd been thinking the same kinds of things I had, wondering whether it made sense to be here. He said the session convinced him. "That's what it was like," he said to me. "I could tell. That's got to be what it was like."

I told him there were more of us, even at first, and more of them, and that it was fifteen years ago. But yes. That was what it was like.

August 5, 1975

A visit from Poppa this morning. He was in his wheel-chair in the visitors' room, looking positively triumphant. The people at the nursing home weren't going to let him come. That was why he had tried to reach Vic. He wanted to hire him to protect his rights. While he was waiting, a short hunger strike had done the trick. That, and playing his stereo at top volume.

It was a little upsetting to see him out of the home. It might have been the strain of the trip over, or just the new surroundings, but he looked older and more frail than ever. He had on an old loose sweater. His head seemed almost lost in it.

I told him how happy I was to see him, but it wasn't a good idea to be bothering Vic right now.

"I've got some other things to discuss with him," he said. Then he made a gesture announcing I'd used up my ration of criticism. He made me help him into a visitor's chair. Once he was settled he motioned me to sit across the table. He leaned forward until our heads were almost touching. "So what's the news?" he said.

He grinned at me just the way I'd grinned at Eileen yesterday and I realized he wasn't visiting his son at all. He was back with his comrades. I began to wonder if this was the only place left in the world where all the old good times were stored. I began to wonder if it was haunted.

I gave him all the news I had. I tried to sound optimistic, but his eyes are still sharp and his ear is trained. "You're getting discouraged," he said.

"I'm having doubts."

"About what?"

I shrugged. "Is this a radical action, Poppa?"

"I'd say so."

"You told me only radical actions win."

He nodded. "I didn't tell you when though. Which reminds me. I called your brother."

"Why does that remind you?"

"Because I'm tired of saying wise things. That's one of the reasons I called him. You always understand me. It was making me soft. I needed some confusion."

"Did you get it?" I asked.

"I congratulated him. Without strings."

"No advice?"

He shook his head proudly.

"That must have confused the hell out of *him*."

"He asked for you."

"What did you tell him?"

"That you're writing him a letter," Poppa said. "Have you finished it yet?"

"Soon, I think. How did he sound?"

"Cautious." He shrugged. "It's to be expected."

"Does he know where I am?"

"He saw you get arrested on television. Said it looked like a circus. And that he hopes you get what you want, but I shouldn't say that publicly. He also sends his love." Which was what I'd been waiting for.

"So it was a nice phone call," I said.

"Momma would have handled it better. That's one thing about this strike, Jackie. People who don't understand each other are trying to. That's something, you know."

"I won't get discouraged," I said.

"Try not to. On the phone Lenny started to offer you help, then he stopped. I thought that was good."

I nodded. It was better than sending your love. And it was just what I needed to get on the stick and tell you about the years on tour.

I've got a session in the library now, but tonight I'm going to get down to it.

Later

Just before dinner. Another good session. More people came to listen. Just thought you might be interested in the enclosed. It was on the bars of my cell when I got back.

Dear Fleischman,

What are you doing in there? I'm a sick man. The music is more important. You know goddamned well I'd never do it for you. I don't know why I'm writing this.

Arthur Quasnosky

((229))

ON TOUR

That visit with Molly happened in the autumn of 1954. You and I didn't see each other again until the spring of 1956, when I played with the Philadelphia Chamber Orchestra. That was the longest stretch apart we'd ever had. Even while you were in the Navy there were always those chance meetings on Friday nights in Brooklyn. They were out of the question now.

You and Cynthia were supposed to come to my senior recital but she phoned at the last minute to let us know you couldn't make it. I didn't expect any surprises this time. Molly and I got married that summer. I sent you an invitation but I knew that would be impossible, too. We were married in the rabbi's office on Nostrand Avenue. Ed was there. It was the day before he left for St. Louis. The only others were Momma, Poppa, Aunt Sarah, and Uncle Meyer. You couldn't come for the same reason you hadn't heard my senior recital. Poppa.

It was a terrible time for him. The poison in the country had finally seeped down to the leather industry. He and about twenty of his friends were laid off without explanation. The union wouldn't touch the case. He'd spent the first couple of months trying to find work at other factories but there were no openings. No, there was no blacklist. No, they didn't know about his political past. They were just looking for younger and less skilled workers. He'd been expecting it for a long time. What made it harder was that it came so late, after the worst of the hysteria had died down, and no one was paying attention anymore.

He had some savings they could live on for a while, and Uncle Meyer would ask Momma to come into his dress shop as a saleslady during heavy times. Soon she was working the slack season, too. It went on for two years. Poppa sank into depression. Momma grew more exhausted, not so much from the work as from trying to keep Poppa going. It was those two years that broke her. When Poppa finally did go back to work, it was as if she could let go and grow as old as the struggle had made her. He wasn't back at work a year before she got sick.

Everything during that time was tinged with bitterness and it was a time when we all had so much to celebrate. The recital, the wedding, your Susan, our Anna. Momma tried to re-create the excitement and the bustle of other celebrations. Poppa tried to laugh. But it always ended in silence and sad assurances about how happy they were. Cynthia had Susan that summer. Momma went down to Philadelphia alone. She tried to get Poppa to go with her. For a while it seemed as if he would, but at the last minute he managed to fall and fracture his ankle. Molly stayed with him so Momma could help with the first grandchild. Momma cut her visit short. "They have a nurse," she said when she got back.

Something had happened between you and Poppa. I didn't find out exactly what it was until we saw each other. All I knew then was that it was eating away at both of you. I would get periodic phone calls from you. There was always a reason. You'd seen an article about me; you had an investment tip; you'd gotten your master's degree or just found out Cynthia was pregnant. I'd ask what was wrong between you and Poppa. You'd say, "Nothing." Then you'd say we all had to get together soon and I'd agree.

In the meantime my career was happening. The Lewises had started making good on their promises. They brought their manager, Robert Hubel, to hear my senior recital. Hubel had been managing people like the Lewises for over

((231   ))

forty years. His father, Michael Hubel, had been doing it for another fifty years before that. Every serious musician dreamed of becoming a Hubel artist. They were the high priests of international music. After the recital he told Mme. Vlady to bring me to his office. I asked if I should bring my violin. Mme. Vlady said, "He has heard you play."

Robert Hubel was in his seventies then. He had been a huge man. In all the pictures I'd ever seen of him he towered over everyone else, and he always wore black opera cloaks that made him even more imposing. The night before, he had sent Mme. Vlady backstage with his message. Now I understood why he hadn't come himself. He'd had a stroke fifteen years earlier that left his legs paralyzed. He greeted us from his wheelchair. I also realized why every picture I'd ever seen showed only his right profile. The left side of his face was scarred from a burn he'd gotten in World War I.

His office turned out to be his apartment, an old duplex on East End Avenue. He used the upstairs only for guests now. He had brought down all his paintings and memorabilia and filled the first floor with them. It was like walking into a hundred years of music.

Even in his wheelchair Robert Hubel was a presence. He seemed to contain everything that the photographs, the posters, the remembrances that covered the tables and desks stood for in his own body. And he was one of the gentlest human beings I've ever met.

Mme. Vlady, all five feet of her, swept past the houseboy and kissed Robert Hubel on the forehead. She introduced me and plunked herself down on a sofa beneath two high Whistler portraits. I wondered if I would ever be able to maneuver so easily in a room like that. Right now I was having a terrible time controlling my ankles.

Robert Hubel took my hand in both of his, then asked me

to sit. For some reason I'd expected a foreign accent. If anything, there was a trace of the Midwest in his voice.

"I enjoyed your recital," he said. I could hear him place it exactly where it belonged in a lifetime of listening. "Did you know I was there?"

I looked at Mme. Vlady to find out how to respond. He caught me at it and smiled. I blushed. "Yes, sir."

"That's even better. You didn't know I was there the other time though."

"What other time?"

"When you played with the Brooklyn Symphony."

Ella Vlady sat up. "You never told me you heard Jack before."

"I didn't know until last night. I'd forgotten your name," he said apologetically. "It was only halfway through the program last night that I remembered."

"You heard me play with the Brooklyn Symphony?"

"You were Laszlo Resnick's student. Don't be so surprised, Mr. Fleischman. The world of music only seems big at the beginning. The longer you dedicate yourself to it, the smaller it becomes. Laszlo Resnick and I were friends for years. He was never a soloist, but he was a great and dedicated teacher. He knew his place. He asked me to come to hear you that night. It was a little premature," he said gently. "You weren't a prodigy. I told him you had promise, but only time could tell if you would work and grow. He was satisfied. He believed in you. He never told you what I said?"

I shook my head.

He closed his eyes lightly. "Of course not. We'll have to talk about him sometime. And now Ella and Daniel bring you to me." He turned to Mme. Vlady. "It's extraordinary, isn't it?"

She said, "Don't dramatize, Robert. Talent is talent. Tell him you want him as a client and get down to work." Only she said "voork."

"I haven't found out yet whether Mr. Fleischman wants me."

"Of course he wants you."

He turned to her again, wearily. "Ella, my darling. I love you beyond anything else in the world. Your hands have the gods in them. But you are not a businesswoman and you have never in your life been able to manage anything except a harpsichord. Which should be enough for any living mortal. Now shut up and let me talk with Mr. Fleischman." He turned back to me and left Mme. Vlady pursing her lips as if she were throwing kisses at the coffee table. "The Hubels don't take on new clients easily," he said.

I told him I knew that. The way he talked about himself as "the Hubels" gave me goose bumps.

"That's because we look for something more in an artist than just talent."

Mme. Vlady made an impatient noise.

"Pay no attention. If you agree to sign with me I want you to be clear about just what it is you're agreeing to. When I invest my time and money in an artist it is not because I believe he will be famous or rich. It is because I believe he will be great and that he will offer something great to the world of music. That's a process that takes years . . ."

"He thinks he's immortal," Mme. Vlady said from her corner.

Robert Hubel disregarded her. "If I wanted, I could book you tomorrow with all the great symphony orchestras in the world. And I believe you would perform well. You have the technical ability, a certain fine sensitivity and intellect. You could make a name for yourself. I hear something else in your work, something I hear in the work of many young people, most less promising than you."

"He's going to tell you about hunger," Ella Vlady said.

"It's understandable. It took me years to name it." He jerked his head toward Mme. Vlady. "She's right. It's a hunger. For fame. For reassurance. It gets in the way. And the most dangerous thing that can happen to a young artist like you is to have it fed."

"You heard that in my music?"

"I've seen it happen too often," he went on. "To some of the finest musicians, ones that the world is acclaiming right now. It's a gradual process. They begin by thinking they're dedicated to music. They believe themselves the most selfless human beings. They don't admit the hunger in time. They never confront it. Until it's too late and they're playing only to have that hunger fed. They will say it's not the money. That will be true. But it is not the music either. That is why they will never be able to give themselves up. Their work is dazzling, but it isn't pure. And they know it."

"How?"

"They are afraid to take risks. They only take what look like risks. If you become my client, Mr. Fleischman, you will commit yourself to a very slow career. You will play with some of the finest musicians in the world. They will not necessarily be the most famous. You'll play with small orchestras in European provinces, with chamber groups; you will give recitals in cities you may not even know have concert halls. And while you're doing that you'll build your repertoire, become impatient, and learn to give up your hunger."

"And then you will become old like me," Ella Vlady said.

Robert Hubel said, "Stop fishing, Ella."

"I'm not."

"Then stop sulking. Eventually you will play with the great symphony orchestras, but only when they mean something quite different to you than they do now."

"Make him an offer, Robert. I haven't had time to work yet today."

"I've already made you the offer," he said to me. "I want you to take some time to think about it."

"I can tell you now," I said.

He smiled. "I know. But that's because you're still hungry. Take the time."

Mme. Vlady clapped her hands and got up. "All right, then. Come, Jack."

"When do you want me to tell you?" I asked.

"When you're sure."

"You make it sound like he's taking holy orders."

He grinned at Mme. Vlady. "Your problem, Ella, is that you've never suffered."

She went to get her cape and left me alone with Robert Hubel. He waited silently for a while. I wandered around his living room pretending to look at the photographs. I could tell he was watching me. Just before Mme. Vlady came back, he said, "Mr. Fleischman, you asked before if I heard that hunger in your music." He said it very softly. "The point, you see, is that the music isn't yours at all."

It took me two weeks to work up the courage to call and say I wanted to sign with him. They were two weeks of agony, as much for Molly as for me.

Robert Hubel had astonished me. All those years I'd puttered along, thinking I was the least ambitious musician I'd ever met. I'd seen ambition in you, in Momma, in all the other students at Juilliard. I wasn't like that. I knew my place. I didn't have to steamroll down any basketball courts.

I had no demons. I was an innocent. And somewhere, deep inside, I carried around a certain smugness about it. But Robert Hubel had heard more than ambition when I played. He had heard hunger. We both knew the music never lied. The musician might lie, but the lie would be there in the music for anyone with ears to hear.

So there I was, suddenly, at twenty-one, with a whole new Jack Fleischman to contend with. A hungry one. And when I looked back on all the hours of practice, on what happened to me with the Lewises, even on what had happened at my bar mitzvah, it made a new kind of sense. I was even more competitive than you, Lenny, could have hoped for me. I thought I was out of it all; I was really just out for higher stakes. The only other person who knew that about me—at least, the only person who'd been honest enough to say it—was Irving Dicks. He'd said I was a hustler.

I was also a maniac to live with during those two weeks. I wandered around the apartment, questioning myself, questioning Ed. I borrowed a tape recorder, practiced, then listened to my practicing to see if I could hear what Robert Hubel had heard. When Ed couldn't stand it anymore he threw me out and I went to Molly.

"I'm running out of pillars and posts, Jack," she said. "What do you want from me?"

I wanted her to tell me I wasn't like that.

"Of course you're not like that. You are that."

"That's terrible," I said. "That's the most terrible thing you've ever said to me."

"I can think of worse."

"You're not taking me seriously."

"I don't have to. You're taking yourself seriously enough for both of us. That means Hubel is right."

"I can't stand it," I groaned. "I can't stand it. I'm just another egotistical, self-centered, brilliant artist. He called me hungry. Hungry!"

"If you were any hungrier you'd be the French Revolution."

I groaned again.

"How can I be great if I'm hungry?"

That was how it went until Molly shouted at me, "Get off the merry-go-round. Call Hubel. Sign with him." So I did.

He booked me in Europe for the whole summer. Molly and I used the trip for our honeymoon. While we were in Athens we flew to Haifa to meet Molly's mother. She was a small, nervous woman. I'm not sure she ever understood what Molly was doing there or who I was. She kept asking if I was Jewish, then if I was Israeli. She asked Molly if she lived in Haifa and seemed apprehensive that Molly might say yes. She never looked at her, and flinched whenever I said anything. We only stayed a day, sitting uncomfortably in the apartment Mrs. Reisdorf shared with her sister. When we left she wept and asked Molly if she needed money. Molly hugged her gently, said, "No, Ma. It's all right. Be happy with Aunt Hannah. It's all right."

That was all I ever saw of Molly's family.

Hubel kept me traveling all that year. I played with chamber groups in Italy, orchestras in Germany, gave recitals in Canada and Panama, and all the time I was discovering new musicians, new approaches, new capacities. I stopped being surprised when Robert said to me, "There is a string quartet in Kansas City . . . a violinist by the name of Flynn . . . they've asked you to join them for a three-week series. I think you'll enjoy it."

Molly was finishing her work at Columbia. At first I was worried. "I'm away so much," I said to her. "It's our first year of marriage. Shouldn't we be adjusting to each other or something?"

She explained we'd been married for three years. The only difference was that now we bought furniture.

Which was true. We'd moved from our furnished apartment to West End Avenue. The new place was big enough for Molly to have an office for private practice. She had brought her desk and books. I brought my music stand. We had to fill in the gaps.

By spring she had finished her dissertation. She started traveling, too. Not with me. She was reading papers at conferences. Our kitchen looked like the information desk at LaGuardia, with suitcases stacked near the door and arrival and departure times taped to the refrigerator. Once I came home from San Francisco and found an announcement:

J. arrive Sat., Apr. 12.
M. flight to Cincinnati pushed back
    to Sunday.
Remarks: Weather conditions and horniness.

April was a busy month. Anna may be one of the few people in the world who knows the date and time of her conception.

Hubel booked me with the Philadelphia Chamber Orchestra in May. It was a small group that had formed from the Philadelphia Orchestra to play special chamber concerts on Sunday nights. That was when you and I saw each other again.

Irving Dicks had the whole ensemble out to your club for dinner, then we all drove back to the city for the concert.

Cynthia was in her seventh month. She looked tired, but determinedly beautiful. Her father clucked around her the whole time, adjusting her shawl and stroking her shoulders.

You and I didn't really get together until after the concert.

I'd invited you and Cynthia up to my hotel room for a drink after the official reception. She was looking drawn, though, by then. Her father offered to drive her home early so you could have some time with me.

The hotel was only a couple of blocks east of Broad Street from the Academy of Music. We decided to walk. Just before we got there you steered me around. "Let's walk some more." We headed west on Locust toward Rittenhouse Square.

It was one of those city spring nights on the near edge of summer, the kind that makes you realize you haven't heard the sound of your shoes on the pavement since August. We listened to that for a long time.

You were changed. Your eyes were steady. They could stay with a person until they were finished looking. Your voice was lower, more intense. Your whole face had the firmness of a man's. You were still only twenty-seven, but in the light of the streetlamps I could see where the lines would be at forty. It was as if you'd taken all that drive, that manic energy that seemed to be a force outside you, and swallowed it so that now it lay smoldering inside. I would have called you subdued, except that there was still that urgency beneath it all. The difference was that it had a direction, one you had chosen and seemed to know why.

Irving Dicks had made you a junior partner in February. For your master's thesis you had worked out a new system for puts and calls on commodities that had impressed your advisor. He started recommending you as a consultant. You were getting used to flying to Washington and New York for lunch. Your name was on the letterheads of five different charities; you were president of the Dicks Foundation, a non-profit organization dedicated to the furtherance of Jewish art; and you were personally managing the money of some friends who didn't have quite enough to be able to use Dicks, Martin and Golden. You'd never been so busy, so in demand, yet you seemed more solid and controlled than in all the years when the only things you had were time and freedom.

You asked after Molly, and Momma and Poppa, as we walked. I asked about Cynthia and Irving Dicks and plans for the baby. The talk between us was low and easy in the empty street. It surprised me. You had a way of surprising me every time we came together. Maybe it was because the times between were getting longer. Each meeting I would leave you and carry around the Lenny of that visit until the next, when our very first greeting exploded the memory. Then I would waste time trying to pick up the fragments and fit them over the new reality. This time even that was different. Your new control and intensity didn't leave room for memory.

You asked about Robert Hubel and wondered why I had played with the chamber group instead of the whole orchestra. I tried to explain. And you tried to understand.

We were quiet again for a long time. Then you said, "You know what our trouble is, Jack?" It was the first time you called me Jack instead of Jackie. "All we ever have is reunions . . . I mean, we have to spend so goddamned much time catching up, we never really get a chance to—"

"I know what you mean." I interrupted before you could finish, partly to reassure you, partly because I was embarrassed. You were trying to open with me in a way I'd always dreamed of. You were thinking the same things I was. It was almost as if I'd come to expect you to disappoint me. To count on it. Now there were signs that you wouldn't. It scared the hell out of me.

"I was sitting there, watching you play tonight, and I thought, He's my brother. He's my brother and I don't even know him. I didn't even feel I had a right to be proud."

((241))

My face flamed. It could have lit the whole street. "I didn't think you cared about stuff like that." I had cleared my throat but it still came out a mumble.

"I guess I'm getting older. You start to think about those things as you get older."

"What things?"

"Family, I suppose."

"You seem more settled."

"So do you."

I gave a little nervous laugh. "I'm all over the place."

"You're going to be Uncle Jack soon."

"Uncle Jack and Aunt Molly. It sounds like we own a furniture store."

You chuckled easily. I got edgier. Anyone watching us drift down Locust Street that night would have thought we were absolutely comfortable with each other. The only thing odd they might notice was that you wore a gray flannel suit and I was still in my dinner jacket. In some ways we really were more relaxed than we'd ever been. In others, though, I was frantic.

"I heard Dad talk to some of the musicians tonight. They think a lot of you. It's funny. I used to think we were different. Maybe we're not so different after all. You're ambitious, Jack. Like me."

"I learned from you." My mouth was moving fine, but I was having a terrible time getting sound.

"How could you learn from me? You always knew what you wanted."

"Didn't you?"

You smiled and shook your head. "I only thought I did."

"Do you know now?"

You didn't answer right away. "It feels funny when I try to say it. I've never put it in words, not even to Cyn."

"You don't have to if you don't want to," I said quickly.

"I do. It's just . . . hard. I always thought I wanted to be rich and powerful. I was ashamed of that. That's why I never got anyplace. I was always getting in my own way because I thought what I wanted was wrong. And, I mean . . . Poppa . . . didn't make that any easier. You know what I mean?"

"What happened between you and Poppa?"

You didn't seem to hear. You really may not have. You were working hard at talking. "But this year . . . with Dad and Cyn . . . I realized what I'm all about, what I really want. It's not just to be rich. It's something else. Something . . . good. You know what I want? Jesus, it's hard to say it." You paused again. "I want to be necessary."

I nodded. "Needed."

"No. Necessary. That's the point. Cyn *needs* me now. And the baby's going to *need* me when it comes. That's all terrific. But if I wasn't around they'd get by. They'd manage. I want to be necessary. To a lot of people. That's what I'm after. I know that now. That's what was eating me up with Margaret and at Holtzman. But Dad is teaching me . . . I can do a million things now and still not feel as if I'm all over the place."

"Necessary," I murmured. "That's a pretty big word."

You nodded and gave another little laugh. "I told you. I'm ambitious. Like you."

"But I don't want to be . . ."

"You don't have to. You've got your music." Your forehead wrinkled. "I don't have one thing like that. Maybe that's why I want everything."

We sat down on one of the benches in Rittenhouse Square. It was a longer walk than I thought. I wondered whether we'd be able to find a cab back at that time of night—and whether you'd be willing to take it.

Here you are, Jack, I was saying to myself. This is the chance you've been waiting for all your life. Your brother's talking to you. And he's ready to listen. Now you can tell him all the things you've always wanted to.

But all I could do was clear my throat and wonder about finding a cab. I raced through all the times I'd thought about what I'd say if I ever really got the chance to open my heart to you. You were giving me every signal you could find. I saw them all, but I was paralyzed. Maybe I'd never really wanted the chance at all, I thought. For all those years, maybe all I'd really wanted to do was to spend just enough time to take away one part of you, one piece each time, one wonderful thing you'd said to me that would make you a hero or one terrible thing to make you a villain. Maybe I wanted anything in the world but for you to become real. And that meant that maybe it had never been you, after all, who had gotten in our way.

I snuck a sideways look at you. You sat forward with your arms on your knees. You'd picked up a dead branch from the locust trees and were peeling it absently. Your hair was short, almost a crew cut. You scanned the dark old houses across the street from the square. "The city's changing," you said absently.

"What happened between you and Poppa?" I said.

You shrugged. "We had a fight."

"What about?"

"He's a proud man." You concentrated on the locust branch. "I wanted to help. When the business happened at the factory . . . when you called and told me about it . . . I wanted to help. I offered . . . I'm making a lot of money now . . . so I offered . . ."

"He didn't take it."

"He got angry. If he'd just said no. . . . O.K. No is no.

But he shouted at me. He said he'd take it from somebody else. Not from someone who was making it happen. I said, 'Poppa, I want to stop it as much as you. That's why . . .' He called me a fascist and I lost my temper."

"He's under a strain," I said.

"Who isn't?" You shook your head. "I don't know what he wants." Then you said something so softly I couldn't hear it.

I said, "What?"

"I can't spend the rest of my life trying to find out." You dropped the branch. "It's getting late. Cyn is going to worry." But you didn't get up right away.

"You think we can find a cab?" I said cautiously.

"I like the walk. You don't mind, do you?"

"No. No." I figured it was the least I could do.

On the way back you said, "Tell me about this Robert Hubel. Do you think he's handling you right?"

I assured you he was.

"I care about you, Jack. You know that."

I nodded. A lot.

You asked about Hubel some more. And about my career. If I hadn't been so preoccupied I would have known you were leading up to something. I was too busy watching my chance with you slip away though. I knew what you were going through. I knew from all the times I was the one who made myself vulnerable, or thought I did, and you seemed to never notice. Now I understood your embarrassment those times, too, and your shame at being embarrassed, and your frustration because you could never figure out just what it was that I wanted. I understood because that was what I was feeling now.

"Does he manage your money, too?" you said.

"He pays me. He finances the tours . . ."

((245   ))

"I mean besides that."

"What else is there? You mean like taxes?"

"Investments," you said.

"I'm a musician, Lenny."

"Has Hubel said anything about incorporating?"

"Incorporating what?"

"Yourself."

I laughed.

"I'm serious."

"Jack Fleischman, Incorporated. It would make me feel like a crowd."

"You're going to be making a lot of money. You need somebody to manage it."

I didn't answer right away. "You want to do that?"

"It's the most dangerous thing in the world. Like a surgeon operating on his own family."

"You don't want to do it."

"But I wouldn't trust anybody else," you said.

"You do want to do it." I thought about my checkbook for a while. I had always mixed up money and sports in my head. I had the idea that you had to be athletic to be rich. "I don't have that much money, you know. Right now it's all tied up in sectionals."

"You will."

"I'd have to talk to Robert about it . . . ." I was doing it again. You were showing faith in me. You were making the kind of offer I'd heard you make in my imagination a thousand times, and I was backing off. Poppa used to say, "Be sure you know what you really want, Jackie. Because you're sure to get it." Who knew he meant an offer of friendship from you?

"A lot of stars have artistic managers and business managers," you said.

"Robert Hubel is different . . ."

"O.K." You dismissed it quickly. I couldn't stand the hurt underneath it.

"Give me some time to think about it. O.K.? How would it work?"

You explained what it meant to become a corporation, how it wouldn't interfere at all with the music. I wouldn't even have to think about it. You would be in charge of making my money work for me and it would mean security for Molly and me.

"When are you going to have time for all this?"

"We're talking about my brother's future," you said. "Besides, I've got time for everything now."

They were vacuuming the carpet in the hotel lobby when we got back. My feet were numb. You said you'd call me in a day or two and we'd work things out. "I'm proud of you, Jack," you said.

I turned into the great American mumbler again. You asked if I was going to see Poppa soon. I told you yes, and waited for more. You just nodded and let it drop.

"You think we'll get to see more of each other now?" I said before you left.

You smiled. "We might get sick of each other."

"That'd be nice."

It was about three in the morning when I hobbled up to my room. Molly was in Boston for the week. I called her. The phone rang a long time before she answered.

"Did I wake you up?" She didn't say anything, but I heard her breathing. "It's Jack."

"It goddamned well better be."

"I'm going to be a corporation."

"What time is it?"

"I don't know," I lied. "How's the conference?"

Molly said, "Jack?"

"I just left Lenny. He's going to be my business manager."

"Wait a minute."

I heard her put down the phone. She was gone a long time. When she got back, I said, "Where were you?"

"I had to brush my teeth."

"It's long distance."

"It's your fault."

I told her everything that had happened. When I finished, she said, "Talk to Robert."

I said, "Sure. But I know it's the right thing."

There was silence on the other end. "What's wrong?"

"When you know something's right you ask me for advice. When you're not sure you make announcements."

"You wouldn't believe the change in Lenny."

"Talk to Robert."

"When are you going to be home?"

"Thursday, I think. Check the refrigerator."

I lay awake a long time. Molly was right. I wasn't as sure as I would have liked to think I was. You'd taken me by surprise. I told myself it was just a business deal. I was growing up. I was a married man. I had a career. I should be able to handle a business proposition. You had assured me it wouldn't interfere with the music. It could only help make me stronger, more worldly and realistic. Besides, I had to be honest. It wasn't just a business deal. It was you. You had noticed me that night the same way you noticed me riding my bike one-handed. I had made a hash of it then and I'd almost botched it again that night when I backed off, but you'd given me another chance. This time I'd handle it. I would call Robert Hubel as soon as I got back to the city. Or the next day. I fell asleep thinking of all the reasons to wait a couple of days before I said anything to him at all.

I did speak to him, finally.

That Wednesday I went to his apartment. He took my hand in both of his the way he always did and told me he'd heard the Philadelphia program was a great success. Then he looked at me more closely. "Is anything wrong?"

I said, "No."

He said, "Sit down and tell me."

I stumbled through an explanation of your offer

"You're free to do whatever you want with your money," he said.

I told him I knew that.

"Then why are you so troubled about telling me?"

I said, "I'm not sure."

"Are you afraid the arrangement will interfere with the music?"

"No," I said quickly. "Not at all. Lenny assured me it wouldn't have anything to do with that. . . . Yes. I'm afraid it will."

"How?"

"I don't know."

"It needn't. It's not inevitable, you know."

"But it could."

He nodded. "You're the only one who knows that." He smiled. "Not a year ago I had another one of my young artists sit where you're sitting now and tell me she was getting married. I don't suppose it ever occurred to you that your marriage might interfere."

I shook my head.

"You see? That young woman—she's going to be a magnificent dramatic soprano—that young woman has had her own private business manager for three years. It never occurred to her it might be dangerous. She knew where the pitfalls lay for her the way you know where they lie for you. For someone else it might be alcohol, or women—or even politics. None of those things needs to interfere. Any of them could, depending on how well you know yourself."

"Did she get married?" I said.

"Who?"

"Your soprano."

"Oh, yes."

"How's she doing?"

He looked at me reproachfully.

"Am I allowed to retract that question?"

He laughed. "You've already decided to accept your brother's offer, haven't you?" he said gently.

I nodded.

"So you're not really asking for advice. Just my blessing." He shook his head, amused. "Ella always accuses me of confusing myself with the pope. Times like these aren't much help. I'd like to meet your brother," he said. "Does he understand music?"

"I think he wants to."

"At least he wants to understand you."

I flushed.

He studied me awhile. "Your work this year has been extraordinary. You know that. I'm sure your brother couldn't have helped but hear the quality."

I hesitated. "I think this is his way of telling me."

"And that's why you're nervous."

"I'm not sure."

"So the danger may not be business at all, but love." I opened my mouth but nothing came out. "If there *is* any danger," he added. "Tell him I'd like to see him. I'll explain our arrangement and do everything I can to help."

You met with him the next week, when you were in town

on some other business. Robert Hubel was impressed. You knew money, he said, and you seemed eager to learn about music. You were impressed, too. "He wants to do right by you, Jack," you said. "We both do."

Then the papers started arriving. Special delivery, every other day for a month, with short notes attached. "Sign at red X. Make sure you hit all of them. Cyn says come down and visit. Love to Molly. L." It was exhilarating. All my doubts fell away. The thick envelopes with long, legal papers made me feel positively legitimate. I bought a special pen and a rolltop desk with all kinds of different-size drawers. Whenever you were in town you'd stop by for a drink, sometimes dinner, and tell me how I was getting along. The two of us would talk business the way I'd seen you talk to Irving Dicks, but underneath there was a current of excitement and wonder for both of us. You were taking me seriously. I was trusting you. We were finding a way to give each other what we'd always wanted.

Molly was suspicious. She admitted you were different from the first time she met you. Certainly I was behaving better, but those things were tricky.

"I'm a client," I said to her. "Think of it that way. He's a businessman and I'm his client."

She was restive. "He doesn't need you as a client."

"Maybe he just wants to do for me what he can't do for Poppa."

She didn't buy it. "Besides," she said, "that makes you different from a client."

There was one thing I never did tell her. That was what you said about wanting to be necessary. I knew that would have been the clue she was looking for. I was afraid if she found it she would convince me to drop the arrangement.

Through the next two years I watched you make yourself necessary to me. I felt as if it was my gift to you and no one, not even Molly, was going to take that chance from me.

We spent a lot of time together, you and Cynthia and Molly and I. We were both new fathers. We thought we were the first in history. You were as excited about Anna as you were about Susan. Every time you came to the city you brought a new toy or a dress or something for Anna's room. You still had that habit of suddenly showing up without warning, but if I was practicing or Molly was with a patient you'd slip away without disturbing us.

Molly became less cautious. You were the only family she had. She admitted that she liked the idea of having in-laws.

Even Poppa thawed. As soon as he was back at work you made some tentative moves toward him. You phoned Momma, then asked to speak to him. You and Cynthia brought Susan to Brooklyn. When Momma was sick you were there as much as you could be. When she died you stayed with us over the whole week of *shiva*.

You were taking care of all my practical affairs. Instead of interfering with the music you helped me to grow. I had your respect and admiration. Whatever impatience or hunger I'd felt before fell away. Wherever I played I felt as secure as if you were lying beside me in the dark, looking out for my future. Just when I'd learned to give up hoping for it, we'd found a way to weave into each other's life.

Robert Hubel died in 1958. That was when the trouble started. Sol Hurok picked up people like the Lewises. Most of Robert's younger artists went over to Vargas Associates. You didn't see any reason for me to sign a new contract with anyone. You'd been learning the business. You could handle the whole thing yourself.

"Where are you going to find the time?" I said.

You laughed. "You asked me that in Philadelphia. Remember?"

"But you've got twice as many things going for you now. And besides . . ."

"What?"

I shook my head. "You've just been doing so much," I said. Sean had been born a couple of months before. I was going to mention him and Susan and Cynthia, but I stopped myself. When you first told us Cynthia was pregnant again you'd announced it with the same excitement and pride you'd had about Susan. But over the next few months you took on more business responsibilities than ever before. You were traveling more, less for Dicks, Martin and Golden, more for your own, private projects. Your surprise visits to New York seemed to double. Sometimes you would call home from our apartment. Your voice was always concerned, but your face would be tight and guarded. Your eyes would dart around the room the way they used to. If you noticed that Molly or I was watching you'd turn your back. The old furious energy was starting to surface again. It was only starting though, and I wasn't about to pay attention to vague signals and risk giving up our arrangement.

"We're a team," you said, and you meant it.

I didn't sign with Vargas.

You had learned more than I ever imagined from Robert Hubel. You put that knowledge together with your own genius for handling commodities and suddenly I was a celebrity. You booked me in just the right place at just the right time. You even had an instinct for putting together the right program.

"Why don't you tackle something more contemporary for Cleveland," you'd say. "That town's just starting to feel as if they're with it. They know just enough to feel insulted if you do all romantic stuff. Nothing too much. Something between Shostakovich and Schoenberg. You know what I mean?"

"How did you learn so goddamned much about music all of a sudden?" I asked you once.

You grinned. "I lived around you and Poppa for a couple of years. Half the trick in my business isn't learning new things. It's using what you've already learned without knowing it. Besides, I've got Edith."

All I knew about Edith then was that she'd started out as your secretary, that she was Vassar '55, and that now she was your executive assistant. It made sense. She was as sharp and high-powered in her way as you were in yours. That was why you could handle as much work as you did. You could leave Philadelphia for weeks at a time and know that when you got back everything would be under control. It was only later, when she started traveling with you, that I realized what was up. Then the phone calls home started making sense, too.

You were pushing me faster than Robert Hubel had planned. I was playing on a much more public circuit. However quick you were, you couldn't possibly have learned the nuance of an artist's development the way Robert knew it. I told you I was a little nervous.

"It sure as hell isn't getting in the way of your playing," you said.

That was true. My work was better than ever. All the publicity and the raves only seemed to add a new kind of energy and tension to my music. I was nervous before every performance, but I was able to use those jitters to serve my concentration, and they would make the triumph afterward that much more exhilarating.

"I work differently from Hubel," you said to me. "I know

that. He was old school. That's why I liked him so much. It was kind of like working with the House of Morgan. You and me though. We're a different generation. That's the way I see it. I take more chances."

"Chances?" I said.

"No. That's the wrong word. I know what I'm doing. I'm just more aggressive. So are you. That's why we work so well together." You grinned at me. "That's what makes you a star."

One of the first things you had done was to hire a publicity agent for the Fleischman Corporation. The advance publicity in every city made my appearances a major event. It was a kick to arrive at a concert hall early and see a line stretch into the street from the box office. Once, in Denver, you happened to be there at the same time I was playing. I dragged you to the concert hall and we stood across the street, watching the crowd mill around the front door.

"That's for me," I said. "They're all waiting to hear me. Isn't that incredible?"

"They wouldn't be there if you weren't worth it," you said.

"They wouldn't be there if it wasn't for you."

You laughed and put your arm around me.

Your reputation in money circles was growing as fast as mine was in music. At the end of our first year together you'd made yourself a partner in the Fleischman Corporation and used it as a base to manage your friends' money. By the second year we were as exclusive as the most exclusive investment corporation on Wall Street. "More exclusive than Holtzman," you would say, and flash a triumphant grin. You left Dicks, Martin and Golden the next year. Cynthia had already filed for divorce.

She had known about Edith long before Molly and I. The

two of you had worked out an arrangement. The marriage was for the children. For their sake, and for Irving Dicks, you would keep up appearances. It had finally become too much for her though, and when your father-in-law figured out what was going on, he blew the whistle.

It was best for all of you, you said. People outgrew each other. You'd been stifled in Philadelphia. You needed the freedom to expand.

Molly said, "Did you ever notice when a man gets divorced he talks as if he's freeing a trapped soul? He usually is. The wife's."

You told us you were going to marry Edith.

"No, he's not," Molly said to me.

"Of course he is. He jumps in and out of those things."

"She's too smart. She won't marry him until he's settled down."

You were anything but settled then. "For five years I've been two hours out of the action," you said to me. Now you were smack in the center. The Fleischman Corporation had offices just off Trinity Square. You were eating lunch at Delmonico's every day.

Once you called me while I was in Montreal.

"Jackie?" You'd started calling me Jackie again. "Get this. I'm having lunch today with Ken Galbraith, people from Jones, and people from Oppenheim, see, and I hear somebody at the bar say, 'Boy, I'd sure as hell like to know what they're talking about at *that* table.' " You chuckled. "That's better than a line outside the box office."

It was a heady, breathless time for all of us. I was on tour eight months out of the year. I saw as much of you and Edith as I did of Molly. I was constantly catching planes, checking in at hotels, racing to the concert hall for rehearsals. You would show up by surprise in Chicago, in Brussels, in London. You started arranging my tours so they'd coincide with your business trips. "That way I don't have to mail you papers," you said.

You had me endorsing vodka and some kind of skin cream for men. You had Edith writing reviews of music books for *The New York Times* under my name. We were moving so fast there was no time to notice what was happening to both of us, how we were changing.

I had always despised prima donnas. All through Juilliard and during those first few years with Robert Hubel I'd seen other musicians throw tantrums or fall apart with fits of sensitivity. It seemed stupid and unnecessary. I promised myself that I would be the nice guy of the world of music, beloved of all. Warm, reasonable, unruffled. I wasn't going to contribute to the myth of the temperamental artist. That was what all the others were doing anyway, living up to some kind of adolescent idea of what a musician *should* be. I never believed it. That was another reason I didn't notice how I was changing. I'd lived so long with the idea that I was sensible and understanding that if I demanded something, if I made a scene, I figured there was a reason for it.

Molly saw the signs. She tried to warn me, gently at first. I would come home, raging at the acoustics of the San Francisco Opera House.

"And they were still letting people in during the first movement of the Bartók. Can you imagine that? I was ready to stop. Just stop playing and walk off until they all got settled."

"You didn't though."

"Of course I didn't. What the hell do you think I am?"

She shrugged.

"But I let them have it afterward. I told them I'd never play there again."

"I'm going to a conference in Miami next week," she said

cautiously. "Poppa's taking Anna. What do you think about going with me? Take a little vacation. Hang around the pool."

"Lenny's got me booked."

You must have seen what was happening, too. Every tour I was on the phone with you, complaining about my billing or the radio interviews you'd set up, or my hotel. Once, when I was playing Washington, I demanded you come down and take care of a mixup about some house seats.

"I'll send Edith," you said.

"No! You!" I shouted.

"I've got business meetings all afternoon."

"I'm not playing tonight unless you're down here."

By the time you arrived I'd calmed down. You were furious.

"All right," you said. "What's the trouble?"

I made something up.

I made up a lot of trouble during that time. I didn't want to face what was really happening. The nerves I'd been able to use at first were getting worse with each performance. The crowds outside a concert hall weren't exciting anymore. They had turned into a monster that pulled itself together every night and sat there waiting for me to slip so it could spring into judgment. I'd delivered myself into its hands. Every concert I depended on it to reassure me that the skill was still there, that I'd made it through another contest. Soon that reassurance wasn't enough. I had to test my value in other ways. So I made demands, irrational ones, to prove my power. I was becoming everything Robert Hubel had warned me about.

My music was dazzling. I was tackling the most astonishing showpieces I could find. I tore into them with a furious energy that kept the audience breathless. But even when they were over and I saw the crowd swell to its feet, I would think that somewhere in there was a Robert Hubel who had heard the agony and the terror, who knew I was growing more and more afraid I would be found out.

I wasn't about to tell that to you. I had barely been able to admit it to myself. Sometimes, in a hotel room, just before I was falling asleep, I would think, If only I could relax. If only the nerves would go away, I'd be able to climb out of this thing and find the pure sweet sound that Robert . . . But the more the nerves tortured me, the more I came to depend on them to get me through a performance. I was afraid to give them up.

I knew what you would say.

"It's what makes you a star, Jackie. The bigger you get, the more you prove you have a right to be where you are. You can handle it. I'll let you know when you can't."

I had delivered myself into your hands, too. And I was growing to hate you as much as I hated the audience. What I wanted, more than anything else in the world during the worst of that time, was to fail. If once an audience had caught me out in the lie, if once I had heard them shuffle and cough the way I'd heard them at my bar mitzvah, my worst fears might have played themselves out. I might have been able to start fresh. But you had convinced them I was an event. They weren't listening to the music any more than Uncle Oscar or Aunt Millie had listened years before. They were hearing me. The only difference was that by then I wanted that, and by then I could make them believe I was delivering. The more they acclaimed me, the more contemptuous I grew. The more you and the managements put up with my outbursts, met my crazy demands, soothed and coddled me, the more contempt I had for you, too. I was doing everything I could to make someone shout "Enough!" or force me to shout it myself, and release me. Nobody did. None of us could afford to.

Molly had been saying it, more and more urgently each year. She never saw me in action on my tours. I don't know what she would have let loose if she had been there when I made them hold the Chicago concert a half hour while an electrician fixed a light that bothered me, or when I demanded they turn off the heating system in Paris in the middle of winter. She only got my reports. She heard enough though, and she was able to see what happened when you and I were together.

Once, very close to the end, you had dropped in to clear up some details on a concert at the Hollywood Bowl. You hadn't been coming to the apartment as much lately. More and more you'd been having Edith take care of things over the phone. Molly was in the other room with Anna, but she heard us.

When you left she came into the living room. She was pregnant with Marty. It was beginning to show. "You forgot to tell him to spit-shine your shoes," she said.

I started to smile, then I realized she was trembling. Her eyes were blazing.

"You have no right, Jack. I don't care who you are. You have no right to talk to anybody the way I heard you talk to your brother."

"We were talking business," I said.

"Giving orders like that. If Anna ever talked like that to me I'd smack her mouth. If your brother wasn't such an idiot that's what he would have done to you."

"Be careful, Molly."

"No. No more careful. No more padding around in my bare feet while the artist practices. No more keeping Anna busy and quiet while the genius rests. No more careful, Jack.

You might end up thinking you can talk to me the way you talk to Lenny."

"We understand each other."

"How could he let you?"

"It's his job."

She drew a sharp breath. "What?"

"You heard me."

"That's it. All right, that's it. It's all over. Get out of your contract. Drop it."

"Stop it, Molly."

"I know you. I've been living with you for five years and I know you. Whatever hell you're going through now, I see what it's doing to you. It's got to stop. Do you understand what I'm saying, Jack?"

"An ultimatum."

"A promise. Get away from Lenny. Get away from the tours. Get away from the violin if you have to. Anything to become a human being again."

I tightened my mouth. I wanted to tell her what was going on inside me with every performance. I'd already become too locked in, too isolated and ashamed. "Lenny needs me."

"He hates you. Some night you'll murder each other in your sleep."

"Leave me alone."

"Get out from under."

"Lenny loves me."

"How do you know? You've been on tour for three years."

"I love him."

"Then get off his back."

"He wants me there."

"Try it and see."

I sprang out of my chair. Molly flinched and drew back,

afraid I was going to hit her. I stormed into my studio and locked the door.

I realized how bad things were when I saw Molly flinch. I stayed in my studio that whole night.

She was right. We hated each other. All that euphoria from the beginning of our arrangement was gone. It had dissipated so gradually and in the middle of so much activity that neither of us had really noticed. By the last couple of months we'd been tearing away at each other as openly as I'd seen you and Margaret do it twelve years before. There was a difference, though. You and Margaret never gave each other what you needed. You and I had. We had both become necessary—and we despised each other for it.

What Molly had heard that afternoon was only my contempt for you. If she'd been in your office a couple of days before, when you announced that you'd booked me at the Hollywood Bowl, she would have heard yours for me. I was exhausted. The notice was too short. I pleaded with you to cancel. You said, "Don't pull that temperamental crap with me. I'm your brother. Remember? You're committed. They love you in Los Angeles. You don't have to be good. You just have to be there. Pull something out of the hat."

It was getting dark in the studio. I lay down on the couch and stared at the ceiling. Molly knocked on the door once.

"Jack?" Her voice was cautious.

"I'm practicing," I said.

"Are you all right?"

"I'm having a nervous breakdown."

She left me alone for the rest of the night. My violin lay on top of a pile of scores near the music stand. I opened the case but I couldn't take it out. I don't know how long I stood there, looking at it with loathing. I was sure I would never pick it up again without revulsion. It had finally come to that. First I'd learned to hate my audiences, then you, then the other musicians who played with me. Now I even hated the music. I waited until it was so dark I couldn't see the instrument before I moved away from it.

Sometime in the early morning I switched on my desk lamp. There was a pile of booking offers on the blotter. Edith always put a little "Yes" or "No" or "Neg" for "negotiate" in the upper right corner. After you worked out my itineraries you left Xerox copies with me. "So you know how many places you turned down," you said to me. "It's an indicator." The pile was two months old. I leafed through it absently until I came to the St. Louis Symphony. There was a little "No" in the corner. I crossed it out, threw all the others away, and waited until it was morning so I could call to accept.

I was ripe for Ed Lewis.

That was 1961. Everything happened very fast after that. I negotiated the St. Louis concert myself and made my own travel arrangements. It was only when you called to ask me if I wanted to play Dallas the night before that I told you about it. You hit the ceiling.

"I've already got you booked."

"Then why'd you ask if I wanted to?"

"Don't start with me, Jack."

"Next time check with me first. For real."

"What do I tell Dallas?"

"Handle it. That's what I pay you for."

I threw my last tantrum in St. Louis. Two weeks later I flew to Atlanta with Ed, and left you to cancel Chicago.

You thought I was going through another temperamental phase. I guess I purposely made it look like that. Neither of us was ready to admit it was really over.

I was scared. Ed, Fred Holland, Reinhold Blesser, and I met with Eileen Simpson and Bob Cross in Atlanta. Their scheme sounded crazy. They were talking about a community orchestra. I had left you to cancel an appearance for five thousand dollars against 10 percent of the gross to talk to some people about a community orchestra. But they were talking about something very different. They tried to help me understand that.

I protected myself with disdain. It was quixotic, I said. I preened on my own experience. I was a soloist. I had to be realistic. Yet they were talking about music and about finding an audience for the music with an enthusiasm, with a faith and a love I hadn't heard for years. It frightened me.

"You're talking about an amateur organization," I said.

"I don't think it's a question of amateur or professional, Mr. Fleischman," Eileen Simpson said quietly. "I think it's a question of serious or not serious."

"I think the whole thing is a big question."

Reinhold Blesser smiled. "You are right, Mr. Fleischman. It is a risk. You are a virtuoso. You know about those."

On the plane back to New York, Ed said, "It's a political move, too, Jack."

"Art isn't political," I snapped.

He laughed. "Everything's political. Your tantrum in St. Louis was political."

I tried to dismiss it.

"Ask your father," he said.

I flushed. I'd been seeing as little as I could of Poppa over the past two years. Every time we got together I would end up with a migraine. He would greet us at the door to the apartment in Brooklyn and his eyes would pierce right through my cashmere suit. He heard me play every time I was in New York. At first we would talk about the concert. He never stopped coming, but he stopped discussing my music. More and more I managed to be busy when Molly arranged to take Anna to Brooklyn or have Poppa uptown for dinner.

He never challenged me directly. Only once, he said, "You're getting a lot of headaches, Jack."

"I'm seeing a doctor."

"Do you think it's physical?"

"It's not psychological."

"It could be political. Headaches are a symptom of the alienation of labor."

"I'm an artist."

He shrugged. "The only difference between artists and workers is that workers know who's oppressing them."

I would have liked to go to Poppa when I got back from Atlanta. Reinhold Blesser had talked to me about risks as if I lived with them every day, but I'd forgotten what a real risk felt like. I'd forgotten the sense of life that went with it, the exhilaration of letting go and giving myself up to the thing outside me, that leap into the moment when all you can do is trust that the skill and the good faith will be there to fill the void. Over the past three years I'd learned how to imitate that, but I'd been away from the real thing too long. The exhilaration felt too much like terror and the trust too much like suspicion. I was ashamed to go to Poppa.

I went to Ella Vlady instead.

She had a recording session that week. She told me to meet her at the studio. When I got there she was cutting one of the Mozart concerti. I slipped into the control room and watched her.

She was wearing slacks and a gray pullover sweater. Her short white hair fit like a little cap. The face underneath it was immobile, except for that habit she had of pursing her lips as she concentrated. A short way into the *menuetto* she stopped and looked up to the control booth.

"I am sorry," she said. "It takes me some time to relax."

The producer flipped a switch and told her it sounded fine.

She shook her head. "All this." She gestured around the studio. "It always makes me feel I have to do it right. I forget to do it well."

"Do you want to hear the first movements?"

"No. Not yet." Mme. Vlady noticed me at the control-room door. "Is that you, Jack?"

The producer turned and recognized me. I stepped back. I was already feeling like an outsider. "Don't let me interfere. I'm sorry."

"No, no, no. We have been recording since one. Mr. Kenton, I will take a little break now anyway. It will help, I think, if I talk with Mr. Fleischman."

He checked his watch. "How much, Ella?"

"Just enough for some tea. All right?"

He called a break and Mme. Vlady summoned me into the studio.

There was a couch with a coffee table set up for her. She had her own little water heater and tea set arranged over the top.

"Come." She took me by the hand. "We'll make believe it's my living room."

"You were playing beautifully," I said.

Ella Vlady shook her head. "Not yet. After the break, perhaps . . ." She started pouring the tea. "Now, what is so urgent . . ." She glanced up and stopped. My eyes had filled with tears. It took us both by surprise. If we'd really been alone in her living room I probably would have been able to control them. The studio was too public and they'd sprung up too suddenly.

It was the way she'd stopped in the *menuetto*, the selfless honesty of her own ear and the grace of her apology that had done it. Ella Vlady was the best of everything I had worked for all those years and I realized I had come to say good-bye to it.

She touched my hand. "When you are ready," she said and went back to the tea.

"I'm leaving the concert stage."

She raised her eyebrows. "To do what?"

"I'm not sure." I tried to tell her what had been happening over the past three years. "I feel as if I've betrayed everyone," I said when I was finished. "You and Daniel, Robert . . ."

She shook her head. "You have not betrayed us. Besides, I do not think this is the time for that kind of judgment. It is too much like another kind of self-indulgence."

"I'm not just throwing another scene."

"I know that. You are going through a crucial phase . . ."

"In my career?" I said wryly.

"In your life as an artist. I have been hearing it in your music. All of us who have also been where you are now could recognize it, the anger and the determination to believe that what you are doing is worthwhile even after you think you have lost belief. It gives the work brilliance and power, but it robs it of clarity."

"If only Robert were here . . ."

"Robert is dead."

". . . it might not have happened."

"It would have happened anyway. You are an artist. You have just discovered you are lonely. Robert would never have been able to help. Not any more than I can. Or beautiful Molly or your nice father or your brother."

"People can help each other," I said.

"We can admit our loneliness and offer to share it. That is all. That is what makes the music worthwhile."

I shook my head.

"You say you have learned to despise your audience."

"They don't hear," I said.

"They are lonely, too. That is why you despise them. They are the image of your loneliness. You will learn to love them. In a new, more honest way."

"You don't believe I'm leaving."

She smiled. "It is inconceivable."

"The music has no meaning," I said.

"Yet you say you don't know what you'll do if you leave."

I hesitated. "There's a group in Atlanta."

"A group of what?"

"Musicians."

"Ah." She nodded. I thought her lips twitched. "Go on."

"They want to try something new." I told her about the idea for a People's Ensemble. I wasn't that clear about it myself then. My explanation was disjointed, but she heard me out. She never took her eyes from me.

"And you think this is something new," she said finally. I nodded.

"Perhaps." Mme. Vlady picked up her tea and sipped it quietly. "You do not sound convinced that it will help you."

"I'm not sure."

"I don't believe it will. Your audience in Georgia will hear no better than the one in New York. At first there will be the excitement, the adventure of experiment. But what will happen after four or five years when you discover nothing has changed? You say the music has no meaning. That is not true. It is simply that you have lost the thread for the moment. To leave now would be a mistake. I do not like it."

"You and Daniel have been very good to me . . ."

She waved her hand impatiently. "We have done no favors. You have no obligation to me. Only to music. And to your own excellence. If you fulfill those you will find an audience."

"My work is selfish."

"But that is only a symptom of doubt. You are capable of finer work than you ever dreamed of."

"Maybe the People's Ensemble is the way."

"That is not the tradition. You must remain among other great musicians, among the ones who can hear. We will challenge you and you will learn from us."

"I have to find out if what I do has any value. Any value at all."

"So you will lose faith in the music, but you will have faith in the people of Georgia."

"I don't have to have faith in them. They're real. Maybe they'll make the music real for me, too."

She paused and thought a moment. "For me it worked the other way."

"How?"

"I never questioned the value of the music, but I did not know the value of my audience. I came to learn it through the music." She spread the fingers of one hand and massaged it gently with the other. The skin was mottled and paper-thin. "Perhaps you are only trying to come to learn the value of the music through the audience. Perhaps. Perhaps the certainty of one generation must always be the doubt of the next." She shrugged. "Perhaps that is why the risks never look the same."

"I haven't taken a risk in a long time," I said.

"You haven't had to. That is why you are in despair. All great risks come out of necessity."

"I've been so unhappy."

Her voice turned sharp. "With all the gifts God has given you, do you demand happiness, too?" She paused. "You are determined."

"I have no choice."

She took another moment. "Then it is a risk. You will not be able to come back. You know that."

"Yes."

"I cannot help you to change your mind."

"No."

She threw me a puzzled look. "Then tell me, Jack. Why did you come to see me?"

I hesitated. "To hear you say everything you have said."

She lowered her eyes. The producer called into the studio over the speaker. "Ready to go, Ella."

"Yes," she said. "One moment more, please." She looked at me. "I will tell you one other thing, Jack, since you are determined to do this. It is a hope that I have. You may only think you are leaving."

"Mme. Vlady . . ."

She shook her head. "No, no, no. Listen to me. You are an artist. I will ask you to be my audience for a moment and to hear the way you want your audiences to hear. I am sixty years old. Music has been my life. So I have been sitting here and drinking tea with you and listening while you tell me that my life has no meaning."

"I didn't mean . . ."

She held up her hand to stop me and clicked her tongue. "That is what you say, Jack. It makes me sad and it makes me a little angry. I think you are foolish. I tell myself you are young and that you are making a mistake you will regret for the rest of your life. To throw away the traditions of hundreds of years when you are so close is an act of waste. I and Daniel are a part of that tradition. So I think it is an insult, and I think it is a threat. But what do you threaten, I ask myself. Not the music. Nothing can threaten that. Even if it were not to be played for a hundred years, nothing could destroy it. Only the *way* of the music. You threaten that. My way. The way I have come to realize the music in my own lifetime, the way I have come to believe in it, in the great cities in front of the great audiences, with the acclaim of the whole world. If that is not your way—and as long as you are an artist—I should not be threatened."

She paused. "Now I will tell you about Ella Vlady at twenty-five. It was a time when Paderewski and Leschetizky and Landowska were playing. I lived among a scruffy, disreputable, barbaric group of unknowns. We thumbed our noses at Paderewski and we thumbed our noses at his audiences. There was no meaning in the music. It was already dead. The audiences did not notice because they did not hear. And they, too, were angry and insulted. Who were these children, they said, to challenge the music? Undisciplined. Ignorant. Unrealistic. But we were not challenging the music, you see, only the way of the music. Ella Vlady, Daniel Lewis, Darius Milhaud—and our friends in the other arts, André Breton, Marcel Duchamp. Upstarts. Unknowns. Angry." She touched my hand again. "And much less gentle than you, Jack. No more or less dedicated, no more or less of a challenge. Only young and passionate and frightened that when we grew old there would be no place in the world for our art. Like you. And now"—she looked around the studio— "we are the tradition. Who would have dreamed that it would look like this?" She laughed. "Look at the harpsichord with the funny little microphone suspended over it, and that window with all the machinery inside, and this sofa and tea set here, in the middle of nowhere. It is like something out of the Dada exhibition, that shocking affair of 1928."

She smiled at me. "And you, because of who you are, you do not thumb your nose; you challenge it sadly while you ask the same questions we did, and make the same pronouncements. 'Absolutely,' and 'Never.' Perhaps. But perhaps you have only found it necessary to make a new way, and in forty years you will find that you have always been a part of the tradition, more than you realized. And that you have helped to keep the tradition alive by changing it. So I am no longer angry or insulted by what you are doing, Jack. You tell me it is necessary, and you tell me with just enough confusion and hesitation to make me believe it. I know you are an artist. That is enough. I do not understand it. I think it is foolish. But you convince me there is still youth in the world and you offer a little of that to me. And you are kinder than we ever were. That is very nice."

She was silent a moment. Then she said, "Now you may speak."

"I won't stop working," I said. "I can promise you that."

She lowered her eyes to acknowledge it.

"I'll tell Ed what you've said."

"No."

"But . . ."

She pursed her lips and shook her head. "Whatever this thing is that you are doing, this People's Ensemble, I know why you are doing it. You have been able to tell me. And I am not frightened or angry that I do not understand. I do not know why Edward is doing it, but I am afraid that I understand. He is my son. I am familiar with his enthusiasms.

They are different from commitment. I would not say the same things to him that I have said to you."

The producer came into the studio. "Ella," he said.

He startled her and she spun around. "Oh, Mr. Kenton. Yes, yes, yes. I am sorry." We both stood up. "Forgive me. Mr. Fleischman and I were planning the future of art." She turned to me. "I must get back to work." She reached up and pulled my head down to kiss me. "You, too," she said.

I followed the producer out. In the control room they flipped on the monitor. "I think now I will do it well," Mme. Vlady said. "Tell me when you are ready."

There was a message to call Edith when I got home. She had a tentative schedule worked out for the next year. She wanted me to come down in the morning to look it over with her. I asked if you would be there.

"He's tied up for the rest of the week, Jack." I recognized her tone. It was bright and concerned and cautious. She was getting ready to handle me.

"I think I have to see Lenny," I said.

"Jack . . ."

"I'm not pulling anything, Edith. This time it's important."

She hesitated.

"Really," I said. "No scenes."

She put me on hold. I've always wondered what she said to you then, how much she had understood from my voice. When she got back she said you'd be able to come in early, say seven o'clock.

She was surprised when I said, "O.K." Even more when I thanked her.

I didn't sleep much that night. I lay there and watched

Molly breathe through her mouth. I told myself she'd had it hard all her life, never having a family. I had no business envying her. Once she turned and the shoulder strap on her nightgown fell. I replaced it gently, but that woman sleeps like she works. Nothing distracts her.

I got out of bed as soon as the light broke. I puttered around the kitchen, lingered over three cups of coffee. Still, I got to your office a half hour early.

You were already there.

Wall Street was as deserted as one of those end-of-the-world movies. I wondered why we never made any of our important decisions during regular working hours.

You were sitting in your recliner, looking out the window. Neither of us said anything about being early.

You said, "This goddamned well better be important, Jack."

I told you it was. You looked up at me. I'd gotten used to your looking at me like that, anticipating trouble, already restraining impatience. I'd gotten so used to the look that I hadn't noticed your face in a long time. Your hair was shot with gray. Your lips were firm without being tight; your eyes were hard without being mean. I don't know what you saw as you looked at me; all I knew was that even as partners, seeing each other every week, every month, even that way we'd managed to lose touch. It was another reunion.

"I'm getting out, Lenny."

You nodded. You'd expected it.

It was going to be harder than I thought. I wanted to explain the past three years, to confess my panic, to make you feel it with me so you could understand. The words in my head were the wrong ones for that. You were sitting there, impassive except for the stored-up anger behind your eyes. It wouldn't do any good to tell you I had betrayed the

((274))

music. Or that the reason I'd been so impossible was that I was afraid for my soul. You made those words sound foolish in my own ears. From the time we'd been kids and you gave me advice in the dark you could always make me mistrust my own reality. Under the colors of love I'd done everything I could to fight that. I'd worshiped you, worried about you, patronized you, found reasons to despise you, everything but make myself vulnerable to you. Now, with the maturity, the intelligence of your face as you waited for me to say more, it was harder than ever. You'd been through your second divorce, you'd built up the Fleischman Corporation, you'd had to deal with me and God knew how many other problems like me, and all the strength that had given you was there in the creases around your eyes. Everything you'd come to understand from the confusion of your own life showed in those creases even while you sat unsmiling. My own face felt like a baby's. I began to wonder if I might not just be pulling another adolescent stunt, if maybe the smartest thing would be to admit you were older, that you'd always been older than I, and put myself back in your hands.

I said, "It just hasn't been working out."

You nodded again. "There have been problems."

I gave a short laugh. "Problems." I sat on the edge of a leather chair.

"You expect things to come easy, Jack. That's always been your trouble." I looked up, startled. "Things always fall into your lap. You'd have been better off if you had to fight a little. Who are you going to sign with? Hurok?" You made a wry face. "You think you won't have problems with him?"

"I'm not signing with anybody."

"You can't handle it all on your own."

"I'm leaving altogether. I'm not going out as a soloist anymore."

"What are you talking about?"

"I'll still be playing," I said quickly. "I might even be able to do some solo performances . . ." I was getting muddled and defensive.

"You don't just walk out on a career like this," you said.

"I have to, Lenny."

You studied me a second. Your mouth had gone tight. You were trying to figure out if this was another of my whims, like Washington. You made me feel as if it was.

"Don't you think it's time you grew up?" you said.

"I'm not pulling temperament this time. I mean it."

"Either way," you said sharply. "Even if you mean it, it's kid stuff. You don't walk out on the kind of career I've built for you. You've got obligations."

"The whole thing's gone wrong, Lenny."

"I can't keep carrying you and your future around on my shoulders."

"I never wanted you to."

"You needed me to. All my life you've needed me to. You and Poppa both. You're both a couple of babies. You live in a world of ideals and art and I'm left to worry about where your next meals are coming from."

"Poppa turned down your money," I said.

"But Momma took it. She just never told him. And when she was sick, who do you think paid the bills for that? Poppa? On his socialist one hundred and forty-eight dollars a week? Momma and I. We were the only ones who could keep the family running. You were always the baby, the artist. I had to look out for you. You think I didn't have things I wanted to do? Dreams like yours? I just wasn't allowed to keep them, that's all. I had to grow up and be realistic because I was the oldest."

"Lenny?" I said softly.

"I couldn't afford to be a rebel," you said bitterly. "I didn't have an older brother to make it easy for me. Well, now you've got some obligations, too. To me. I've put you on your feet so I don't have to worry about you anymore and you can't throw it away for another whim."

"You wanted to manage me, Lenny. You asked me . . ."

"Because you needed me."

"That's not true. Robert Hubel . . ."

"You'd never be where you are today without me."

"Where am I, Lenny?"

"You're a great violinist."

I shook my head. "I'm a famous one."

We held each other's eyes. All the stored-up anger, the resentment that had started out as concern in the dark in our room in Brooklyn blazed in yours. The whole crazy process that had brought us together that morning began to make sense. It would have been easier, it would have come clear so much sooner if we'd just kept wrestling for thirty years, the way we'd started on Saturday mornings, struggling for power over each other until we fell apart, exhausted, and realized neither could win. All those years when you'd needed to explain the world to me and needed me to believe without question so that you could be sure you were right; all those years when I needed you to approve of me, when I wanted to believe because then your reality would be in my hands; all those years we had simply refused to admit our anger, our frustration and confusion over the fact that we could never be the same person, that I had been born into a world where you already existed, and you had been born into a world where I arrived as a stranger, that we were separate and lonely and would never, ever be able to tell each other who we really were.

"You still need me," you said.

((277))

I nodded. "That's why I've got to get out."

"You have no idea of the things I've protected you from."

"I guess I'm old enough to find out."

"I gave you the chance to move right into the real world where you have to take some responsibility for your own talent instead of just sitting around and dreaming. I gave you a chance to test yourself where it counted and it scares you."

"Not as much as leaving you scares me."

"I left Dicks, Martin and Golden to take care of you," you said angrily.

"You left Dicks, Martin and Golden because you were ready to leave and I was the opportunity. You know that."

"No, I don't." You'd gotten up and you were standing by the window. I could barely make out your face against the light outside.

"Then maybe I've been protecting you from a couple of things, too," I said. There was a pause. "You resent me all you want, Lenny. For being the baby, for making demands, for cutting into your life. But don't use me as an excuse for doing the things you wanted to do yourself."

"You're an ungrateful son of a bitch."

"You're my brother, Lenny. And I think I love you. I can't be sure of that right now. I haven't been able to be sure for the last couple of years because my eyes have been filled with such anger. I've hated you for protecting me from all those things you say you've protected me from. But you must have hated me, too, for protecting you from yourself. I let you use me for that. Be honest, Lenny. That's very important now. You left Dicks, Martin and Golden because you wanted to. And you built the Fleischman Corporation because you wanted something of your own. Don't say you did it for me."

"I did."

"Then why don't you want to let go now?"

"You're my brother."

"I don't know what that means."

"It means we've got a responsibility to each other!" you shouted.

"No, Lenny." The sharpness in my voice stopped you. "This way is easy. We use each other, we feed our resentment and contempt for the way we let ourselves be used, and we call that being brothers. We just make it look hard to avoid the real work of knowing each other. And to do that we have to let go of each other first."

"If you walk out I'm not going to be around for you to come back to," you said softly. "You understand me?"

"Yes."

"You're on your own."

"That's better than a blessing, Lenny. For both of us. You don't know that yet, but it is."

The light behind you was starting to glare. I had to look away. I thought for a minute about what would have happened if I hadn't played Philadelphia five years before, or if I had and we'd just been able to admit we never understood each other instead of trying to force ourselves into each other's life. It wouldn't have mattered. We still would have had to finally say good-bye like this, even if it was only to the brother we carried around in our heads.

"Hey, Lenny?" I said. "You want to hear something funny? I think we're going to find out what it really means to be brothers. We're going to stop working so hard at being what brothers are supposed to be and find out what we really are. I think we may end up liking each other."

"What if we don't?"

I looked up in spite of the glare. "Then at least we won't be afraid of it anymore."

((279))

You came away from the window. Your eyes had that same mixture of confusion and anger and sadness I remembered from the day of my bar mitzvah, when you found me in the back room. You'd said the right thing then. You were groping for the right thing to say now. I think you wanted to tell me you were trying to understand. That you were trying to love me. I think you'd been wanting to tell me that for a long time, but you hadn't yet found the right way and you were frightened of being wrong again.

There was a long silence, like the kind I used to use in the dark to mull over your advice after you'd fallen asleep.

It never stops, I wanted to tell you. Music and love. They're always a risk.

"There'll be a lot of papers and stuff," you said softly. "We have to decide . . ."

"I can go over it all with Edith, if you want."

You said, "I'll do it myself."

"Come for dinner?"

You hesitated.

"Bring Edith."

You said, "O.K."

August 6
Early afternoon

I guess I'll have to finish this letter now and try to make some sense of this whole crazy business. I'll admit it, Lenny. I'm a little disappointed. I wanted to end it back home on a note of triumph, but I don't know how long I'm going to be in here and it doesn't make much sense to hang on to it. Besides, the prospects for triumph get slimmer every day.

Everything's at a standstill. The only thing that keeps us going is our sessions in the library. Even those are starting to pall. They're fine for in here, but after that first high all of us started wondering what they have to do with the world outside. We spend a lot of time feeling each other out, waiting for someone to be the first to ask if we're licked.

Ed was in this morning with Dowd and Gwynne. Maybe that's why I'm so depressed. I spent all last night writing you about St. Louis and Atlanta, remembering what Ed was like in those days. Then I met with him this morning in the visitors' room. He kept talking to Phil and Dudley, trying to avoid Eileen and me. Mainly me. Phil and Dudley told him about the first day we played in the library though. Then he didn't look at anybody.

The board is going to give us another three days. If we

don't play next week they're going to have a financial excuse to close the season. Then they'll reorganize the whole symphony. Ed pleaded with us to compromise.

"You've got no support," he kept saying. He was acting more strangely than I've ever seen him, distracted and indecisive.

"You don't believe that," I said.

"Please, Jack . . . for your own good. For everyone's good." He seemed to want me to understand more than he was saying.

The four of us managed to look staunch. It would have been easier if Ed had been tough. What I couldn't stand was the way he begged us to be reasonable. Dowd and Gwynne just looked smug.

Vic had to be in Atlanta for the past two days. We told Ed he was coming back tomorrow. We'd consult with him then.

Maybe I'll wait until after that before I sign off on this letter. I've told you everything about us, about you and me, I mean, but it still feels unfinished. This strike is so much a part of everything I've been trying to say to you. I don't want to leave it hanging.

It's just about time for our session in the library, anyway. It feels as if we've become an institution here already, the way everybody looks forward to it. I mentioned that to Dudley. He said, "Yeah. Give us another week and we'll get subsidized. Then they'll build us our own room—and start telling us what to play." Everybody's down.

I'll let you know what Vic says.

Later

Molly's back.

We were in the middle of a Handel sonata when Buck

((282))

Howells came in to tell me I had a visitor. I thought it was probably Poppa and I planned to yell at him for wearing himself out. For one crazy minute I even suspected it might be you. I never dreamed it was Molly.

But there she was, leaning on her elbow at the visitors' table with her chin cupped in one hand, waiting for me to come through the prisoners' door. She was grinning.

"You always wanted to be John Garfield," she said.

I hugged her and kissed her the way I had wanted to four days ago. "What are you doing back so soon? Did you know I was here?"

"It's all over Europe."

"It's not." For a moment I believed her. That made her grin more.

"Poppa sent me a telegram. He made it sound like you were a political prisoner."

"When did you get back?"

"A couple of hours ago. I landed in Atlanta last night, then I drove home this morning."

I kissed her again. We kept pecking at each other until the guard asked us to stop. He said it was against the rules. I think he just couldn't handle two middle-aged people carrying on like that. He told us it would be all right if we sat down and held hands across the table. For some reason he didn't think that would look as grotesque.

I asked about Europe, mainly so I could watch Molly's dimple as she talked.

"I can tell you about that when you're home," she said. "What's going on with you?"

I told her what had happened since she left.

She nodded. "I saw Vic last night."

"What did he tell you?"

"Pretty much the same story. Only he was more optimistic."

I snorted. "Did he tell you why?"

"He believes in what you're doing." She studied me. "Do you?"

I shrugged.

"Uh-oh."

"I'm glad you're back," I said.

"What's doing?"

"I don't know. Maybe it's this place. You lose perspective . . ."

"What's doing, Jack?"

"I'm having second thoughts."

"You don't believe in the strike?"

"Sure." She looked relieved. "I'm just not sure we can win."

"Is that all?"

"Well, what the hell good is believing in something if you can't do anything about it?" I burst out. I stopped myself. "I'm sorry. I didn't realize I was so angry."

"Better angry than depressed."

"Analyst."

"You're on strike," she said. "You're waiting for Lefty, not Godot. Talk to me."

I let go of her hand and slumped back in my chair. "I have too much time to think in here."

"What about?"

"Where we'll be if we lose this thing."

"That's not very realistic."

"It's a possibility."

"That's why it's not realistic. You're still fighting. You don't think about losing while you're still fighting."

"It doesn't feel much like a fight in here."

"What do you want? A steaming sword?"

"That's very Freudian."

"Don't be an amateur."

"I'm thinking about leaving the Gainesville Symphony, Molly."

She shook her head to dismiss it.

"I'm serious. We're turning into another fancy community orchestra. I might as well have stayed with Lenny if that's all we are. Even if we win. I don't know if we can ever get back to where we were."

"Of course you can't."

"Then maybe I should start again somewhere else."

"Where? You think the same thing wouldn't happen there that happened here?"

"We could learn from our mistakes."

"Leave that to the younger ones. They can learn from your successes, too. You know how many small ensembles and orchestras have started outside of New York since the People's Symphony."

"That's the trouble. They all expect to be big successes like us. We didn't expect anything when we started. They're not getting the point. Nobody's gotten the point."

"How do you know what point they're getting? What do you want to do? Run around to everyone and tell them what the right point is? That's the curse on the house of Fleischman. You don't trust anybody. Your job is to make your point. Let the others worry about getting it."

"Have you seen Poppa yet?"

"Later," she said. "One old man at a time. And don't change the subject. No leaving, Jack."

"The situation's getting worse."

"All the more reason to stay."

"How come you didn't say that to me when I left Lenny?"

"You were too wrapped up in yourself then. Leaving Lenny got you out of that. Leaving Gainesville would just put you right back into it."

"Do you know what's going to happen if we lose?"

"Will it be as bad as what would have happened if you didn't fight at all?"

"I didn't think of that."

"Maybe it'd be a good thing if you lost. People get soft from winning all the time. They forget what they're fighting for."

"So I'll go back and tell the others everything's fine. We stand a good chance of losing."

"I tell you what, Jack. You leave the Gainesville Symphony because it's getting worse. And I'll go back to rats and gerbils because people are getting crazier. We'll both show 'em."

"Are you sure you haven't seen Poppa?"

She grinned again and reached across the table for my hand. "I came straight to you." The guard wasn't looking so we kissed again. "You need to get laid," she whispered. "That's why you're brooding."

"You think that's it?"

"Even if it's not . . ."

"I really am glad you're back."

"In the nick of time, too. No more nonsense about leaving."

I shook my head.

"I'm going to see Poppa now."

"Don't tell him how I'm feeling."

"You think he doesn't know?" She stood up. "Which reminds me. Next time you go to jail remember to run the dishwasher."

The others were finishing up when I got back. The news about Molly gave us all a lift. In spirit anyway. The outlook for the strike is still grim enough.

New developments.

Vic Jenkins was supposed to get here at one o'clock this afternoon. We're in the civil-offenders section of the jail. Our cells have little windows that look out on Main Street. The commotion started a little before noon. Dudley was the first to notice. He yelled to Phil and me to look out our windows.

There was a small crowd gathered on the steps.

"I thought it was just a bunch of people waiting for a bus," Dudley said. "But the buses are letting them off."

I had to stand on a chair to see comfortably. About forty or fifty people dotted the steps and the sidewalk. A few of them leaned against the police cars parked in front of the building.

Dudley asked if anyone had seen last night's paper. None of us had. We thought maybe someone had been picked up overnight or there'd been a disturbance in another wing.

The crowd started spilling into the street. Buck Howells came out with a troop of men. Two of them directed traffic at each end of Main. The others set up sawhorses.

"Nobody's wearing riot equipment," Phil said. "Just short-sleeved shirts. What the hell's going on?"

The WGGA news truck pulled in.

Dudley yelled, "Jesus Christ! My wife's out there. She's got the kids."

Phil spotted Reinhold Blesser and his wife. Then Mel Sandler.

The television reporter found Buck Howells. Buck pointed up at us, then at a window in the women's wing.

"It's for us!" Phil said. "It's a fucking demonstration for us!"

Dudley's wife saw Buck Howells point toward us. She spotted Dudley and started waving. Dudley shouted back and waved. She kneeled down to show the kids where he was and told them to wave. Fred Holland saw us and pointed us out to Bob Cross. They waved and shouted, too.

People were pouring in from the side streets. Signs popped up in the crowd.

"Does Eileen know what's happening?" I said.

"How the hell can she miss it?"

The shouts and the waving swelled with the crowd.

"You think this was Vic's idea?" Dudley said.

"He's been out of town. He couldn't have . . ."

"Maybe Reinhold and Mel," Phil said. "There must be a couple of hundred people down there."

"More," Dudley said. "A thousand at least. I'm an expert at counting crowds."

"They're still coming."

Somebody tested a loudspeaker. They had set up microphones at the top of the steps. We couldn't see them from our angle. A voice said, "Test . . . test . . ." and tapped the air.

I looked for Molly but I couldn't find her. The crowd was spread out to both ends of Main Street. They were starting to pack together.

"They're on the roof across the street, too," Dudley said.

Music came over the loudspeakers. It was the jazz ensemble from the symphony.

"It's Frank," Phil shouted. "They must be up on the steps. Who's on the bass? Can anyone see?"

"It sounds like Bramberg."

"Yeah. He's a little stiff."

The special bus from the rest home pulled up, the same one I'd seen so often at the Arts Center. They set down the portable ramp and opened the side doors. Molly came out, wheeling Poppa. Behind them were the others, some in wheelchairs, others helped by aides. Poppa looked around at the crowd. I couldn't make out his face, but I saw his head go up, scanning the front of the jail. I knew he was wondering if I could see what was happening. Molly wheeled him up the ramp at the side of the steps until they were out of sight.

Three buses from the Orange Street Baptist Church inched through the crowd. Reverend Parker got out with a hundred members of his congregation. He went up the steps of the jail.

A couple of minutes later the music stopped. Reverend Parker said a little prayer, thanked Buck Howells for his cooperation, and reminded everyone this was a peaceful demonstration. He said it was a tribute to the Gainesville Symphony that there should be so many people here. Plans for the demonstration had begun only three days before and the only official public announcement had appeared last night in the *Gainesville Star*. That was something to note, he said. He launched into a history of the Orange Street Baptist Church, including the arrival of the People's Ensemble. He talked too long. He always does. He took the opportunity to invite everyone to service that Sunday. "If you like the Gainesville Symphony," he said, "you're sure to enjoy our gospel singers who have appeared with them many times in the past. But I want to be brief. There are others up here with me who want to speak a few words. Now I'm going to introduce the man who is most responsible for this gathering. Mr. Seymour Fleischman."

Dudley and Phil yelled over the crowd, "Sy! It was Sy's idea!"

My head had turned into a huge conch shell. I could hear the ocean in it.

There was a lot of scraping and static over the loudspeakers while they adjusted the microphone for the wheelchair. Then Poppa's voice came through, clear and young enough to fill the air over the whole street.

"I hope the four of you can hear us in there," he said. There was another cheer and some whistling. Jerry Frank gave us an A on the trumpet. "We're making some noise out here because there's a bunch of people around who have been making music for us for a long time. It's a good thing to let people know you appreciate that. And it's interesting what's happening here. For a couple of days there's been four people inside there for us. Now there's a lot of us outside here for them. That's maybe how it should be if you're a real community. Now I can't talk too long and I don't have to because you've all had a chance to read about what's been doing with this strike. You know what the musicians want. A lot of you also know that my son Jack is in there along with the others. And for those of you who didn't know that, I'll tell you now. So he should know how proud I am. But I'll tell you something else. I'm just as proud for Dudley Rogers and Phil Carnovsky and Eileen Simpson. And I'll tell you why. Because they're a part of the Gainesville Symphony, and that's something we can all be proud of. And I'll tell you something else. They know what's doing.

"I live at the Gainesville Rest Home. That's because I'm an old man. And I live there with a lot of other old people. Some of them are my friends. Some of them are not such friends. But all of us can tell you, the members of the Gainesville Symphony know what's doing. Because they voted to go on strike so a man like us, a man named Arthur Quasnosky, should be able to live his last few months and weeks with his comrades." I could practically hear Momma. "No Trotsky, Sy." "That's something special," Poppa said. "And I only mention it because there's a lot of you don't know yet how important that is. What's a miracle is how the musicians know it. But they do. So that's why I can tell you they know what's doing. And that's why we started this demonstration to help the symphony. Some of you may have other reasons. What's important is that we all want to help."

There was a little pause. "Now, I'm getting a little tired up here because I've been busy for the last couple of days. So I'm going to let Mrs. Dudley Rogers make the important speech. The thing I want to tell you is that this demonstration is a very wonderful thing. But it's not enough if we really want to help. That's why Mrs. Rogers is going to tell you about the boycott."

The crowd had doubled by then. There must have been close to three thousand people filling the street. There was applause and more static. None of us said anything. It had grown very quiet inside.

Leona Rogers got right down to business. Her voice was crisp and direct.

"The members of the board of trustees of the Gainesville Symphony have a direct or indirect financial investment in the following Gainesville business establishments," she said. "Clarence McCallum, President of the Gainesville National Bank; Seth Bryant, owner of the Gainesville *Ledger;* Elmer Johnson, the Gainesville Mills Clothing Outlet; Harvey Gulden, owner of the Shop 'n' Save food chain; Darrell Politis, Great South Contractors, with a large interest in the mill and the bank." She read the names of all twelve members and their businesses. She asked everyone to boycott those establishments in support of the striking musicians until a settlement was announced. She said that she had already gone to the Gainesville National Bank and told them that if a settlement was not reached within three days, she would withdraw her savings and deposit them in the Georgia Savings. She had, that morning, canceled her subscription to the *Ledger*. She asked everyone who advertised in the *Ledger* to cancel that, too. And she called for a general boycott of the other businesses. She read the list again, without the names of the owners.

There were a couple more speeches. Reinhold Blesser thanked everyone for their support. Fred Holland talked a little about artistic control and why it was so important to everyone. A couple of patrons who weren't board members reminisced and announced their support. They also mentioned their businesses. Somebody read a terrible poem about music. Reverend Parker said a closing prayer and the jazz ensemble played Dixie.

It took a good hour for the crowd to thin out. Phil kept saying, "Son of a bitch. Son of a fucking bitch." His mouth hadn't been so foul in days.

((292))

We noticed friends and pointed them out. There were some I'd forgotten from the days of the Orange Street Baptist Church, people Dudley and Phil had never heard of. Molly wheeled Poppa down the ramp. She turned him around before they got on the bus. He looked up at us once, said something to Molly. She threw her head back and laughed.

Phil asked if I thought the boycott was Poppa's idea.

"It's his style," I said. Molly wheeled him up the ramp to the bus. He'd always said to me, "If your cause is good, Jackie, go for the kishkas. The economic kishkas." Now I knew what he meant.

"The man's a genius," Phil said.

I smiled. "He misses the music." He must have been working his tail off for three days. I'm still worried about the toll it's taken. Molly's probably with him now. I won't know how he is until tomorrow.

They called us to the visitors' room while we were watching the last stragglers. Eileen was already there with Vic. So was Ed Lewis. All three of them beamed at us.

Vic and Ed had both known about the demonstration. Poppa had organized it out of the rest home. He'd turned the residents into a phone corps, gotten Reverend Parker to mobilize his congregation, and Leona Rogers to work on publicity and coordination. He'd also made everyone swear not to tell us. He was afraid I would worry about his health, maybe try to stop him. As it was, Ed had been terrified. He was sure if the activity didn't kill Poppa, the disappointment would.

Nobody dreamed the demonstration would be so impressive. Vic thinks it will move the board. "It's the boycott," Ed said. "They've got to feel it. Even if only a third of that crowd honors it. And they know it."

Eileen said, "I had no idea Darrell Politis had investments

in the bank and the mill. I didn't know a lot of the things Leona said." She was puzzled. "And if I didn't know it, Sy Fleischman didn't know it." She turned to Vic. "Where did they get all that information?"

He grinned and shrugged. I looked at Ed. He stared back impassively.

"We don't get to see enough of each other," I said.

"I told you that a week ago."

We got down to business. Ed told us what he thinks he can get from the board now. We told Vic to focus in on artistic control and Arthur Quasnosky. Fred Holland's standing by to call a meeting.

I'll let you know what happens.

August 11
Early morning

Back home. It's six o'clock in the morning. Molly's still asleep. I can hear her breathing behind me. If I look up I can see the top of her head through the mirror. It makes her pillow look like the floor of Eddie's Barbershop on Nostrand Avenue.

I've got rehearsal in four hours. Concert tonight.

The board has agreed to increments based on the union audit. We're setting up an Artists' and Repertory Committee to sit in on auditions and plan out the winter season with Ed and Maestro Kleinhaus. And on my way to rehearsal I have to pick up Arthur Quasnosky. Vic says the Quasnosky issue was the first to come up at the meeting on Saturday night. It was the easiest to resolve. They think he's too sick to make it, anyway. They don't know him. I'll guarantee that the bastard plays the whole summer season. I called him after the membership meeting to let him know the results.

"I want to be on that Artist and Repertory Committee," he said. "Can't trust any of you hacks to keep up the standards." I told him I'd gotten his note in jail and thanked him for thinking of us. He called me an asshole and told me to pick him up on time.

Molly met me at the jail when they released us. We went straight to Poppa but he was asleep. The rest of the place was buzzing. People kept stopping me, asking for news, telling me what they did during the campaign. I finally got to see him yesterday, after the membership meeting. He was still in bed, but he was awake. He said he felt young again. "But I'll tell you something, Jackie. Feeling young at my age could kill you."

I gave him the news. "You should be pleased, Poppa."

He nodded. "It was a good risk."

"You had a lot of people worried."

"I'll tell you how I saw the situation. You get to my age, you think about leaving a little something for your children. Everybody thinks cash. I figured a working symphony isn't such a bad thing either. Besides, that's for everybody."

He's not strong enough to come to the concert tonight. Maybe next week.

Now comes the hard part.

You called last night just after dinner. I'm going to tell you about it. That way you can check me out on this whole letter. If my version of the conversation is anything like yours, then maybe my version of the rest of us is close, too.

Molly answered the phone in the kitchen. After twenty-two years of marriage I know who's calling from the way she says, "Hello." I took the extension in the bedroom. By the time I got on she was telling you what Europe thinks about your new boss.

You said, "Jack? Are you on?"

I said, "Hey, Lenny."

Molly said, "I'm hanging up," and clicked off.

"I called to congratulate you."

"How did you find out so soon?" I said.

"They ran shots of the demonstration at the end of the news Saturday night."

"In Washington?"

"I'm in New York right now. But I saw the news in Chicago."

"You're still running around like that?"

"Wrapping things up," you said. "Anyway, they showed Poppa. I called the home to find out how he was. They told me the strike news."

"They're pretty excited about it down there."

"How's Poppa?"

"Exhausted. But I think he's O.K."

"I'd like to come down and see him."

"I wish you would, Lenny."

You hesitated. ". . . Maybe even stay with you and Molly." You gave a nervous little laugh. "Hotels, you know. After a while . . ."

"I'll make Wheaties for breakfast. You can read the box first." There was a little pause. "I never called to congratulate *you*."

"Poppa said you wrote me a letter. I never got it."

"I haven't sent it yet."

"Well, for chrissake . . . put it in an envelope."

"I need a box."

"What?"

"You'll have it. Special delivery."

"Jack? You sound funny."

"It's the connection." It wasn't. Everything I've been trying to say in this letter just crowded into my throat at once. It didn't leave much room for my voice. I wanted to say that I'd started writing to you three weeks before and that once I'd started I hadn't stopped, not even during the most frantic and desperate times of the strike. That was how much you meant to me. I wanted to tell you that when I started I was sure I knew what it meant to be your kid brother, what it had always meant, but that I had discovered some precious surprises along the way, some secrets and some mysteries. I found out how much you're a part of everything I hold dear in my life, Lenny. You always said you'd look out for me and you kept your promise, but not in the way we both thought. You gave me advice in the dark about love. The information was wrong, but the anguish of all your mistakes —with Margaret, with Cynthia—the things you could never say to me because you had an image to keep up in front of your kid brother, the confusion that lined your bewildered face, they were what led me to Molly. You explained to me about Poppa's weakness and how I could learn from his failure. But I watched you try to offer the trappings of manhood to him and I watched the two of you struggle so fiercely with his rejections and I learned his value from that. You told me the only way I could ever be sure of success was by counting the number of people around me. I watched you build that number around yourself, I helped you build it around me, I learned what it meant to be torn apart by a hunger for reassurance and I learned to embrace my own loneliness.

Those were gifts, Lenny. Gifts from you. But when I tried to return them, to share them in my own way, I turned clumsy and stupid. I didn't know then they were your gifts in the first place and that because they were yours in the first place, the real gifts of an older brother, they were the ones you understood least.

Sitting there on the bed, talking to you long-distance, I wondered what gifts I might have given you in the same, blind way and what offers to share in return I'd never recognized. I knew my conscious gifts as well as you knew yours. You gave me advice in the dark and it seemed to you that I never took it. I gave you music and it seemed to me that you never heard. Every time I prepared my bow, every time I turned a peg, every time I found my tone, it was for you, Lenny. You've always been my audience. I've always known what I played for you; I've never known what you heard. I know now you will never understand what I do. You can never hear my music the way I play it. You may never know the mystery that made me able to write this cockamamy letter to you. But I've done and I've played and I'm writing right now.

For fourteen years we lived together in the same room, fell asleep against the same dark walls, woke up to the same blank ceiling. For fourteen years we talked and wrestled, learned each other's habits and believed they were the way of the world. And for fourteen years, without our knowing it, we were really learning loneliness, our own and the shape of each other's. That's in the music, Lenny. It comes from you. But now, in a world without miracles, I know better than to ask if you hear it.

So I said, "It's the connection," and wondered if you believed it.

You said, "Hey, listen. When would be a good time to come down?"

"As soon as you can," I said. "Try to make it so you can hear us play."

"I'd like that."

"Tuesday through Saturday." There was another little pause. "Hey, Lenny? What does an economic advisor do?"

"Well, it's pretty complicated. I don't know if you'd . . ." You stopped yourself. "I'll tell you when I see you. It'll take a whole night."

"I'll get plenty of rest."

"Hey, Jack?"

"What?"

"I had an idea. With all the publicity you guys have gotten down there, I could book you all over the country."

I froze, then I heard you laugh on the other end.

I said, "Lenny?" and it bubbled out of me and grew and fed on itself the way it used to around the dinner table until the two of us roared long-distance and our laughter sang across the wires. It must have met somewhere in Virginia.

You said, "I have to get off. Did you get what you wanted from the strike?"

I said, "You'll read about it."

Molly's awake now. She's put the coffee up. I can smell it. I've got just enough time for a cup.

I'll drop this at the post office on my way to pick up Arthur. Then I've got to go make music.

                                                    Love,
                                                    Jack